FROM WALLFLOWER TO COUNTESS

Janice Preston

MILLS
BOON

Published in Great Britain 2015
by Mills & Boon, an imprint of Harlequin (UK) Limited,
Eton House, 18-24 Paradise Road, Richmond, Surrey, TW9 1SR

© 2015 Janice Preston

ISBN: 978-0-263-24773-2

Harlequin (UK) Limited's policy is to use papers that are natural,
renewable and recyclable products and made from wood grown in
sustainable forests. The logging and manufacturing processes conform
to the legal environmental regulations of the country of origin.

Printed and bound in Spain
by CPI, Barcelona

'Do not make fun of me, sir. I may be a spinster, and therefore in your eyes a poor, undesired thing, but I have feelings and I have pride.'

'Felicity, I promise I intended no slight. The thought never crossed my mind that you might think I was making fun of you. I was… Oh, confound it! Come here.'

He had run out of words. He clasped her shoulders and drew her close. A finger beneath her chin tilted her face to his. He searched her eyes. They were shuttered. She was rigid in his arms. Was she scared? Had she never known a man's kiss? The thought, strangely, pleased him: knowing his wife had never experienced another man's touch. But he must take care not to frighten her. He lowered his head, slowly, and put his lips to hers.

He almost recoiled in shock. He had expected ice. What he felt was fire.

AUTHOR NOTE

I first met Richard, Earl of Stanton, many years ago, when he was a drop-dead gorgeous secondary character in my first ever attempt at writing a Regency romance. That attempt has not yet seen the light of day, but I always knew Richard would have his own story. I had no idea which lucky lady would share his journey, until one day he ran up the stairs in his shirtsleeves and came face-to-face with an unprepossessing but sparky spinster who had absolutely no intention of ever getting married.

One year on from that meeting Lady Felicity Weston's fear of unrequited love is as strong as ever, but her circumstances have changed. She begs her mother to find her a quiet, unremarkable gentleman with whom she might be content, little realising she will end up with society's most eligible bachelor.

I hope you will enjoy reading about the arranged marriage between Richard and Felicity, and about how they help each other to reveal and ultimately resolve their emotional conflicts on their journey to true love.

I had a lot of fun writing their story, and I'm sure both Richard and Felicity will pop up from time to time in my future Regencies.

Janice Preston grew up in Wembley, North London, with a love of reading, writing stories and animals. In the past she has worked as a farmer, a police call-handler and a university administrator. She now lives in the West Midlands with her husband and two cats and has a part-time job with a weight management counsellor (vainly trying to control her own weight despite her love of chocolate!).

Books by Janice Preston

Mills & Boon® Historical Romance

Mary and the Marquis
From Wallflower to Countess

Visit the author profile page at millsandboon.co.uk

To my friend Morton Gray.
We've shared an exciting, unpredictable journey
since we first met on the steps of Birmingham Library.
Thank you for your generosity, your support
and your wonderful imagination!

Prologue

August 1810

The single state had much to recommend it, Lady Felicity Weston mused as she crossed the landing of Cheriton Abbey on her way downstairs for dinner. She was beholden to no man: no man to criticize her appearance; no man to dictate her activities; and, most important of all, no man to threaten the barriers she had erected around her heart.

Her life was content.

As she reached the head of the imposing staircase, Felicity froze. A man, dressed in shirt and breeches, was bounding up the stairs two at a time. His shirtsleeves were rolled up, exposing tanned, muscular forearms. He wore no neckcloth, his open shirt collar exposing the strong column of his neck. With his thick brown hair wet and dishevelled he looked virile and slightly dangerous. Felicity's mouth dried. Just two steps down from where she stood, he glanced up and slammed to a halt.

Felicity's stomach flipped as she recognized the Earl of Stanton.

One of the most eligible bachelors of the *ton*, Stanton was a catch coveted by zealous mamas and ambitious daughters alike. And admired even by disregarded, unprepossessing spinsters who had watched his star from afar and had once—for one brief, uncharacteristic flight of fancy—wondered what it might be like to catch the attention of such a man.

Of all the men in the *ton*, it was Stanton who had drawn her eye, time and again, during her come-out five years before. But he had never noticed her.

Never asked her to dance.

Never escorted her to supper.

And that had suited her—even then—perfectly. She had seen little of him in the intervening years but she might have guessed Stanton would be amongst the guests at Cousin Leo's house party. They were close friends.

His chest expanded as he hauled in a breath, his chocolate-brown eyes regarding her with apology but no hint of recognition.

'I beg your pardon.' His voice was a rich baritone. 'I'm aware I am a little late, but I did not think anyone would be coming downstairs for dinner quite yet.'

He swept long fingers through his hair then climbed the remaining stairs to Felicity's level.

Up close, he smelled of rain and horses and leather...and very *male*. Felicity stepped back involuntarily. His lips twitched.

'I apologize for my unkempt appearance. I was drenched coming up from the stables and I left my coat downstairs, where it might drip with impunity.' He sketched a bow. 'Stanton, Miss...?'

A craven impulse to proffer a false name was swiftly quashed. Much good that would do her if they were to spend the weekend at the same gathering. Besides, Felicity was in no mind to turn into a simpering miss over an attractive gentleman in his shirtsleeves. Her gaze lowered without volition, drinking in the breadth of his shoulders and the strength of those arms. She raised her eyes to his, and caught his expression of wry amusement.

She straightened, lifting her chin. *Arrogant wretch*. She would do well to remember arrogance was a trait that often went hand in hand with wealth, status and a handsome face.

'Felicity Weston, my lord.'

She was unsurprised by his perplexed frown. She attended society events rarely now and knew she had faded from memory. She had become accustomed to such a reaction upon introduction and it no longer embarrassed or hurt her, it simply was. People inevitably struggled to place her within the Weston family, not quite believing she was so closely related to her handsome parents and siblings.

Her sense of the ridiculous bubbled to the

surface, prompting her to bestow a kindly smile upon his lordship.

'It is a thankless task, I fear, to try and second-guess my position within the Weston clan. Allow me to enlighten you: I am the sister of Ambrose, Earl of Baverstock.'

'Sister?'

'I am afraid so. Quite shocking, is it not?'

'Not at all,' came the swift rejoinder. 'My apologies for my shocking lapse in memory.'

'Oh, I do not take offence, I can assure you. Yours is a reaction I am quite accustomed to. Indeed, I believe I should almost miss it if I failed to provoke such a response. For otherwise, you see, I might be *quite* overlooked.'

Stanton held Felicity's gaze in silence, then his eyes narrowed. 'You are—'

'Unbecomingly frank?' Felicity tilted her head and raised her brows.

'Frank, yes. Unbecoming?' He stepped closer, his gaze locked on to hers. His voice deepened. 'Hmmm. Unusual, perhaps.'

Felicity battled her instinct to retreat, ignoring the flutter deep in her belly, knowing this kind of intimate verbal sparring was a game to men like Lord Stanton.

'I shall accept that as a compliment, my lord. After all, one would not wish to be considered in the common way.'

His eyes crinkled as he laughed. 'No, indeed, Lady Felicity. No doubt I shall see you later, when

I am more appropriately attired. My apologies once again for my appearance.'

'Unnecessary, I assure you, although…it did cross my mind to wonder…'

He raised one dark brow.

'…is it the new *mode* for gentlemen to dispense with neckcloths? I am quite out of touch, I fear. And also—' she added quickly as his mouth opened, '—is the rolled-up sleeve now quite the thing? Or might they both, perhaps, be an affectation restricted to sporting gentlemen, much like the Belcher neckerchief?'

Stanton's lips firmed. For a split second, Felicity feared she might have prodded his lordship too far. After all, many men did not take kindly to being teased, but then she recognized the glint in his—quite beautiful, now she came to think about it—velvety-brown eyes. A muscle in his jaw bunched, then he threw his head back and laughed. Felicity's gaze snapped to the dark curls exposed by the open neck of his shirt. An involuntary shiver trembled through her.

'I shall add incorrigible to unusual, Lady Felicity. If you wish to know why I am more *déshabillé* than the mere removal of my coat might indicate, why not ask?'

'Sir!' Felicity raised the back of one hand to her forehead in mock horror. 'How could you suggest such a thing? It would be *most* improper for a lady to quiz a gentleman she barely knows about his activities.'

'Indeed it would. However, as you have made

so bold as to raise the subject, I shall enlighten you. I was assisting my groom in the stables with a poultice.'

Felicity sobered. 'One of your horses is lame? I am sorry to hear it. I hope he will soon recover.'

Stanton smiled. 'Thank you. It is merely a precaution. I am sure there is no cause for alarm.' He bowed. 'My apologies once again, Lady Felicity.'

'That is quite all right, Lord Stanton, you were not to know I would have the audacity to appear before the allotted time for dinner. You may rest assured your lapse in standards will not become public knowledge.'

Felicity bent a gracious smile upon his lordship and then sailed down the stairs, her head high. One thing she had learned during her brief sorties into polite society was to do the unexpected and, always, to walk away first. That way, she was never the one left standing, open-mouthed.

Chapter One

Late August 1811—Bath

'Mama, I should like you to arrange a marriage for me.'

Felicity held her breath as she leant back against the solid strength of her mother's sitting-room door. Lady Katherine Farlowe reclined upon a rose-coloured sofa, clad in a pale pink chiffon robe trimmed with swansdown. Her already huge blue eyes widened as she stared at her only surviving daughter.

'Oh, my *darling* girl. I am so happy for you.' Lady Katherine arose elegantly and wafted across the room to Felicity. 'Who is the lucky man?'

Felicity braced herself as her mother enveloped her in a scented embrace. 'I don't know.' Her voice was muffled against her mother's breast; the swansdown tickled her nose. 'That is why I am asking you to arrange it.'

Lady Katherine released Felicity and stepped

back, a frown creasing her soft white skin. 'But…I do not understand. Why? What about love? Do you not want to be happy in your marriage?'

Felicity bit back her cynical riposte. Her mother was an incurable romantic. Felicity knew better. Love, particularly unrequited love, was agony. She had seen it with her sister. She had lived it with her mother—a woman who was adept at closing her eyes and her mind against all unpleasantness. No, she was determined to never feel anything for her husband other than friendship. She would not, like the other women in her family, fall victim to the heartache of unrequited love.

Besides, at four-and-twenty, and after having been on the marriage mart for nigh on six years, the chances of Felicity making a love match were close to zero. She could not recall any man showing her particular attention, despite being the daughter of an earl and possessing a respectable dowry. She had lived her life overshadowed by the beauty of her mother and of her older sister, Emma, before she died.

'I would like my own household,' she said, in reply to her mother's incredulous questions, 'and, eventually, children.'

She felt the heat building in her cheeks as she said the words. She had never admitted that dream out loud before, not even to Beanie, her old nursemaid, but at least her desire for children made this previously unthinkable decision more tolerable. She would wed—if her mother could find her someone suitable. Marriage had become the best of a poor set of options available to her.

'Come and sit by me, Felicity.'

Mama was clearly overjoyed, despite the further proof of her daughter's lack of feminine attributes. She had long despaired over Felicity's sad lack of looks, of her inability to make the best of what she had and of her consistent refusal to pander to the mores of society and the expectations of a young woman by seeking a husband. As time had passed, and as Felicity had aged, Lady Katherine had expected less and less of her. And that had suited Felicity perfectly.

Until this past year.

Felicity banished all thought of her new stepfather, Mr Quentin Farlowe: the sole reason for this drastic step. She could never admit that to her mother—the slightest criticism of the latest love of Lady Katherine's life would be met with tears and reproaches and, ultimately, stubborn denial.

Lady Katherine took Felicity's hand, turning it over in her own lily-white hands.

'Tsk. I declare, Felicity, if only you would use Bloom of Ninon on your skin, as I have begged you to do, time without number, you would have hands to be proud of. Like mine,' she added, with satisfaction, as she extended her arm and splayed her plump, bejewelled fingers. 'You will want your husband to be proud you wear his ring, will you not?'

Will I? 'Well, Mama? Will you arrange a marriage for me?'

Lady Katherine sighed. 'How I can have given birth to an unromantic soul like you, my darling, I have no idea. Even your dear Papa, God rest his soul, was more romantic, and that is not saying a great deal.'

Felicity pondered this observation of her late father's character. She had watched her parents' marriage: her mother, hopelessly besotted; her father, benignly indulgent of his wife—as long as she did not interfere with his pleasures. Her mother had been deeply hurt by her father's careless neglect and by his affaires. And now, as for her mother's new husband... Felicity clamped down her stewing resentment. It seemed it was the way of aristocratic gentlemen—to pursue their own pleasures, including other women, without regard for the pain it caused.

'Now, who is there?' Lady Katherine tapped one finger against her perfect Cupid's bow. 'There's young Avon. You've always been close, and he is heir to the duke.'

'No! I beg your pardon, Mama, but I should prefer an older man. Not only is Dominic younger than me, he is like a brother. I could never marry him, even if he were ready to settle down, which he is not. No, I do not want young, or handsome, or popular. I want *ordinary.*'

I cannot marry a man I might fall in love with. I will not risk that.

She could not delude herself that her husband would love her. If neither Mama nor Emma, with all their beauty, could engender such feelings in the men they had loved, what chance did Felicity have?

Felicity watched as her mother visibly swallowed her disappointment. 'Well, it all sounds most unsatisfactory. However, I am sure you know your own mind, Felicity. You always have been an odd girl. Not like my poor, dear Emma...' The all-too-ready tears brimmed over, spilling down Lady Katherine's smooth cheeks. She heaved a sigh, raising a hand to her chest as it swelled. 'Very well, Felicity. I shall consult with the duke. He will surely know of someone. I shall write to him immediately.'

The Duke of Cheriton—Cousin Leo—was Felicity's joint guardian, together with her mother, until such time as she married or reached the age of thirty, whichever came sooner.

Felicity must hope he would find some pleasant, unremarkable gentleman with whom she might be content.

Chapter Two

'Stan. Good to see you.'

Leo Beauchamp, Duke of Cheriton, clasped the hand of Richard Durant, Earl of Stanton, in a firm grip as they met in the elegant hall at Fernley Park in the County of Hampshire, Richard's family seat.

'Your Grace,' Richard said, grinning, fully aware Leo hated his friends to stand on ceremony. 'Have you come up from Cheriton today?'

'No. Bath, as a matter of fact.'

Richard raised his brows. 'Bath? I had not thought you were in your dotage quite yet, old chap.'

Leo cuffed Richard playfully on the ear. 'Enough of your cheek, pup,' he said, although he was only seven years older. 'I was not there to partake of the waters.'

'Care to enlighten me as to why you went there?'

'I was summoned by my cousin Baverstock's widow on family business.'

Richard knit his brow. 'Baverstock? Oh, yes… quite the beauty, his widow, if I remember rightly.'

'Yes, she was…is… She remarried in April. Farlowe.'

Richard whistled. 'Went to welcome him into the family, did you?'

Leo snorted. 'Hardly. I tried to warn her off, but she was as determined to have him as he was to secure her. Her income alone will be enough to allow him to live like a nabob.'

'Fortunate fellow, falling on his feet like that. I could wish Charles such luck. Mayhap a wealthy widow would remove him from my back.'

Charles Durant, a distant cousin, was Richard's heir, and regularly applied to Richard to settle his debts. Richard thrust aside his momentary qualm at the thought of Charles ever inheriting the title and the estates. He was fit and healthy and had every intention of living a long time.

A footman opened the salon door as they approached and they dropped the subject as they joined Richard's other guests—gathered for the first evening of a shooting party. It was an all-male event, as Richard's mother was away from home, visiting an old friend.

The messenger arrived as dusk fell on the second day of the shoot. The weather had remained fine, the birds were plentiful, and beaters and shooters alike were happily exhausted after a successful day. The news of the death of Lord Craven—an old school friend of Richard's—in a fall whilst out hunting shook them all but, for Richard, it was particularly painful, resurrecting the dark, agonising time when his older brother, Adam, had been killed in a shooting accident sixteen years before. Richard had been away at school at the time and, poignantly, it had been Craven who had comforted him when he heard the news.

He had returned home to find his parents changed beyond recognition: his father almost mad with grief, scarcely eating or sleeping, and his mother bitter and withdrawn. His parents had barely communicated with each other or with him. Richard had inherited the earldom at the tender age of seventeen, after his father had followed Adam into the grave and, since then, it seemed to Richard that his mother's only interest in him was as a means to secure the succession of the title.

Many an argument had raged over his refusal to contemplate marriage to protect the title and estates, but he had held fast. He was one of the most accomplished sportsmen in the *ton*. He led a full and active life and was universally admired and feted for his prowess on a horse, his precision with the ribbons, his expertise with an *épée*, his shooting skills, and even his invincibility in the ring. He was in no hurry to don leg shackles. The only obstacle to his contentment was his mother's persistent harassment about the risks he took, and her refusal to retire to the dower house until there was a new mistress to run Fernley Park.

But now…Craven's death made Richard question his stand. If he did nothing, might his mother's great fear of Charles laying waste to the estates be realized?

The atmosphere after dinner that evening was sombre. Most of his guests settled down to play cards after dinner, but Richard declined to join them, in no mood to play the convivial host. He wandered into the library, where he found Leo, alone, pushing chess pieces around a board in a desultory manner.

'Care for a game?'

Richard shrugged, and pulled up a chair. Preoccupied and uneasy, he found it nigh on impossible to concentrate on the game, his thoughts dominated by his mother's diatribes about sporting activities and premature death.

He moved his bishop and cursed under his breath as Leo swooped with his knight to seize the piece. He looked up to meet Leo's quizzical gaze.

'Things on your mind, Stan?'

'Craven; hard to believe, isn't it?'

'Sad business. It must bring back unpleasant memories for you.'

'It does.'

Leo had been a close friend of Adam's and a frequent visitor to Fernley Park during his youth. He had supported Richard through those lonely years after his father's death, having experienced for himself the pressures of inheriting such power and wealth at an early age. They had been friends ever since.

Richard reached for a bishop, hesitated, then withdrew his hand. Moving it would expose his queen.

'How old was he? Thirtyish?'

'Two-and-thirty: the same age as me. We were at Eton together.' Richard fell silent, still contemplating his next move. He reached for a pawn. 'It's brought home my responsibilities, though. There's no shying away from it: I've decided it's time to settle the future.'

Now the words were out in the open, Richard, paradoxically, felt better. The tension that had plagued him throughout the evening began to dissipate.

Besides, marrying will have the added bonus of removing Mother to the Lodge.

The thought of Fernley Park without his mother made even marriage seem appealing. Her presence constantly reminded him of his failure as a son and he was conscious he avoided coming home, leaving more and more of the business to Elliott, his bailiff. Remorse filled him at his antipathy towards his own mother: all he could feel for her was filial duty and responsibility. Since Adam's death, she had withdrawn any hint of affection for him. And then his father had… He swallowed hard. If only he had tried harder. Been a better son.

Could I have stopped him? Would he still be here?

His father's death had rocked what remained of their family and shifted their world on its axis. Scandal had been avoided but neither he nor his mother had been the same since.

'Much as I like Charles,' he added, placing his pawn on a square at random, 'I cannot risk him running the estate to ruin.'

'Indeed. He is a somewhat profligate young man.' Leo moved his queen, capturing the pawn Richard had just moved. 'I hear the duns are sniffing at his heels again.'

'So soon? I only bailed him out last year. I thought his debts were all cleared.'

'I have no doubt they were. I believe I cautioned you at the time not to throw good money after bad.'

'You did, and I should have heeded your advice. You've never steered me wrong yet.'

Leo smiled. 'I like to think I still have some uses,' he murmured, moving a rook. 'So, you are thinking of marriage. Might I enquire as to the identity of the lucky lady?'

Richard huffed a mirthless laugh. 'I have no idea. There is no one who springs immediately to mind. As long as she's well born, is of an amiable and compliant nature, and is not minded to interfere with my life, I am sure I can find someone to suit.' He picked up his bishop, hesitated, then took one of Leo's pawns.

'Aha,' Leo said, with satisfaction, as he swooped on Richard's queen. 'Mine, I believe.'

Richard sighed. His mind was definitely not

on the game. They had barely begun but, studying the pieces left on the board, he could see he was in trouble.

'A marriage of convenience?' Leo said. 'Are you certain that is what you want? A compliant wife?'

'Why ever not? I have no interest in a love match and, if I crave excitement, I can find plenty outside my domestic arrangements. No. A nice, compliant lady, content to run a comfortable household and to look after my children—that will suit me very well.'

'In that case,' Leo said, 'I might know just the girl for you.

'Checkmate.'

Chapter Three

Mid-September 1811

Felicity sat before the mirror in her bedchamber at Cheriton Abbey as the maid loaned to her by Cousin Cecily—the duke's younger, unmarried sister, who had raised his children after the death of his wife—dressed her hair. It was hard to garner any enthusiasm over Anna's efforts, although Felicity did silently admit—with a twinge of guilt at her disloyalty—that the result was an improvement on poor Beanie's usual effort.

Miss Bean, nursemaid to all three Weston children, had acted as Felicity's maid since her sixteenth birthday, but her advancing age and failing eyesight had made travelling to Cousin Leo's estate impossible. It was time, Felicity had finally accepted, for her beloved Beanie—more of a mother to her than her own mother had ever been—to retire.

The house party had been organized for the

duke's seventeen-year-old daughter, Olivia, in preparation for her *début* the following spring. A party of fourteen, plus the family, Cecily had told Felicity when they arrived from Bath an hour ago. Felicity was stomach-churningly aware, however, that she was also to meet her prospective husband.

'There, milady, you're ready,' Anna said. 'I must go now and help Lady Cecily—the family usually gather in the drawing room at six o'clock.'

'Thank you for your help, Anna. Have all the guests arrived?'

'I believe so, ma'am.'

Felicity's palms turned clammy and her stomach seemed to rise up. How she wished she could simply turn up at church one day to find a stranger awaiting her at the altar. Surely that would be preferable to this wretched charade? She forced her thoughts away from the ordeal to come, recalling that Dominic, Lord Avon—Cousin Leo's eldest son and Felicity's childhood playmate—would arrive tomorrow. Buried in Bath, as she had been for the past six months, she was eager for news from Westfield, the orphan asylum in London both she and Dominic supported whenever they could.

A thought struck her. What if her husband disapproved of her charitable activities? Might he ban her from involvement with Westfield, as her stepfather had tried? He would have that right—the right to command and control her. A chill raced over her skin, raising gooseflesh on her arms.

It is nerves. You will feel better once you have met him.

Fretting over something to come was the worst part: it was the lack of action—the sense of being tossed and turned by events without any control, like a piece of driftwood caught in a current— that allowed such fears to tease her. She could stay alone with her thoughts no longer. Dragging in a breath, Felicity left the sanctuary of her bedchamber and headed for the stairs.

At the head of the magnificent staircase, she looked down and pictured *that* scene a year before. Stanton. A pleasurable feeling coiled in her belly at the mental image of his lordship in his shirt sleeves and breeches. Would he be here this weekend? It was likely, she realized, with a shiver of anticipation she swiftly banished. Despite their encounter on the stairs, Stanton had barely noticed her again as he had flirted with and charmed the other guests during the remainder of that weekend, living up to his rakish reputation.

Whoever her prospective husband might be he would be bound to show to disadvantage against the earl. Most men did.

And is that not precisely what you want? Did you not stipulate a quiet, ordinary gentleman for your husband?

She swallowed the nerves playing havoc with her insides as she descended the stairs and entered the drawing room to await the other guests and her future.

* * *

Leo ushered Richard to one end of his magnificent library, where a small leather-upholstered sofa and two matching armchairs were placed invitingly around a stone-carved fireplace in which logs crackled merrily.

'Well? Are you going to tell me who she is?'

All through dinner Richard had been trying to guess the identity of his prospective bride. Why on earth had he not demanded to know before travelling all the way to Devon? All he knew was that she had asked her mother to arrange a match for her.

Leo's silver-grey eyes gleamed. 'Patience, dear boy.'

Richard glared at Leo, who met his look with raised eyebrows and a bland smile. *He's enjoying this, the wretch.* They had been friends for fifteen years—Richard knew that look. Biting back his irritation, he sat on the sofa whilst Leo poured them both a brandy before settling into one of the armchairs. Richard tipped his glass, savouring the warmth of the fiery spirit, waiting.

'My ward, Lady Felicity Weston.'

As he digested Leo's words, Richard conjured up a mental image of Lady Felicity. They had not been neighbours at dinner and so had not conversed, but she had appeared monosyllabic and subdued throughout. Perhaps it was nerves, knowing she was to meet her future husband? He dredged up the memory of their encounter last year, but this girl had shown none of the spark and wit she had exhibited then.

Her mother, in contrast, was the life and soul of the gathering, but too loud and foolish for his taste. The other daughter—she had died young, he recalled—had inherited her mother's beauty, but not so Lady Felicity. No wonder she had jested about being overlooked, for it was no more than the truth. Certainly, next to her flamboyant parent, she slipped into anonymity.

A further image arose, from his perusal of the occupants of the drawing room before the meal. Lady Felicity—head to one side, eyes bright, hands animated—had been chatting with Leo's sister, Cecily, who had clearly found it hard to contain her giggles. Then Felicity had looked up. Their eyes met, and immediately all her liveliness had leached away. He had barely noticed at the time.

He chose his words with care. Leo, he knew, was fond of her.

'She is a little insipid, is she not?'

An image of his mistress of the past year materialized in his mind's eye. Harriet—now *there* was a woman: curvaceous, experienced, uncomplicated, fun. He frowned into the amber liquid swirling in his goblet. What had been his stipulations for his future wife? *Well born, of an amiable and compliant nature, and not minded to interfere with my life.* He had said nothing about appearance and, indeed, why should her looks matter? She was not ugly. She was...plain.

'She doesn't show to advantage next to her mother,' Leo said, 'but she's a good girl, she has a kind heart, she wants a family, and she's the daughter of an earl. And Lady Katherine's father was a marquis, so her breeding on both sides is impeccable. Or have you changed your mind, and now desire a love match?'

Richard glared at Leo, who met his eyes with a grin. He leaned forward and gripped Richard's knee.

'Are you sure you want this, Stan? Neither Felicity nor her parents know your identity, and need never know if you do not wish to proceed.'

Was he sure he wanted this?

No. He had not thought to wed for several years to come.

But Craven's death weighed on his mind, as did the premature deaths of his father and his brother. He was loath to agree with his mother but, if anything *should* happen to him... It was not about what he wanted any longer.

It was his responsibility.

His duty.

His decision.

'My mind is made up. I must secure the future of the title and estates.'

Leo leaned back. 'So, given that you are still minded to wed, how do you wish to proceed? Is it to be Lady Felicity?'

He had a choice. He could either choose to settle the matter now or he must seek another bride. The thought of suffering the matchmaking efforts of determined mothers and importunate fathers during the coming months in London was enough to bring him out in hives. Which left…

'She is very young.'

'She is almost five and twenty; older than she appears.'

Richard felt his brows lift. He had thought her younger. At least she had a spark of personality, although her dress sense was appalling—that pale-pink gown she was wearing tonight had done her no favours, and her figure, probably the reason he had thought her so young, was almost boyish. But, on balance, would he prefer someone like her mother—beautiful, but empty-headed and fluttery? No, that would drive him demented in a trice. At least Felicity had demonstrated a sense of humour and a down-to-earth manner he could countenance.

As long as she did not entertain girlish notions of his falling in love with his own wife, he thought Lady Felicity Weston would suit nicely.

'Very well, Lady Felicity it is. At least I can deal with you, and not Farlowe, over the settlements and so forth.'

Leo grinned and gripped Richard's hand. 'Welcome to the family, Stan. I will go and extract Felicity and Katherine from the throng, hopefully without causing too much speculation.'

It was not long before he returned with Felicity and her mother. Richard stretched his lips into a smile as he stood up, pushing a hand through his hair, smoothing the unruly curls back.

He hoped he concealed his true feelings with more success than Lady Felicity. Her expression as she came through the door, and their eyes met, was one of sheer horror.

What was so very special about Lady Felicity Weston to suggest the Earl of Stanton was not a good enough match for her?

Chapter Four

Richard had no further opportunity to study his bride-to-be. Lady Katherine sailed past her daughter and captured his hands, standing so close her floral scent made his nostrils twitch. She gazed up at him through fluttering eyelashes. Already knocked off balance by Felicity's reaction to him, Richard's muscles quivered with the effort not to snatch his hands from her mother's soft, moist grasp. From the corner of his eye he caught the resigned look that passed between Leo and Felicity. Mayhap he was not the only person who found Lady Katherine a touch overwhelming.

'My dear, dear Stanton. Such joy…oh!' She giggled breathlessly. 'How droll am I? Joy is my dear girl's middle name: Felicity Joy. Does that not suit her a treat, Stanton? I am certain she will bring you as much joy as she has brought to me and her dearest papa—God rest his soul—and now to my beloved Farlowe.'

Richard extricated his hands. 'Indeed.' He shot

a baleful look at Leo, who shrugged and grinned before manoeuvring Lady Katherine to the sofa facing the fire. He then proceeded to engage her in conversation, leaving Richard to get to know his intended.

Which proved to be as difficult as drawing blood from the proverbial stone. Felicity, her face quite colourless, had taken her place beside her mother, her attention firmly on the flames as Richard sank into the nearest chair. Her expression was hard to read but her rigid posture and tight fists told their own story. Something—something about him, he must conclude—was not to her liking. Contrarily, her seeming reluctance fanned his determination to proceed with the marriage.

'Well, Lady Felicity, who could have guessed when we met on the stairs last year that we would be here now, discussing our forthcoming marriage?'

'Indeed, my lord.' Still she avoided eye contact, staring into the fire.

Richard, momentarily nonplussed, continued to study her. Nondescript was the most fitting adjective he could conjure up. She was a touch taller than average, with a slight build. Another woman of her stature might be described as willowy, but, somehow, Felicity was not quite tall enough, and not quite slender enough, to earn that accolade. Her features were regular, her complexion dull. Her oval face was a shade too long and her chin a touch too determined, for delicacy. Her nose was straight, but a little too strong to be considered dainty, and her mouth was… Richard paused in his appraisal. The compression of her lips did little to disguise their rosy fullness. They, at least, could be declared alluring.

Her brown hair was pinned up in the Grecian style, with curls—already wilting—framing her face. Her eyes were a striking amber and, at this moment in time, they stared dully ahead as Felicity sat straight-backed, her hands white-knuckled in her lap.

What was she thinking? According to Leo, Felicity had asked her mother to find her a husband, but her reaction to Richard almost suggested she would be entering the union against her will. Richard hoped not. Now he had made his decision he was impatient to proceed. He vowed to win her over.

'It's a pleasant evening, Lady Felicity. Would you care to stroll on the terrace?'

She looked directly at him for the first time since she entered the room. Try as he might, he could not read her expression. Before she could answer him, though, Lady Katherine intervened.

'Of course she would, Stanton. Go along, Felicity. I am sure you do not need chaperoning if you are with your intended. I declare I have never been so happy in my life—except, of course, when my dear Farlowe proposed. Who would have thought that I would be mama-in-law to the Earl of Stanton. I shall be the envy of everyone. I cannot wait to see their—'

'Mama, please.' Felicity cut across her mother's monologue as she stood up.

Richard rose to his feet with a guilty start. He had been on the brink of becoming mesmerized by Lady Katherine's inane chatter.

Felicity, cheeks splashed with colour, shot a glance at him before lowering her gaze. 'Thank you. I should enjoy a breath of fresh air.'

She took his arm and they left the library via one of the French doors. It was dark outside on the terrace, but lamps at intervals along the balustrade cast weak pools of light to soften the shadows.

Richard placed his hand over Felicity's, where it lay on his arm. It was chilled, despite the mildness of the evening.

'You are chilled, Lady Felicity. Shall I fetch your shawl?'

'I am warm enough, thank you, my lord.'

'Richard. Please. We need not stand on ceremony with one another; unless, of course, you have doubts about our marriage?'

Her eyes flicked to his face, then returned to their contemplation of the flagstones at their feet. Richard stopped beneath one of the lamps and took her hands in his.

'Forgive my blunt speaking, but you do not appear happy. Am I ousting a preferred suitor?'

'No, there is no other, although I had not thought... I did not realize... Oh, heavens, I cannot find the words.'

Felicity tugged her hands free and turned to

stare into the darkness of the surrounding gardens. Her arms were wrapped around her waist and she looked somehow very vulnerable, standing there alone. It crossed Richard's mind that she was self-contained: she gave the impression she was used to relying on her own resources. He shook his head in self-deprecation. Harriet *would* be impressed. She was forever castigating him about his lack of insight and yet, here he was, analysing his bride-to-be as though he had known her for years. He thrust away all thought of his mistress. It felt, somehow, disloyal to think of her whilst in the company of his future wife.

He put his hands on Felicity's shoulders, the bones fragile beneath his fingers. 'Try. I won't bite, you know. I should prefer to start off with honesty between us, if we are to live together with any degree of comfort.'

Her shoulders tensed as she inhaled. Then she turned, and regarded him, her eyes as rueful as her smile.

'This is ridiculous. You are right. If we are to wed, we need to understand one another. And, I admit I have doubts. Not about you. Well, that is...' She paused, her brows drawn together in a frown. 'No, that is untrue. It *is* about you, but it is about me, also. You and me. Together. You see, I hadn't thought...I never presumed to be presented with such a...such a...*catch*, if you do not object to my calling you that?'

Richard bit back a smile. He had been called a catch many times, he was aware, but never to his face before. And never by an earnest-faced female who appeared to believe herself unworthy of a 'catch' such as he.

'You may call me what you will,' he said, 'as long as you promise not to use such insultingly offensive terms that I shall be forced to take umbrage.'

She laughed, revealing a glimpse of white teeth. 'Umbrage? I always thought that to be a state applied to elderly dowagers. Do you sporting gentlemen consider it a fittingly masculine trait, my lord?'

This was better. The spirited girl he remembered from last year had surfaced, her face alive with laughter, her eyes bright.

'Perhaps umbrage does not quite convey the precise meaning I hoped to convey,' he conceded. 'Which word, in your opinion, should I have used, if I am to portray a suitably manly image to my future wife?'

Disquiet skimmed her expression, then vanished. Had he imagined it? Was it the bald reminder that she would be his wife that had disturbed her? Her countenance was now neutral, but her eyes remained watchful and she made no attempt to answer him.

'Would you have preferred me to use "offence" perhaps, or "exception"?' He leaned closer to her, and said, 'I do not, you notice, suggest "outrage" for that, I fear, would not meet with your approval any more than "umbrage". It is too synonymous with spinsters, would you not—?'

Felicity stiffened. 'Do not make fun of me, sir. I may be a spinster and, therefore, in your eyes, a poor, undesired thing, but I have feelings and I have pride.'

'Felicity, I promise I intended no slight. The thought never crossed my mind that you might think I was making fun of you. I was…I was… Oh, confound it! Come here.'

He had run out of words. He clasped her shoulders and drew her close. A finger beneath her chin tilted her face to his. He searched her eyes. They were shuttered. She was rigid in his arms. Was she scared? Had she never known a man's kiss? The thought, strangely, pleased him: knowing his wife had never experienced another man's touch. But he must take care not to frighten her. He lowered his head, slowly, and put his lips to hers.

He almost recoiled in shock. He had expected ice. What he felt was fire.

Chapter Five

Felicity's heart clamoured in her chest as Richard's lips claimed hers. One arm swept around her back, the other hand cupped her head. His lips were warm, surprisingly soft and tasted of brandy. They slid, slowly, tantalizingly, over hers and she felt her own lips soften and respond. A tingling thrill shot through her, all the way to her toes. Her fingers tightened on his sleeve as her belly squeezed in a strange but not unpleasant way. That kiss ended too soon for Felicity and as the reality sunk in—that this man would indeed be her husband, would be entitled to kiss her and caress her and much more—her heart faltered.

How could she resist falling in love with such a man? She was under no illusion that he might ever love her. Unrequited love had caused far more beautiful women than she to suffer. She saw an image of her future—lonely and desperate—stretching before her.

Richard smiled down at her. She searched his

face. It confirmed her fears. Even in this dim light, she could read the amusement that lurked in the depths of those velvety eyes. And why would he not be amused? A naive spinster and the experienced man about town: would that not set the precedent for their marriage? Could she protect her heart? Through the lit windows of the library she could see her mother and the duke, deep in conversation. She must tell them as soon as possible that she could not marry Lord Stanton. She peeked at him again. He looked bored. That settled it, then.

'Perhaps we should go back inside. Mama will be wondering where we are.'

His lips twitched as he glanced through the window. Felicity felt a lick of heat, deep inside, remembering their warm, silken caress.

'I suspect your mama has forgotten our existence for the moment.'

Nothing would prevail upon Felicity to admit he was right. 'Nevertheless, I think we have been out here long enough.'

Richard sketched a bow. 'As you wish, my lady.'

Felicity studied him surreptitiously as she took his arm. Starkly handsome, his close-fitting black tailcoat and trousers emphasized his masculinity. Not only was Stanton one of society's most eligible bachelors, but Felicity was aware he was also widely acclaimed for his sporting prowess. The hard muscle of his arm under her hand attested to his strength.

He seemed not unkind.
He had a sense of humour.
He was nigh on the perfect man.
Just not for her.

Felicity wrapped her shawl closer around her and knocked on her mother's bedchamber door. She glanced along the corridor, praying no one would see her. The sick dread churning the pit of her stomach would not go away. She must speak with Mama and tell her of her decision, or she would never be able to sleep that night. The sooner she halted Lady Katherine's inevitable runaway enthusiasm for this match, the better.

She heard a faint voice from within, and entered. Lady Katherine was in the massive four-poster, reclining in a sultry pose against the stacked pillows. When she saw her daughter, she sat up, pouting.

'Felicity. I thought you were my darling Farlowe. What is it? Will it take long?'

Thank goodness her stepfather was still downstairs with the other men. It would be hard enough to persuade Mama to understand without Farlowe there to stir the pot.

Felicity perched on the edge of Mama's bed.

'Mama, I cannot marry Lord Stanton.'

'What?'

Felicity flinched, her mother's piercing shriek loud in her ears.

'I am sorry…'

'*Sorry?* You are the most ungrateful little…

Why? You asked me to arrange a marriage, and I have set up an alliance with *the* most eligible bachelor of our acquaintance, and you have the *boldness* to suggest he is not good enough for you? Oh! Where are my salts? You *infuriating, stubborn* girl…'

Lady Katherine's face was pink with fury. Felicity found her mother's smelling salts and watched her wave them beneath her nose.

'Mama, I am sorry to distress you, but if you will listen to me—'

'Listen to you? I listened when you asked me to arrange your marriage. Finally, I thought…*finally*, Felicity is behaving as a modest young woman ought. But I was mistaken. You still imagine you are too good! Too good for the likes of Stanton, of all people.'

'I do not believe I am too good for him,' Felicity said, heart sinking. Once Lady Katherine had worked herself into such a state, she was unlikely to heed anything other than her own point of view. How Felicity wished Beanie was here to confide in.

'Well, I should think not. Now, if it was poor, dear Emma who had caught the eye of such a man…mayhap *she* could believe herself too good for him.'

Felicity thrust down the pain of once again being unfavourably compared to her sister.

'May we discuss this in the morning, Mama?' *When you are calmer.* 'I am sorry to upset you, but I would try to make you understand why I must refuse Stanton.'

Lady Katherine straightened in the bed, sparks shooting from her blue eyes. 'I do believe you are serious, you ungrateful chit. You always were stubborn, and unbecomingly *forward* with your opinions. Well, we shall see what Farlowe has to say about *this*.'

'My stepfather can have no opinion on my betrothal,' Felicity retorted. *If only you had never married him, I wouldn't be obliged to marry* anyone. 'The decision is mine. You cannot *force* me to accept Stanton.'

'But *why*, Felicity, darling?' Her mother changed tack, wheedling. 'I don't understand. Most girls would *swoon* at the thought of catching such a man.'

'The problem is that he is *too* good a catch, Mama.'

'Too good? How can a man be too *good* a catch?'

Felicity struggled to find the words. How could she possibly explain without insulting her mother and dragging Emma's name into the argument? Her mother would—and not for the first time— accuse her of jealousy.

'I wish for a quiet, retiring gentleman, Mama. Lord Stanton is popular. He is always the centre of attention. Please try to understand.'

I am afraid I will fall in love with him.

The words she could not say near choked her. A man like Stanton, in an arranged marriage, would develop the same carelessness her father had demonstrated towards her mother; the same indifference Farlowe was now beginning to demonstrate, a mere six months into their marriage. Such indifference in a marriage of convenience would be tolerable. But that *same* indifference, if she were to fall in love with her husband... A handsome face with warm brown eyes materialized in her mind's eye and her lips tingled in memory of his kiss. She could never resist him. She knew it as surely as she knew her own name.

Stanton was one of the most attractive men she had ever seen, with his dark brown, wavy hair, his deep, soulful eyes, and his fine figure. Since their encounter last year, she had added those strong, muscular arms and the glimpse of dark chest hair to the tally of his attractions. And now she had experienced his kiss—how could she ever withstand such an onslaught? She might be inexperienced, but she suspected that kiss had triggered only the merest hint of the passion buried deep within her. No, she dare not expose her heart to such a man. That way, for sure, would result in heartbreak and despair.

'Well, I do *not* understand, you provoking girl. Oh, where is Farlowe when I need him? I need his support. No one understands my trials.'

'Please, Mama, may we speak again in the morning, before the betrothal is announced?'

'The duke and Lord Stanton have agreed to announce the betrothal after dinner, tomorrow evening. But do not think the delay will favour your case, my girl, for my mind is quite made up. Just think, I shall be the envy of all, when our news becomes known.'

'Mama, I cannot marry a man merely in order that you can boast to your acquaintances.'

'Oh! You would make me sound the most uncaring parent in the world, Felicity. Have I not always put your welfare and happiness at the very top of my priorities?' Lady Katherine sank back against the pillows and waved her salts beneath her nose again, her eyes closed. Then they snapped open and she sat up, nailing Felicity with a triumphant stare. 'The duke has approved the match. He believes you and Stanton will suit very well. Do you dare to question *his* authority?'

If her mother was to start invoking the duke's authority, Felicity knew she must concede her argument for now and try again tomorrow.

'Goodnight, Mama. I hope you sleep well. I shall come to see you in the morning. Please try to understand—I want to be content in my marriage but I cannot believe Stanton will prove a *comfortable* husband.'

She bent and kissed her mother.

'Do not think I shall yield on this, Felicity. There are times when you must realize that your elders have more worldly experience than you and know what is best.'

Chapter Six

A bright morning saw Felicity up and about early, her determination not to wed Lord Stanton stronger than ever. He had prowled through her restless dreams, stirring strange and unwelcome yearnings deep within her. She had woken from those dreams, her heart racing, her skin hot and damp. And that was merely the result of a single kiss.

As she made her way downstairs it was apparent there was no one else up, other than servants, but that suited Felicity: the only person she wished to speak to was her mother, unlikely to be awake at this hour. Felicity crossed the library and let herself out on to the terrace, where she had strolled with Lord Stanton the previous evening.

She paused at the spot where they had kissed. Her pulse quickened at the memory even as the ever-present fear wormed through her belly. Unrequited love. She could not, would not risk it. It was unrequited love that had so wrecked Emma's life that she had climbed to the roof of Baverstock Court and…

Felicity turned abruptly from the spot and headed for the flight of stone steps that led down into the garden, laid out in a formal style dissected by stone-flagged paths. There were gardeners already at work, weeding and collecting leaves, so she did not linger but followed the central pathway to an arched gap cut into a tall beech hedge. Through the gap was another pathway, and she turned left, knowing the stables were to the right. They, like the garden, would be a beehive of activity at this time of the morning.

A short distance along the path she reached the small rustic gate she remembered from her childhood. It led to a grass path that wound through a copse of ornamental trees before opening on to a vista of Cousin Leo's lake. Water always soothed her. When she eventually wed she would have, if not a lake, then at the very least a pond, preferably near to the house, so she could see it every day; a large pond, with water lilies, and fish, and a bench to sit on. Daydreaming pleasantly, Felicity continued towards the lake.

'Good morning, Felicity Joy.' The deep voice startled her from her reverie.

'Oh!' Her heart leapt into her throat as she looked around.

Lounging at one side of the path, broad shoulders propped against the trunk of a copper beech, was Lord Stanton.

Felicity felt her face heat. *Why must I blush*

now? She could never blush prettily, like her mother or Emma. Then she gritted her teeth. Why should she care how she blushed? She could never impress Stanton with her appearance, and she was not about to try. Besides, had she not already decided he was not for her?

'Good morning, my lord. You are up early. I had not expected to see anyone out and about quite yet.'

'I am sorry if I startled you. I had a restless night. It is not every day a man meets his future wife for the first time.'

Felicity eyed him with suspicion. Was he poking fun at her? 'It is not too late to change your mind.'

His dark brows snapped together. 'And what, precisely, do you mean by that, Felicity Joy?'

He pushed away from the tree and prowled towards Felicity, his attention never leaving her face. She resisted the urge to retreat.

'You sound as though you might welcome a change of heart.'

'Why were you leaning against that tree?' Felicity asked. 'Are you waiting for someone?'

'You.' Stanton was close now, gazing down at her.

She held his gaze, her heart pumping a little too fast to be explained away by her walk. He was so handsome. Too handsome.

'What do you mean?' Her voice sounded breathless. It reminded her of her mother, which fuelled her irritation. She had no wish to flutter every time a man paid her any attention. She cleared her throat. 'You could not possibly have known I would be walking here.'

He grinned. 'I was returning from a stroll by the lake. I saw you coming from a distance, so I thought I might wait for you. And see when—indeed, *if*—you would notice my presence. It seems I am not the only one who is preoccupied. You, too, appear to have much on your mind, and not all of it pleasant, judging by your expression.'

'And if I maintain that is my normal expression?'

Stanton crooked his arm. It would surely be churlish not to take it. They continued towards the lake.

'Then I should say that your life is, perhaps, not very content. I should like to see a smile on your face always, Felicity Joy.'

He halted, tugging her around to face him. He lifted her chin with one finger, and Felicity was instantly transported back to the night before. She tensed. Was he going to kiss her again? His sensual lips curved, and she tore her gaze from them with an effort. His head dipped. If she was not marrying him, she should pull away, and yet… without volition, she swayed closer, relishing the heat radiating from his body. Her entire body softened as she breathed in his scent: a heady mixture of soap, fresh air and maleness.

He studied her, his expression serious.

Goodness, what must I look like? She really had not expected to meet anyone this early. She had splashed cold water on her face, pulled on the closest gown to hand and dragged a comb through her hair before roughly plaiting it, too preoccupied with her dilemma to worry about her appearance. How she wished it was possible to return to her childhood, when she had visited Cheriton Abbey and spent many carefree days exploring the grounds without a care as to how she looked.

The gentle sweep of Stanton's thumb beneath her eye broke into her thoughts.

'It appears I was not the only one who slept ill last night. What is it that troubles you? I can tell you are not overjoyed at the prospect of marrying me, but I confess I am at a loss to understand it. It seems to me we should make a successful partnership. We both, as I understand it, want children. Will you not confide in me about your doubts? I have no wish for a wife who feels she has been pressured into a union she actively dislikes.'

Her heart stuttered. 'It is not that I would dislike being married to you.' Far from it, if she was truthful. She recalled her words to her mother the night before. There was enough truth to sound believable. 'I have seen you enough times in London, sir. You are popular. You are always at the centre of attention. I specifically asked Mama to find a quiet, retiring gentleman for my husband.'

Stanton's brows drew together. 'Do you mean you wish to retire to the country entirely?'

'No. I enjoy country life, but I also enjoy spending time in London as I have interests there.

I take little pleasure in society balls and parties, however.'

'Then I see no reason why our union should not prove mutually beneficial, Felicity. I would never insist we live in each other's pockets, particularly once an heir is born. Many marriages are conducted in such a fashion, with discretion. I would be happy for our marriage to be the same.'

But I would not. Not with you.

She was so afraid she would grow to love him, particularly now, when he had shown such gentle—and unexpected—understanding. And his words—his expectations of their marriage merely reinforced her fears. She was to be used as a vessel to produce an heir. And, without doubt, a spare. Like a brood mare. None of which she really objected to. Indeed, it was what she wanted: a quiet husband to live on the periphery of her life. But Stanton was not, and never could be, he.

'What do you say, Felicity Joy? May I pay my addresses to you? I should like to propose in the customary manner—and to hear your reply—and not just drift into an understanding.'

Chapter Seven

Felicity bit her lip. She would regret her decision either way, but better to suffer disappointment now, and be done with it, than to live in lonely suffering and heartache for the rest of her days. She did, however, need to talk to her mother again first.

'I am sorry to be indecisive, but might I give you my answer later? I should like time to think about what you have said.'

Stanton stepped back and bowed. 'Of course you may. I would not for the world wish to rush you. It is a momentous decision.'

'Thank you. If you do not object, I shall return to the Abbey now. And I will give you my answer later this morning, if that will suit you?'

'Of course.'

Felicity walked back along the path through the trees. She rounded the bend, and her heart sank. Her stepfather, Quentin Farlowe, had just stepped through the gate into the copse. It was too late to turn back, for he saw her almost immediately.

'There you are, miss,' he called.

Felicity cursed under her breath. He strode towards her, frowning, his thin lips barely visible.

As he reached her she lifted her chin. 'I am on my way to see Mama. There was no need to search for me.'

'I disagree. You have worked your mother into the devil of a state. What can you possibly object to in Stanton?'

'I will discuss it with Mama and my guardian.'

Farlowe's fingers bit into her arm. 'We will settle this now. I will not have your mother upset.'

No, of course you won't. No doubt it disturbed your sleep. How Felicity longed to throw those words at her stepfather, but she refused to stoop so low. 'I have no wish to upset Mama either. I am sure we will reach some accord.'

He dragged her close, glaring down at her through narrowed eyes. Felicity coughed as a wave of Farlowe's pungent hair oil pervaded her nostrils. The sickly smell contrasted sharply with Stanton's fresh, spicy scent.

'You've been a thorn in my side ever since I married your mother, looking down your nose at me. Why do you not want Stanton?' He bent his head close to hers, his breath hot against her skin as he whispered in her ear. 'Is he too much the man for you, miss? Are you scared of your wedding night? Mayhap I can be of assistance? Provide a little tutoring so you will not—'

'Let me go!' Felicity struggled against his

viselike grip on her arm. 'When Mama hears what you—'

Farlowe laughed. 'But she won't find out, will she? You forget—I know you, *Lady* Felicity. You won't say a word to your mama because you hate to upset anyone—'

'Farlowe!' Stanton's voice cut through the air like a whip.

Farlowe looked round, but did not release Felicity as Richard strode towards them, fury pounding his veins.

'Merely a familial misunderstanding, Stanton; nothing for you to concern yourself with.'

The rogue didn't even have the grace to look ashamed. Richard wondered what he had whispered to Felicity. Judging by her expression, he had not been sharing a friendly word of advice.

'Oh, but I am concerned, Farlowe. Anything that distresses Felicity distresses me. Take your hands from her.'

'We have not finished—'

'Yes, we have.' Felicity twisted her arm free. 'I told you, sir, that I will discuss the matter with my mother and the duke. They are my guardians, not you.'

Richard levelled a long look at Farlowe, who blanched. Good. The savage anger in his breast must be reflected in his expression. He would have dearly loved to draw the scoundrel's cork, but would not do so in front of Felicity. Next time they met, though, Mr Quentin Farlowe would have a few questions to answer.

Glancing at Felicity, Richard was struck once more by her forlorn expression. Much as he would like to place all the blame for her dejection at Farlowe's door, he could not deny she had been troubled even before the incident with her stepfather. Was Leo mistaken? Was a marriage of convenience not Felicity's choice, but at the instigation of her parents?

'Would you be so good as to escort me to my mother, Lord Stanton?'

'My pleasure, Lady Felicity.'

When she took his arm, Richard noticed she leant on it a little more heavily than before as they headed back to the Abbey.

'Are you quite well, Felicity? Farlowe…he looked a little rough back there.'

Felicity's fingers tightened on his sleeve. 'He is not a particularly nice man,' she said. 'It is one of the reasons I asked Mama to find me a husband.'

So it *was* her choice. Her doubts, then, were definitely about him.

'Your mama is happy with him, though? He is not…cruel in any way?'

The faintest of sighs murmured past his ears and he had to tilt his head to catch her words. 'No, not overtly cruel. But there is cruelty and there is cruelty.'

Richard pondered that statement. After half a minute, when he was no wiser, he said, 'I fear that statement is a little obscure for this early in the morning. What do you mean?'

Felicity's head snapped round, her eyes stricken. 'Oh,' she gasped, 'I am sorry, I had quite forgot…that is…what I mean is that Mama has high expectations of my stepfather. I do not think he has the character to meet those expectations. Does that make sense?'

'I suppose it does. Your mother, if you will forgive me for saying so, is a lady who would re-quire her husband to dance attendance on her. I surmise, from your explanation, that Farlowe does not view his role in quite the same way?'

'No, indeed. His role—in his opinion—is to live as high as possible, doing precisely what he wishes, with Mama's money. Oh! I do beg your pardon. That was most unbecoming in me… I'm afraid my stepfather brings out the very worst in me, despite my best intentions to let his shortcom-ings fly over my head without comment. Some-how—' she smiled, ruefully '—my basest nature seems to rear its head whenever he is involved. I think we shall never live comfortably together.'

'Which is why, as you say, you seek a hus-band. And, yet, you seem reluctant to accept my suit. I am beginning to feel quite deflated, Lady Felicity.'

'Oh, no.' She stopped walking and turned to Richard, her eyes big with concern. 'Please, no, I do not want you to think…to believe… Oh.' Her protestations ceased and her eyes narrowed. 'This is quite ridiculous as well you know, my lord. We both know very well that no other woman would view your suit with the slightest hesitation. The reasons for my indecision are…well, they are… Oh, I cannot say more than I have already. You said you would wait for my answer until later this morning, and I must ask you to honour that.

'Thank you for your escort. I shall be quite safe from here.'

Richard stood at the bottom of the main staircase, watching as Felicity climbed the sweep to the next floor.

'Good morning, Stan. Enjoying the morning air with your betrothed?'

Richard did not turn to look at Leo. 'I am not sure "enjoying" is quite the right word, Leo. And neither, if I read the lady correctly, is "betrothed". I must confess to a certain bemusement. Lady Felicity—if I have understood our, at times, quite muddled conversation correctly—is about to turn me down flat.'

Chapter Eight

'Now hear this, young lady, and hear it well.'

Lady Katherine stalked up and down her bed-chamber, gesticulating. Until this very minute, Felicity had not dreamed she might fail in her attempt to avoid marriage to Lord Stanton. She sank onto a chair by the window, her legs unaccountably shaky, as her mother continued to pace.

'You asked me to find you a husband.'

'Yes, that is true, but—'

'No buts. I have found you an eminently eligible man, one who must be far beyond anyone you could have hoped for.'

'Yes, but—'

Her mother quelled her with one look. A feeling of unreality washed over Felicity. This determination in her normally persuadable mother was new, and she knew who to thank for it. *Why, oh, why did Mama marry that man?*

'I have spoken with the duke this morning— yes, already, at this unearthly hour—and he has confirmed his belief that you and Stanton will suit. He knows you both. He will hardly match one of his closest friends with someone unsuitable.'

'I do not believe Stanton and I will be compatible, Mama.'

'I have discussed this with Farlowe…'

Felicity sprang to her feet. 'I might have known *he* was—'

Her mother continued as though Felicity had not spoken. '…and we are agreed. You have a choice.'

'A choice?' Felicity stared at her mother, hope stirring. 'Who?'

'Not who. What. Our conversation last night left me vastly unsettled, Felicity, and I was still awake when my dear Farlowe retired. I told him of your stubbornness, and he suggested—'

'Did I hear my name mentioned?'

'Farlowe. My darling. Such a valiant but wasted effort on your part, searching for this wretched girl. But no matter, for she is here now, and I am about to reveal her options.'

Felicity caught Farlowe's smirk. Cold sweat prickled over her back. He wanted her out of their lives as much as she did. What was her mother's alternative? A nunnery?

Oh, please. We are not living in the pages of a Gothic novel. 'Very well, Mama. What is my alternative?'

'You said you wanted a family and we have found you a perfectly eligible suitor. You either accept Stanton or you will never wed. You will end your days living with us as my companion and, after I have gone, you must depend on the charity of your dear brother. You will forever be the poor relation.'

Felicity's knees threatened to buckle. She grabbed the back of a chair.

'You cannot prevent me finding a husband of my own,' she said.

'And you have proven yourself oh-so-successful in that endeavour to date, have you not, Felicity?' Farlowe said. 'And do not think you will be permitted to squander good money on those urchins and thieves you are so fond of. You will have no need of such a generous allowance as your mother's companion.'

She could not win. In order to find herself a husband, she would have to allow herself to be courted. She must risk her heart whichever way she chose. The alternative: remaining with her mother and Farlowe—to have to endure his leers and his constant crude remarks about virgins— was simply intolerable. And she would not even have the release of involvement with Westfield.

She must capitulate. Her choice was, in reality, no choice. But she would move mountains in order to protect her heart. On one thing she was adamant: she must *never* fall in love with Lord Stanton.

Richard turned from his contemplation of the portrait hung over the mantel and watched Felicity approach.

'Lady Felicity. I am honoured you have consented to hear my address.'

He scanned her features. She looked no more enthusiastic than she had earlier. Her eyes refused to meet his as she curtsied.

'The honour is all mine, my lord.'

Richard gave himself leave to doubt that. The hopeless resignation in her voice matched her whole demeanour. He felt a scowl crease his brow and hastily smoothed it away. Not that she'd noticed; her eyes were fixed on a point somewhere beyond his right ear.

Why not end this farce now? There are plenty of girls available who would swoon at the idea of marrying you. Why tie yourself to a woman who doesn't want you? Haven't you experienced enough rejection from your own mother?

Was it the challenge? Part of his determination to marry Felicity was precisely *because* of her indifference. The other part... In his mind's eye, he saw Felicity struggling against Farlowe's grip. Could he really abandon her to life with that rogue?

She was well born, compliant and desirous of a family. Leo was convinced they would suit one another and Dominic—Leo's twenty-year-old son and heir, who had arrived home earlier that afternoon—had even sung Felicity's praises, assuring Richard there was more to her than might be apparent on the surface.

He thrust aside his doubts. There would be time enough once they were wed to discover what she feared. She would not be here if she was completely averse to him personally. Would she?

He took Felicity's hands: fragile, the bones delicate in his grasp, the skin chilled. He felt a tremor wash through her, and squeezed reassuringly. Whatever her doubts, she was not shy, she had proved an entertaining conversationalist, and the way she had returned his kiss suggested she would be neither afraid nor reluctant to explore the physical side of marriage. That kiss! His loins stirred as his gaze dropped to her mouth without volition. He studied her full, shapely lips. She was not as insipid as he had first thought—Leo was right, she merely did not show to advantage beside her mother. She had a neat figure and her smile was infectious, lighting her whole face.

He was sure this marriage was the right decision for him, and that he and Felicity would rub along well together. His life was full and satisfying. He boasted a wide circle of like-minded friends with whom he shared an interest in a variety of sports. And, once he was wed, his mother would remove to the Lodge and he would happily spend more of his time at Fernley attending to the estate.

What he was less certain of was if it was the right decision for Felicity, standing quietly, her hands limp in his. Richard focused on her.

'Lady Felicity, would you do me the very great honour of accepting my hand in marriage?'

Her features appeared carved out of rock. Not even an eyelash flickered.

'Yes. Thank you.'

Her voice was as colourless as her complexion. His jaw clenched. He moved closer. She stepped back. He tightened his grip and tugged until her body was pressed full length against his. Another tremor ran through her as he wrapped one arm around her waist. But she did not look away. She held his gaze as he lowered his lips to hers.

Her lips were sweet and soft and relaxed as he kissed her and they opened readily enough. She allowed him to explore her mouth but she made no attempt to kiss him in return. She merely permitted the kiss. Dissatisfied, Richard was about to tear his lips from hers when he registered her tension. It was as though he held a statue in his embrace. Despite his earlier thoughts, he wondered if she was, after all, wary of the intimate side of marriage.

'Relax,' he whispered against her lips. 'This is meant to be enjoyable.'

He feathered butterfly-light kisses over her cheeks, her brows, along her jaw then nudged her head to one side to nibble at her earlobe. Suddenly, she exhaled with a *whoosh*, and the long rigid muscles down her back softened under his hands. Her body relaxed against his and she lifted her hands to his chest and pushed.

'I am sorry. This is hard for me. I wonder… might we wait until after we are married? Someone might come in.'

'We are newly betrothed, Felicity. We should be allowed a celebratory kiss, do you not think?'

Again, her expression eluded him as she wiped her hands down her skirts. Nerves? He would give much to understand what was going through her mind right now.

'Very well,' he said. 'We will wait until after the wedding. Speaking of which, I am minded to wed as soon as possible, if that is agreeable to you?'

He quashed the thought he was being unfair. He couldn't escape the feeling that, if given time, Felicity would renege on her acceptance, and he was suddenly determined not to afford her the opportunity.

'If you return to Bath tomorrow, I shall call in the Bishop's Office at Wells on my way through and procure a Common Licence. We will not then have to wait for the banns to be read, and we could marry by the end of the week.' His sense of fair play intervened, forcing him to add, with reluctance, 'Or do you need more time to prepare?'

Felicity straightened. 'No. That will not be necessary.' Finally, there was a hint of conviction in her tone. 'I shall go and inform Mama of our plans. Thank you for understanding,'

Understanding? Richard wasn't sure he understood anything about his bride-to-be.

Chapter Nine

'My lords, ladies and gentlemen.'

The hubbub of conversation faded as the assembled guests turned their attention to the plinth set up at one end of the huge ballroom to accommodate the musicians. That evening had seen the surrounding families invited to Cheriton Abbey for a ball. Felicity had dressed, with a little more attention to her appearance than usual, in her favourite evening gown of primrose silk, knowing all eyes would be on her at some point during the evening.

The duke stood impassively on the plinth, awaiting the undivided attention of his guests whilst Stanton cupped Felicity's elbow and guided her to the front and side of the throng. Despite her fears, Felicity could not suppress a *frisson* of excitement at the thought of marrying such a man. He was in his element, here in the ballroom. It was unfortunate she was not.

Her mouth dried as Cousin Leo began to speak

and heads turned in her direction. Her lips clung to her teeth, foiling her attempt to smile.

'You might at least attempt to look happy.'

Stanton's breath scorched her ear. Felicity inhaled, his spicy male scent pervading every cell of her body. She pushed her thick tongue between her lips and her teeth in an attempt to moisten them. She was vaguely aware of a murmured exchange between Stanton and Cousin Cecily, who stood nearby. A glass was thrust into her hand.

'Here. Take a sip. It will help.' A large hand settled—comfortingly—at the small of her back, its heat penetrating the delicate silk of her dress, warming her even as a shiver of awareness snaked down her spine.

She registered only an occasional word of Cousin Leo's speech as she sipped the punch. She glanced sideways at Stanton and smiled her thanks just as Cousin Leo said, 'I am sure you will all join me in wishing them every happiness in their life together.'

A low hum swept the room and then people were surrounding them, smiling, congratulating, shaking Stanton by the hand but also eyeing Felicity: speculating, slightly incredulous. She stood tall, steadying her nerves, aware this was but a tiny taste of the attention she would experience in London. She had a choice to make; a choice that might inform the future of this union with Stanton.

She could either shrivel or she could bloom.

She inhaled, braced her shoulders and curved

her lips as she responded to their many well-wishers, grateful for the comforting presence of Stanton by her side, deflecting much of the attention away from her, protecting her, until people were distracted by the musicians tuning their instruments.

'Well, Fliss. It's official now. You are to be a married lady.' Felicity spun round in delighted response to the familiar voice in her ear.

'Dominic! I did not see you there.' She lowered her voice. 'It still feels unreal. I never wanted to marry...oh! I dare say I should not have said that.' She glanced round apprehensively.

Stanton, engaged in conversation with Cecily, appeared not to have heard.

Dominic, Lord Avon, laughed. He was a younger version of his father: tall, elegant and suave with the same black hair and silver-grey eyes. 'Well, I think it will be the making of you.' He raised his voice. 'Congratulations, Stan. Mind you take care of my favourite cousin.'

'Oh, I will,' Stanton said as they shook hands.

'Have you come down from London, Dom?' Felicity asked. 'It is such an age since I was there. Tell me, how do they go on at Westfield?'

'What, and where, is Westfield?' Stanton enquired.

Felicity's mother and stepfather joined the group at that moment and, hearing Stanton's question, Lady Katherine immediately claimed his attention.

'Oh, it is merely some nonsense of Felicity's,

Stanton. Nothing for you to concern yourself with for I am persuaded Felicity will have vastly more important matters to occupy her once she is married.'

Before Felicity could respond, Stanton said, 'You may indeed be confident of Felicity's future preferences, my lady—and I bow to your superior knowledge of your daughter —but I do find in myself a desire to know what Felicity has to say on the subject.'

His voice held the perfect hint of apology, and Felicity could not be quite sure if he had just delivered a most elegant setdown to her mother. As she pondered, he glanced at her and she caught the devilish glint in his eye. She pursed her lips, trying to suppress the laugh that bubbled in her chest.

'My dear, would you care to enlighten me?' Stanton's voice and expression were suitably grave as he tilted his head and raised a brow. 'I asked you about Westfield, if you recall.'

'It is a haven for thieves and pickpockets,' Farlowe interjected. 'That is what it is. A waste of good money. It shouldn't be allowed, that's what I say.'

Her stepfather had never struck Felicity as a perceptive man, and now he sank to new depths in her estimation. How could the man be so blithely oblivious to Stanton's scowl?

'It is my allowance, sir, and I spend it how I please,' she said.

'Felicity! Do not put dear Farlowe down in that

unbecoming manner. Why, whatever will Stanton think—'

'Stanton,' interrupted a silky-smooth voice, 'thinks his future wife has her own opinion and should be allowed to voice it without interruption.'

'Oh, good man, Stan. Well said,' Dominic said, laughing.

'Dominic—' Cecily grabbed her nephew's arm '—the dancing is about to start. Would you be so good as to stand up with your elderly aunt for the first?'

'Oh, transparent, dear aunt. Come then, let us leave the newly betrothed and their relatives to play at happy families.'

Cecily led Dominic away and Felicity breathed easier, knowing he was more than capable of adding further fuel to an already fraught situation.

'Westfield—' she turned to Stanton '—is an asylum in Islington for orphans and destitute children. I've supported it for five years, and Dominic became involved about a year ago.'

'And will you tell Stanton where you find these *orphans* and *destitutes*?' Farlowe's voice rose in anger. 'The criminals you willingly consort with?

'I tried to talk some sense into her, Stanton, I promise you, but the provoking girl would not listen to me. Mayhap you will have more success in curbing her wayward tendencies.'

'Wayward tendencies?' Dark brown eyes turned to Felicity, appraising her. Heat washed over her skin. He bent his head, his lips close to her ear. 'I am intrigued, Felicity Joy. Positively intrigued.'

Felicity suppressed her tremor as the small hairs on the back of her neck stood on end, swallowing past the sudden constriction in her throat.

'They are children.' She struggled to keep her attention on Farlowe, 'They cannot help the things they must do to survive.'

'Pshaw!'

'Well, what would you do, Mr Farlowe, if you were starving?' Felicity's customary caution vanished. 'Might you not be tempted to steal a loaf of bread? Or pick a coin from someone's pocket?'

Farlowe bristled. 'Might I remind you, miss—'

'Come, my darling.' Lady Katherine, after one look at Stanton, tugged at Farlowe's arm. 'Let us dance.' She pouted and cajoled and finally succeeded in dragging her husband to join a reel forming in the centre of the room.

Felicity's heart sank. Why on earth had she risen to Farlowe's provocation? She glanced up at Stanton. Would he be appalled by her lapse in manners? He was staring after his future parents-in-law, his expression a study in perplexity. He switched his attention to her and raised one dark brow.

'Thieves and pickpockets, Felicity Joy?' One corner of his mouth quirked up. 'Might I enquire what other dens of iniquity you frequent?'

Chapter Ten

He was neither appalled nor, it seemed, dismayed that Felicity had argued with Farlowe. It appeared he was diverted.

Felicity swallowed her giggle. 'Do not tease me, Stanton, I beg of you.'

She could cope with Stanton in this playful mood. But when his voice deepened, and his eyes fixed on her in that particular way…intense…the heat of promise swirling in their depths…another shiver caressed her skin as her insides looped in a most peculiar way. She willed her voice not to tremble.

'Did you ever hear such nonsense? What infuriates my dear step-papa, of course, are the donations I make to the school. He even, would you believe, suggested I should pay him rent for living under his roof instead of contributing to the living costs of the children.'

'His roof?'

'Indeed. As soon as he and Mama wed he made

it very clear to me upon whom my future depended. Which is why—'

'Which is why you are willing to marry me?' Stanton looked around the ballroom, then grabbed Felicity's hand. 'Come. Let us go somewhere quieter. I am curious to discover something of those wayward tendencies your mama warned me about.'

Felicity's insides swooped again but the thought of being alone with Stanton made her hang back. She wasn't ready. She needed to harden her heart against him, prepare herself for the intimacies to come. He stopped and looked round. Studied her face, then smiled, his eyes crinkling as he shook his head.

'Felicity Joy, whatever am I to do with you? Come. Shall we dance?' He sketched a bow and, at her nod, led her to join a nearby set.

The energetic country dance afforded them scant opportunity or, indeed, breath to talk further and it was not until supper that they continued their conversation. The other guests—in a rare show of consideration—allowed the newly betrothed couple to eat their food in relative privacy.

'We have much to discuss.' Stanton deposited a plate piled high with food in front of Felicity.

'I find I am not very hungry, sir,' Felicity said, her stomach clenching at the sight and smell of the food. 'What do you wish to discuss?'

'The wedding itself is in hand. Leo and I

met with your mother and Farlowe earlier and it has been agreed the wedding will take place on Thursday morning, as long as the rector is available to perform the ceremony. Will that give you enough time to prepare? Your mother was anxious about your dress.'

'I have a suitable dress I can wear, my lord.'

'Good. Farlowe has undertaken to speak to the rector as soon as you arrive home tomorrow and, as I already told you, I shall call on the Bishop of Bath and Wells to procure the licence on my way to Bath. As long as the rector has some spare time before noon on Thursday there is no reason why we cannot be married on that day. If not, we shall have to wait until we can be fitted in.'

It all sounds so businesslike and unromantic.

Of course it is, you fool. It is an arranged marriage. Sentiment and romance do not come into it.

She buried any hint of regret deep inside. She did not want love. It was her decision. Love hurt. Love destroyed. She watched as Stanton played with his wine glass, his long fingers stroking the stem. Was he not quite as composed as she imagined? He must be like granite if he did not feel some emotion. Marriage, even a marriage of convenience, was not to be entered into lightly.

And yet, here they were, two virtual strangers, planning their wedding. She gazed around the room. The chatter of the other guests intruded, dispersing the haze of unreality that had enveloped her.

'Will you tell me more about Westfield? How did you become involved in such a place?'

She tensed. Would he disapprove? His question reminded her of the power this man would wield over her. He was, surely, more open-minded and charitable than Farlowe? She gripped her hands in her lap.

'It was established by my childhood friend, Jane Whittaker, and her husband, Peter, who is a schoolmaster. Jane inherited a large house and some money from her great-aunt, and they set up a school to help the children of the poor better themselves.'

'It is a school, then.'

'That was the original intention, but Mr Whittaker's brother is a magistrate and he told them how many orphans were brought up before him, so they decided to provide a home for orphans too. The children are taught their letters and numbers and, as they get older, we find them placements with tradespeople and in households, where they are trained to become useful members of society.'

'Which trades?'

There was no denying the genuine interest in his voice.

'Any and every trade you may imagine. Shoemakers, coopers, butchers, tailors, milliners—we try to match the child to some trade they have an interest in or aptitude for. That, I must confess, is where both Dominic and I can help, as well as collecting donations, of course. We can be most persuasive. We seldom meet with a flat refusal to take a child.'

'I was astonished to hear of Avon's involvement.'

'He was very young when his mother died and that experience nurtured in him a kinship, of sorts, with children who are orphaned. However painful his loss, how much worse would it be to lose both parents and to have no family or wealth or position to fall back on? When he heard about Westfield, he was eager to help.'

Felicity paused, studying Stanton's expression. She might as well tackle the subject now. It would ease at least one of her worries.

As if he could read her mind, Stanton said, 'I should like to visit this place with you, after we are married, Felicity. And, in case you were worrying I might be of the same opinion as Farlowe, allow me to set your mind at rest. I shall not raise any objections to your involvement with Westfield, as long as you do not put yourself in any danger.'

Felicity's tension eased. 'Thank you.'

Chapter Eleven

On her wedding day Felicity rose early, unable to sleep despite the exhaustion of travelling up from Cheriton the day before. She sat by the window, mind and stomach churning with equal intensity.

The ceremony did not worry her. But the afterwards…the afterwards was the rest of her life. That did not merely worry her, it terrified her.

A tap at the door broke into her reverie and Beanie's familiar, smiling face, deep cracks fanning out from the corners of her faded brown eyes, appeared.

'You are awake,' she said, shuffling into the room, followed by the kitchen maid carrying a tray. 'I said you would be. There you are, Nell, put the tray down and off you go. Did you manage to get any sleep, my lamb?'

Felicity's throat tightened at the familiar endearment. How would she manage without Beanie? She had raised Felicity, been more of a mother to her than her own had ever been. And the other servants were like members of her family.

'Are you sure you won't come with me…us, Beanie?'

'Bless you, dear. If only I was ten years younger. But I am too old now to get used to a new home and fresh faces and strange ways of going on. I am content here in Sydney Place. I shall miss you but at least it will oblige you to take on a trained lady's maid at last.'

'Oh, Beanie, as if I care for that. You know I would much prefer you. Do not forget, I shall be in an unfamiliar place full of strangers, too.'

'Ah, but you will be the mistress. And you will have your new husband by your side. And you are young. No, my lamb, I will not change my mind, but I shall enjoy seeing you when you visit. Come now, drink your chocolate and try to eat some bread and butter.'

Felicity picked up the cup of chocolate and wrapped her hands around it. 'This will be enough. I cannot face—'

'Or I've brought up a slice of Cook's apple cake, if that might tempt your appetite?' Beanie picked up the plate and followed Felicity to her chair by the hearth. 'I know you, Lady Felicity. At the first hurdle, your appetite flies away with the fairies. You must eat something. You do not want your stomach gurgling in the church because you haven't eaten, do you?'

Felicity burst into laughter. 'Oh, Beanie, I am going to miss you. Gurgling stomach, indeed.'

But she did as she was bid and, after sipping the warm chocolate, she nibbled on the cake and the hollow swooping inside eased to a flutter. Not perfect, but better.

After Felicity bathed and dried her hair by the fire, Beanie helped her to dress. Her gown was of fine white muslin and she would wear a lace-trimmed cap on her head. Her delicate silk shawl, white shot with primrose, and a pair of dainty primrose slippers, would complete the ensemble.

'You look lovely, my dove.'

Later, after Beanie had dressed her hair, Felicity stood before her mirror scarcely able to believe what was happening. She…Felicity…always the plain, overlooked member of the family…was about to wed society's most eligible and desirable bachelor. She pinched at her cheeks to bring some colour to her face. That was better. She tried a smile. Better still. As long as she did not forget to smile, she could at least look attractive for her wedding, and for Stanton.

'Darling.'

Felicity started. She hadn't heard her mother come in, so lost in her thoughts had she been.

'Let me look at you.'

At Lady Katherine's prompting, Felicity twirled a circle.

'You look very well, my dear. Oh, to think of it. Lady Stanton. I never dared to believe you would make such a match, Felicity. Now, if had been Emma…' Her voiced faded into silence and she sighed before continuing in a determinedly bright tone: 'Still, it is your future we must look forward to now, dearest. Except…' She moved closer and began to fiddle with Felicity's hair. 'Oh, dear, I knew I should have sent Wilkins to you but, as dear Farlowe said, who then would have helped with *my toilette*? It is important I should look at my best, as mother of the bride. We do not want Stanton to think he is marrying into a family of peasants, do we?'

Felicity stepped back, out of the reach of her mother's fidgety fingers. 'Please, Mama, do not fret about my hair.'

'Oh, you have ever been a tiresome girl, Felicity. Tiresome and stubborn. Now, the carriage will be outside in twenty minutes—darling Farlowe bespoke it last night after he saw the rector. What a truly attentive and selfless stepfather he has been to you, has he not?' She paused, regarding Felicity with raised brow.

'Indeed, Mama.'

Words cost nothing, particularly as she would no longer reside under the same roof as Farlowe. That was reason enough for the step she was about to take. She was rewarded with a glorious smile.

'Mama, there is something…before we go. Tonight…' Felicity hesitated, feeling her cheeks glow. She had never spoken on such intimate subjects with her mother before. 'Tonight…what will it be like? What should I do?'

'*Do?*' Lady Katherine's cheeks grew pink.

'Why, Felicity, I cannot believe you wish to discuss such matters with me. It is for your husband to instruct you. Do as he says and, remember, it is your duty to please your husband at all times in such matters. That is all you need to know.'

Richard sat in the front pew of the Abbey Church next to Leo. The rector was searching through the Bible on the lectern, the sound of shuffling pages loud in the near-empty church.

Richard reviewed the messages he would send the minute their nuptials were complete. The *Bath Chronicle* and *The Times* would publish formal announcements and he had written letters ready to be taken by courier to his mother at Fernley Park and to the London address of his heir, his distant cousin, Charles Durant.

He had also penned a more personal letter to his mistress of the past six months, Harriet, Lady Brierley. Harriet's image formed in his mind's eye—soft, voluptuous, enticing—and a pang of regret speared him at the knowledge he would never again… He cursed silently, then cast a guilty look at the rector. Thinking about his mistress on the morning of his wedding was bad enough but blasphemous thoughts in church…? He offered a silent apology to God and vowed to exercise tighter control over his thoughts.

His letter to Harriet, besides informing her of his marriage, had ended their *affaire*. The impulse to walk away surprised him—had he not deliberately sought a marriage of convenience in order not to change his life? Harriet was discreet and their *affaire* was not common knowledge but still he had felt honour-bound to end it out of respect for Felicity. He consoled himself with the thought he could always take another mistress in the future, once his heir was born.

'You are quiet.' Leo's voice dragged him from his thoughts.

'Merely ensuring I have not forgotten anything,' Richard replied. 'Announcements and so forth.'

'You are still minded to leave for Fernley Park immediately after the ceremony?'

'I am. I apologize for the lack of a wedding breakfast, but the thought of accepting Farlowe's hospitality...' Richard shuddered.

'Indeed. And it would be a poor start if you knocked your new father-in-law senseless before the ink is dry on the register, would it not? Do you intend to travel all the way home today?'

'I do. I want our first night as a married couple to be under my...our...roof. I have no wish to spend our wedding night in some inn by the wayside.'

'You will both be exhausted by the time you arrive, after travelling all day yesterday as well.'

The bells began to strike the hour and the door at the back of the church creaked open to admit Lady Katherine. She wafted down the aisle, alternately smiling and tearful, flourishing a delicate, lace-edged scrap of a handkerchief with which she dabbed at her eyes. As she settled in the pew opposite his, Richard bent his head, concentrating on his hands, clenched into fists between his knees. The fuss and the flutter eventually subsided and he looked up in time to see the rector signal to someone at the back of the church.

This is it.

His insides quaked in an unfamiliar way and he experienced a sudden urge to flee which he quashed ruthlessly. He was doing the right thing for all the right reasons.

'Nervous?' Leo's whisper was accompanied by a steady hand on his shoulder.

'No.'

He stood up and turned to watch his bride glide down the aisle on her stepfather's arm. His breathing—which only now did he realize had quickened—steadied and slowed. As Felicity neared, her attention fixed firmly on the rector, Richard recognized that his brief attack of nerves must be as nothing compared with hers. He willed her to look at him and was rewarded when, only a few feet away, she did.

Her eyes were shadowed, and her lips compressed. Doubt emanated from her and Richard's own doubts re-emerged. If the match was so distasteful, why was she here?

And yet…and yet…he recalled their conversations; their kiss. She was not indifferent to him. She wanted—she had said as much—to wed, and to get away from her stepfather. He would make sure she did not regret their union. She was to be his wife.

His. To have and to hold. He would protect her, and care for her.

He would fulfil his part of the bargain.

He reached for her hand, to reassure her. She flashed a grateful smile, transforming her face, and his own nerves settled. Her fingers twitched within his grasp, then curled around the edge of his palm. As one, they turned to face the rector.

Chapter Twelve

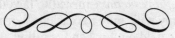

A small crowd gathered around the three carriages as they lined up outside the Abbey. Richard and Felicity emerged to a muted cheer, followed by a swell of speculation as Felicity's name was passed from onlooker to onlooker. The crowd pressed closer, and Richard heard Leo's name mentioned, followed by his own as the speculation got louder.

Leo, Lady Katherine and Mr Farlowe were close behind them, followed by the few friends and servants who had been in the church to witness their wedding.

'How handsome you looked, walking down the aisle, Farlowe.' Lady Katherine's voice rang out. 'And you, dearest Felicity, you looked very nice, as you came into the church. It is a shame you were seen to such disadvantage next to your stepfather, do you not agree, Stanton?'

'My love, I beg of you,' Farlowe interjected hastily. Richard had caught the man's eye and glared at him with such intent that Farlowe had paled. 'This is Felicity's day—'

'Oh, Felicity is used to me running on, aren't you, darling? She isn't a girl to take offence.'

'I take offence,' Richard said quietly. *Blast the woman. Why must she continually undermine Felicity? She clearly believes the only characteristic of any virtue is beauty.* 'If you will excuse us, my wife and I have a long journey ahead of us.' He held out his hand, smiling at Felicity. 'Come, my dear.'

Felicity shot Richard such a furious look, he stared. Did she not want him—her husband—to speak out and protect her? A glance at Leo only elicited a resigned shrug.

'She is my mother. She loves me in her own way,' Felicity hissed before turning to her mother, who rushed to embrace her.

'Oh, Felicity, I did not mean anything by it, you know I did not. You know how I rattle on sometimes. I shall miss you so much, my darling.' Lady Katherine's eyes brimmed with tears as she flung her arms around her daughter.

'And I shall miss you too, Mama.' Felicity's voice was thick with emotion.

Not for the first time Richard realized that his upbringing, and his current relationship with his mother, had ill prepared him to understand the subtleties of other people's families. He only had to think of Leo's large, boisterous brood to comprehend what he had missed in his childhood. Mayhap Richard could learn something of family from his new bride, and top of that list appeared to be forgiveness. Richard vowed that, as his wife, Felicity would get all the support and kindness she deserved. Then his own children would grow up secure and happy in a contented household such as every child surely deserved.

Felicity said her goodbyes to the rest of the congregation, speaking to each one in turn. The last, an elderly, stooped lady, got a hug and a kiss.

'Stanton?' Felicity beckoned him.

Richard felt his brows contract. Stanton? She should call him Richard. Everyone else called him Stanton.

An uncertain expression crossed Felicity's face and Richard smiled, to show her he was not annoyed. How little they knew of each other—negotiating their relationship at the moment was akin to walking over swampy ground, not knowing where the soft, treacherous patches might lie. He must be more mindful, pick his way more carefully, until he knew her better.

'Yes, my dear?'

'May I present Miss Bean? She was our governess and, since we all grew up, she has shouldered the thankless task of being my maid.'

'Oh, nonsense, Lady Felicity; I mean, Lady Stanton,' the old lady quavered. 'You are the least demanding person I know.' Her eyes were red and swollen; as she stared up at him, Richard recognized the milky cast that spoke of failing sight.

He clasped her outstretched hand. 'I am

pleased to meet you,' he said, and was rewarded by a grateful smile from Felicity.

'You see, Beanie? He is quite normal, and I shall be quite safe with him.'

A tear tracked down Beanie's cheek as she clasped Felicity's face between her gnarled hands and kissed her on the cheek.

'Goodbye, my dove.'

On the brink of mounting the steps into the carriage, Felicity turned to her mother. 'Mama, promise me you will take care of Beanie.'

'Why, Felicity, of course I shall. Hurry along, now. Whatever will Stanton think of you, keeping him waiting over your maid's welfare?'

Richard thought, but did not say, that he was rather proud of his new wife for caring for the elderly woman. He handed Felicity into the carriage, and climbed in behind her, after shaking Leo's hand. They waved, and soon left the City of Bath behind.

After a few lacklustre attempts at conversation, Felicity said, 'I do apologize, Stanton, but...'

'Richard,' he said.

A rueful smile crossed her face. 'Ever since my come-out I have known of you as Stanton. I fear it will take me some time to get used to calling you Richard, but I assure you I do not intend any slight if I forget once in a while.'

'In that case, I shall promise not to feel slighted. What were you about to say?'

We are as two strangers, the politeness in the way we converse, the way we glance at each other and look away as if fearful of catching the other's eye.

'I was about to say I am so weary I fear I shall be quite unable to keep up my end of any conversation. Would you think me dreadfully rag-mannered if I try to sleep?'

'Not at all. We shall stop for refreshments at the Old George at Salisbury. I shall wake you then.'

He was, if anything, relieved. He settled in the corner of the carriage, then beckoned. Her eyes rounded.

'You will be perfectly safe, Lady Stanton. I am not about to ravish you in a moving carriage, no matter how well sprung.'

Felicity's lips twitched. 'Such a relief.'

'Come, sit here, next to me. You can rest your head on my shoulder. It will be more comfortable.'

A slight hesitation, then she shifted along until their thighs touched. Richard put his arm around her shoulders, manoeuvring her until she was leaning against him. Several minutes passed.

'You can relax, Felicity Joy. I shall do nothing other than hold you, you have my word.'

A few more minutes and then a quiet huff of breath, followed by the softening of the wooden figure next to him indicated that she had, at last, relaxed.

After several weary hours and only one brief stop after Salisbury, other than to change the horses, the carriage drew to a halt. Richard stirred, biting back a groan as pins and needles coursed through his arm. He peered through the window. Fernley Park. Stiff muscles forgotten, he disentangled his arm from Felicity and eased her upright.

'Welcome to your new home, Lady Stanton.'

'What? I mean, I beg your pardon?' Her voice was muffled and, from what he could see of her face in the dim light cast by the oil lamps either side of the steps leading up to the front door, she looked bleary-eyed.

'We are home,' he repeated. 'Fernley Park.'

'Home?' She straightened and her hands flew to her head, patting at her hair. 'Where is my bonnet?' Felicity's bonnet, and a warm cloak, had been placed in the carriage before their wedding, ready for their journey.

Biting back a grin at her agitation, Richard grabbed the bonnet from the opposite seat.

'Allow me,' he said, and she sat obediently whilst he pinned the hat on to her head and tucked stray hairs neatly away.

The carriage door opened. Beyond the coachman, Richard could see Trick silhouetted in the front entrance. He climbed out of the carriage, stretched, then turned to hand down his wife.

His wife. How strange that sounded.

'Trick, this is your new mistress, Lady Stanton. My dear, this is Trick, the butler.'

'Good evening, Trick,' Felicity said with a smile.

'Good evening, milord, milady. I trust you had a pleasant journey.

Richard laughed. '"Pleasant" is not quite the word I should choose, but it was uneventful.'

'Which is all one can hope for,' Felicity commented as she entered the hall and gazed around.

'Indeed.' Richard eyed his bride. It was their wedding night. She looked exhausted and he felt no less fatigued. 'Is my mother in the salon?'

'Yes, milord.' Trick crossed the foyer and entered the salon. Richard led Felicity in his wake. 'His lordship and Lady Stanton have arrived, milady.'

His mother, impeccably dressed as always, stood to greet them, poker straight, unsmiling. Richard silently mocked himself for daring to hope his marriage might have softened her; might have, somehow, bridged the chasm that had yawned between them ever since his father's death. She had never been a relaxed and loving parent—a result of her strict upbringing—but neither had she been this aloof.

How had they become virtual strangers?

'Stanton. You are home.'

His mother scrutinized Felicity from head to toe and Richard knew, with a sinking certainty, she would find much to disapprove of in his actual marriage, despite her constant nagging at him to wed.

As Felicity's fingers tightened on his, the familiar, complicated muddle of emotions he always experienced in his mother's presence continued to churn deep in his gut.

Chapter Thirteen

Felicity battled her fatigue, sensing this first meeting with her mother-in-law could be crucial to their future relationship. Lady Stanton, tall and slim, her steel-grey hair scraped back from her face, stood erect and unsmiling, her eyes raking Felicity. Determined not to be intimidated, Felicity squared her shoulders and lifted her chin.

'Mother, I should like to present to you my wife, Felicity. Felicity, this is my mother, Lady Stanton.'

Felicity curtsied and smiled. 'I am pleased to meet you, my lady.'

'You may address me as Mother.' No words of welcome. No congratulations. No smile. 'You had better sit down.'

Mother! Something close to hysteria bubbled and swirled inside and Felicity clamped her teeth shut lest it escape. Richard squeezed her hand, and she steadied. Was her mother-in-law really so indifferent to her son's marriage? Cousin Leo had suggested Lady Stanton would be delighted her son had finally wed, but the reality appeared somewhat different.

'We have come to pay our respects, Mother. Felicity is exhausted and will retire immediately. There will be time tomorrow for better acquaintance.'

Felicity stared at Richard's clipped, formal tone. Why were they so awkward and formal with each other?

'Come along, my dear.'

Felicity resisted Richard's attempt to turn her around. Despite her tiredness, she had every intention of establishing her own relationship with her mother-in-law: she would not become a mere extension of her husband, with no opinions of her own.

She held the dowager's steely gaze. 'Goodnight, Mother,' she said. 'I apologize, but Richard is right. I am very tired and I am, I fear, incapable of conversing in anything approaching an intelligible manner tonight. Please forgive me.'

She then allowed Richard to escort her to the door.

'One moment.'

They paused. The dowager glided towards them. 'Stanton. There is a matter I wish to discuss, before you retire.'

'Of course, Mother. Allow me to ensure Felicity is cared for first.'

A kind-eyed, middle-aged woman awaited them in the hall.

'Mrs Jakeway, please take Lady Stanton to the Countess's suite. My dear, Mrs Jakeway is the housekeeper here.'

Mrs Jakeway bobbed a curtsy. 'Welcome to Stanton, my lady.'

Felicity smiled, murmuring her thanks.

'Your luggage arrived an hour since, milady, so it is all unpacked ready for you. Would you like a bite to eat in your room? Shall I ask Cook to send something up?'

Mrs Jakeway glanced at Richard as she spoke, and he said, 'I am sure her ladyship can manage a little something. Please do so.'

While Mrs Jakeway sent a message to the kitchen, Richard drew Felicity aside. She suddenly realized, with a resounding thump of her heart, that it was her wedding night and that this man could now visit her in her bed whenever he pleased. Her suddenly sensitive skin glowed, and her mouth was sucked dry as fear and anticipation swirled in a heady mix.

'Felicity?' Richard bent his knees, bringing his face level with hers. 'I will see you soon.' He held her gaze until she nodded her understanding. He smiled, lifted her hand and pressed warm lips against her skin.

As Felicity followed Mrs Jakeway up the long, curving sweep of the stairs, she glanced behind her. The dowager had joined Richard in the hall and they stood face to face, postures identically strained. They made no attempt to lower their voices.

'Where is her maid?'

'Indisposed.'

'Shocking! Jaunting around the countryside without a maid in attendance. Do you expect one of the household staff to fill the gap?'

'For a day or two only, Mother. I shall send to Winchester tomorrow to appoint a lady's maid. I am sure the house can spare one of the maids for so short a time.'

Felicity paused on the landing. It was wrong to eavesdrop, but they were being so indiscreet she had no compunction in listening to more.

'Lady Felicity Weston. Baverstock's daughter. And how old is she? Not in the first flush of youth, by the look of her.'

Her mother-in-law's voice dropped, but Felicity still caught some of her comments.

'…expected you to do better…dab of a girl… well bred, I suppose…'

'That is enough! You will kindly not criticize my wife, either to me or to anyone else.'

They disappeared inside the salon. Felicity joined Mrs Jakeway, waiting along the landing.

The Countess's bedchamber was spacious, decorated in restful shades of cream and blue, with tall, south-facing windows. The fireplace had a carved oak surround and the room was furnished with elegant rosewood furniture. The bed itself was massive, as wide as it was long, with posts at each corner, and a tester overhead, but no hangings to draw around for privacy and warmth as there would have been in earlier times. The bed dated, Mrs Jakeway informed Felicity, from the sixteenth century, and countless generations of Countesses of Stanton had slept there.

Two doors led from the bedchamber and Mrs Jakeway led her first to an adjoining sitting room with a chaise longue by one of the three windows and a sofa before the fire. There was a delicate escritoire, for correspondence, and a small round table with two chairs was set before the centre window.

'When the old master was alive, Lady Stanton spent much of her time up here,' Mrs Jakeway said.

'I do hope Lady Stanton was not obliged to vacate these rooms on my account?'

'Oh, no, milady. Don't you be fretting about that. Her ladyship moved out after the old master passed away, and insisted his lordship moved into his father's apartments immediately. He was barely seventeen, poor lad. It was…' The housekeeper clamped her lips shut. 'Come, I will show you the bathroom.'

She led the way across the bedchamber and through the other door into a small antechamber, dominated by a large bathtub, half-full of water. Steam gently curled into the air, scenting it with violets and a fire flamed in the grate, a wooden airer hung with towels nearby.

Felicity eyed the warm water longingly. 'Is that for me?'

'His lordship's orders,' Mrs Jakeway said. 'He sent word from Bath as to what time to expect you. The bed is aired and ready, however, if you prefer not to bathe tonight?'

'Oh, no, Mrs Jakeway, it is *just* what I need. Thank you for going to all this trouble. Could you send a maid to assist me, please? I'm afraid my own maid was unable to travel.'

'No need for that, milady. I shall help you tonight.'

Felicity was soon undressed and sank with muscle-soothing gratitude into the bath. She leaned her head back against the rim and closed her eyes, sighing with pleasure.

'My hair was washed this morning, Mrs Jakeway, so I can manage now, thank you.'

'Very well, milady.'

Felicity heard the door open and close again. Her mind drifted, veering away whenever her thoughts ranged near Richard and the coming night. She did not want to think. She simply wanted to be. She slipped a little lower into the water, every inch of her from the neck down bathed in scented heat. She felt underwater for the linen washcloth and spread it, sopping wet, across her face. If only she could remain here and if only the water would stay this warm. She breathed slowly and deliberately, the washcloth moving in time with her breaths. It was already cooling. Reluctantly, she reached for it and pulled it from her face.

A tap at the door behind her brought her crashing back to the here and now.

'Who is it?' *Please let it be Mrs Jakeway or one of the maids.*

'Would you like your back scrubbed, Felicity Joy?'

Her heart scrambled into her throat. Her arms thrashed, attempting to cover her nakedness, even though she knew he could see nothing.

Yet.

He had only to step a little further into the room. Her stomach churned as her flustered brain sought an escape, but there was no cover within reach.

Nothing.

Chapter Fourteen

'Felicity!'

The sharp command penetrated Felicity's panic and she stilled.

'If I had wanted to spy on you in your bath, I could have done so,' Richard said. 'However, I did, as you will recall, knock at the door.'

He sounded amused, but was that also a hint of exasperation in his tone? Felicity peeked over her shoulder. He was in the open doorway, shoulders propped against the jamb, arms folded across his chest. He smiled at her, shaking his head.

'I am not your enemy, Felicity. I did not intend to scare you. I met Mrs Jakeway on her way to fetch your supper and I came to see if you required any help.'

His voice and his words were patient and soothing, much as one might speak to a horse set into a panic. Had she overreacted? From Richard's point of view, no doubt she had done exactly that. They were man and wife. And yet…and yet…

'Thank you.' Her voice croaked and she coughed. 'I believe I can manage.'

'Shall I pass you a towel?'

'I am not yet ready, thank you. I have not finished washing.' Truth be told, she had yet to begin.

'I shall ask again, in that case. Would you like me to wash your back for you? I can avert my eyes, if it will make you easier.'

'I don't...' Felicity's voice failed.

'You don't trust me? Very well.'

There was a rustle and a muffled grunt behind her. Felicity risked another glance over her shoulder. Richard held her gaze as he tugged his neckcloth from around his neck. *Oh, my goodness. Surely he is not...?* He closed the door and held the neckcloth out, grinning.

'Here. You can tie this around my eyes so I cannot cheat.'

A squirm of heat snaked from the pit of her belly to the juncture of her thighs and she felt her nipples harden. Heavens. If the mere thought of him being close to her naked body could prompt such a reaction, how would it feel to lie together?

The water sloshed around the bath as Felicity sat up. She hugged her knees close to her chest. 'Very well.' This time, her voice squeaked. From a frog to a mouse, she thought wildly, clamping down the urge to laugh, certain it would sound hysterical were she to allow it to escape.

Richard shrugged out of his coat, and knelt by the bathtub, presenting his back. He lifted the neckcloth to cover his eyes and then reached behind his head to offer the ends to Felicity. She grasped them and tied a firm knot. He swivelled round to face her, and rolled up his sleeves. Felicity eyed his hair-roughened arms with hungry fascination. They were sinewy and lightly tanned—so different from her own pale, thin limbs.

'Hand me the soap, Felicity.'

His voice was husky. He reached out, palm up, and Felicity gave him the soap. Then he groped for, and found, her back and she saw his lips stretch into a sensual smile. Excitement spiralled through her body and her heart pounded as he began to stroke, his hand gliding over her wet, soapy skin.

'So very delicate,' he murmured, running one finger down her spine.

Her lids drifted shut as Richard lathered her back, fingers spread, palm flat and gentle as he traced her ribcage around, under her arm, until the tips of his fingers rested against the gentle swell of her breast.

'Relax.' The whisper danced across her moist skin, raising gooseflesh.

Relax? How could she relax? She wanted… she needed…she did not know what she wanted, aware only that her mind was at war with her body.

She heard him move, and his lips were on her hair. They traced a path to her ear and, with the tip of his tongue, he outlined the shell before soft lips nibbled at the lobe. Her head tilted, and he trailed warm, open-mouthed kisses down her neck to her collarbone as his hand slid across her torso, brushing the sensitive skin beneath her breasts.

The urge to lie back was strong. Was she really about to succumb to his seduction so readily? But why should she not? If her body could take pleasure in his lovemaking, why should she not relax and enjoy it? It did not mean she must relinquish her heart.

Her sigh murmured as she relaxed back, her thighs parting of their own volition. He could not see her. He had all the experience. Let him teach her of the pleasures of the flesh.

'Give me your hand.'

He pressed a kiss to her palm before washing her arm from wrist to shoulder, his touch gentle, mouth firm with concentration. As his hand moved across her chest, Felicity closed her eyes. He soaped each breast in turn, kneading. Her back arched, pressing into his touch, an unusual sensation tugging deep inside. Long sweeps of his hand soaped down the side of her body, along her ribcage, over the jut of her hip and down the length of her thigh. She drifted in a sensual haze, aware only of his touch, as he raised each leg in turn to soap them before lowering them back into the water. He lifted her foot, stroking the instep until her foot arched. Each toe in turn was enveloped by warm lips, and sucked gently.

A breathy groan sounded loud in the quiet of the room. Hers. Felicity tensed.

'Sssssshhhhh, relax.' The soothing murmur hung in the air and her body responded.

A large hand circled her stomach, the pressure increasing fractionally each time it neared the triangle of curls at the apex of her thighs. Her need climbed. His hand drifted up again, skimming around her breasts, barely touching the peaked, aching nipples. Despite the cooling water, Felicity's blood pumped hot. Then he took one nipple between finger and thumb and rolled it, gently tugging. Desire streaked through her, setting her blood aflame, and she shifted restlessly.

His lips were on her face again, feathery, butterfly-light kisses caressing her skin as his hand slid over her belly again to slip between her legs, caressing and probing the swollen folds. Her body arched, pressing into his touch. He stroked, and she whimpered.

Then Richard leaned towards her. 'Kiss me.' A request, not a demand.

Dreamily she half-rose from the water and met his lips. Soft, searching, sensual, his kiss inflamed her further. It was exquisite but it was not enough. Not nearly enough. She wanted passion. She *needed* passion…and she needed…need.

His need.

She wanted him to feel the same urgency that gripped her. She cupped his face in her hands and took control. He started in surprise, then responded and deepened the kiss, his tongue sweeping between her parted lips. She wound her arms around his neck, urging him on wordlessly. One arm swept around her, half-lifting her, moulding her wet, naked body to him.

The fine lawn of his shirt did nothing to shield her from the heat of his skin. Felicity tangled her fingers through his hair, her fingertips exploring the solid strength of his skull. She hesitated over the knot in the neckcloth that still covered his eyes, but she did not loosen it. She felt a strange kind of power, being naked with this man, this stranger, with him unable to see. She need not feel shame, or doubt, or inadequacy. She could just enjoy. For the moment.

Her thighs opened wider as his fingers caressed and stroked the sensitive flesh between. Her head fell back as she abandoned herself to the sensations that whirled and intensified inside her until she felt she would shatter if she didn't move, and shatter if she did. She trembled as hot lips nibbled the delicate skin of her neck then froze momentarily as Richard's finger circled her entrance and dipped inside. *Goodness.* His finger slid full length inside her, withdrew, and was joined by another and Felicity abandoned herself to pleasure.

As his fingers began to move Felicity kissed him again, clinging as she urged him on. His tongue and his fingers joined in rhythm, driving Felicity on, spiralling ever higher. He pressed lightly with his thumb and she gasped, the sound swallowed within the joining of their lips. All thought suspended as her spiralling passion wound tighter and tighter. She reached and reached, yearning, straining.

'Let it come, sweetheart.' The whisper barely registered but the gathering, squeezing sensation at her very core climbed…building…building…until it peaked, exploding in wave after pulsing wave of pure ecstasy.

Strong arms swept her out of the water and Felicity was dimly aware of being cradled like a baby as Richard stood up. Her eyes stayed tight shut as she clung to his neck. He was moving—striding—across the room. His eyes could no longer be covered. Even as the final waves throbbed at her core, she shivered, cringing, as her mind caught up with reality. A door clicked open then banged shut.

A peep through her lashes confirmed they were in her bedchamber. The bed loomed large, dominating her restricted view. What would he do now? She could barely take in what had just happened to her. She had never imagined—how could she?—such ecstasy could exist. And now…would he want to take his own pleasure with her, straight away? She had a vague idea of what would happen—shortly before she died, Emma had confided her shame and heartbreak at having been seduced and abandoned by the man she loved. Nausea mushroomed from Felicity's chest into her throat. She swallowed convulsively, banishing all thoughts of her sister, focusing her attention on to her husband.

Chapter Fifteen

Richard moved again and heat from the flames caressed her skin. Slowly, he released her, her damp skin clinging to the fabric of his shirt as her toes stretched for the floor. He steadied her, his warm hand splayed between her shoulder blades. Then she felt the sweep of a towel across her shoulders and around her back: enveloping her, swaddling her, shielding her from his gaze. She forced open her eyes. He was smiling down at her. Her belly performed a twisty loop and her mouth flooded with saliva.

'Felicity Joy.'

His voice was a deep, comforting purr. He removed the pins, one by one, from her hair until it flowed loose. He swept her hair from her face, then bent to kiss her still-tingling lips. Her legs quaked and her knees sagged. He chuckled, scooped her up and placed her in one of the chairs by the fire.

Only then did Felicity see the tray of food on the table next to the chairs.

'You must be hungry,' he said, sitting in the other chair. 'I know I am. Come, let us eat.'

'I thought…I thought…'

'There is no hurry, sweetheart. We have all night.'

Felicity's stomach swooped again, and the flesh between her legs pulsed in an echo of pleasure.

'You have much to get used to, and I wish to discover what pleases you.' He reached for a plate, and selected a pastry. He leaned forward and held it to her lips. 'Taste, tell me, help me to learn.'

Does he mean the food, or…? Nerves jangling, she bit into the pastry, and buttery sweetness flooded her mouth: honey, almonds, and a hint of cinnamon.

'Mmmmm.' She savoured the sweetmeat as Richard popped the remainder in his own mouth.

They sat by the fire and ate their fill of the bread and cheese, delicate pastries and fruit, washed down with wine. Felicity began to relax, the mundane activity of eating distracting her from what was to come. Eventually, Richard sat back with a sigh, glass in hand, and gazed into the flames. Felicity took the opportunity to study him as the firelight played across his features. He was so very handsome. She felt as though she were in a fairy tale, the handsome prince having whisked her away from her humdrum life. But this was real life, and soon… As though he could hear her thoughts, Richard switched his attention to her, his eyes penetrating, a half smile playing around his sensuous lips.

'Have you had enough to eat?'

'Yes. Thank you.'

'Some more wine?'

Felicity held out her glass, and he filled it, then stood, holding out his hand. As if in a dream, Felicity placed her hand in his. He led her to the bed and took her wine glass, placing it on the bedside table.

He smoothed her hair from her face and pressed warm lips to her temple.

'I will snuff the candles. You get into bed, and we will drink our wine together, you and I.'

He swept the bedcovers down before crossing to the fireplace to snuff out the candles. Felicity released her grip on the towel and slid into the bed, pulling the covers right up to her chin. The room now in semi-darkness, lit only by the fire, Richard rounded the bed and began to undress. That chest. Broad, tantalizingly sculpted, dusted with dark hair.

He reached for the buttons on his trousers. She groped blindly for her wine glass, hand trembling as she raised it to her lips. The bed dipped as he sat on the edge then bent forward to finish taking off his trousers, his broad back smooth, muscles rippling. Her blood raced around her body, heart thundering in her ears, nipples tight and aching, the flesh between her thighs yearning for his touch.

She put her glass down and reached for him.

A hair's breadth from the skin of his back, she hesitated, registering the heat of his body as it warmed her palm. *Should I? Will he be shocked? Disgusted?* The wine made her bold. She splayed her fingers, and placed her hand on his back. He stilled. She waited.

'It's all right to explore, Felicity Joy.' His back vibrated with the deep rumble of his voice. 'I certainly intend to explore you.'

Her insides quivered. Her fingers trickled down his spine. He did not move. Emboldened, she knelt; crept a little closer; swept both hands up the solid planes of his back until her fingers curved over his shoulders. She kneaded with her thumbs.

'Aaaaaahh, that feels good. You have magic in your fingers, sweetheart.' He stretched his torso, rolling his shoulders.

How had he pleasured her? His neck. Shuffling closer still, until the tips of her breasts brushed his back, she pressed her lips to the side of his neck. Musky maleness flooded her senses. She was rewarded by a deep shudder and a quiet groan. She took his earlobe into her mouth and sucked. Then nipped.

'Ooh. You little…'

Laughing, he turned his head. His lips were inches from hers. Warm, wine-scented breath fanned her skin, raising a *frisson* of pleasure. She closed the gap, pressing her lips to his, reaching for his chest. Rough hair teased her fingertips as she stroked, fascinated by the difference between his skin and hers. She played with his nipple, and he moaned, deep in his chest. She slicked her tongue over his lips: they parted, tongues met, entwined, withdrew, touched again.

He swung round, took control, cupping her head as he eased her down. He lay beside her, half covering her, as he deepened the kiss. His arousal pressed into her thigh. Felicity closed her eyes, concentrating on *what* was happening rather than on *who* was stoking this wonderful, exciting, glorious maelstrom of need. Every other sense was on heightened alert. She luxuriated in his scent: spicy, musky, arousing; the texture of his hair-roughened skin as he moved over her; the moist heat of skin against skin; every inch of her—caressed by skilled fingers and questing tongue—a thousand times more alive than ever before.

'Touch me, sweetheart.' His voice was ragged, urgent with need.

She reached, marvelling at the silken skin that slid over his hot, solid length. She closed her fingers, heard his intake of breath, squeezed. His hand covered hers, guiding her even as long fingers penetrated her most intimate place. She arched, whimpering, and then he moved, covering her, easing her thighs wider. She felt the nudge at her entrance, and tensed.

'Sssshhh. Relax. It might hurt this first time, but not for long. I promise.'

A steady push, and she stretched, and stretched

until she could take no more. He was too big, she
was too small, how…?

'Richaaaard.'

Her protest lost in a cry as he forged into her,
the pain sharp, but brief. He lay still. Impaled, she
waited. Then he began to move, and the yearning ache grew and grew, radiating out from the
place they were joined until every muscle in her
body strained to reach the pinnacle that seemed
forever just beyond her reach.

Frantic fingers clawed at broad shoulders.
Lips kissed and teeth nipped at every inch of
skin within reach. Legs wrapped, and held, urging him on. He took her mouth in a searing kiss
as he reached between them, and stroked. She
flew over that pinnacle in a glorious burst of ecstasy that cascaded through her, shaking her to
her core.

He began to move faster, penetrate deeper.
Cool air washed between them. She cranked open
a weighty eyelid. He was braced up on corded
arms, eyes closed, his face a mask of concentration until, with a primal roar, he reached his
release. She felt his seed empty into her and he
collapsed on to her, rolling a little so as not to
crush her, panting. They lay together, his leg
straddling hers, arm across her waist. Felicity—
tired, sated, content—could have stayed like that
all night.

'Are you all right?' His breathing had slowed
and he caressed her cheek as he spoke.

'Yes. Of course.'

What should one say, at a time like this? His question dissolved her pleasant haze of exhaustion as the sun disperses early morning mist. Words formed in Felicity's head, but were dismissed as too trite or too grateful; gushing, even. One could hardly thank one's husband for... She bit at her lip. Was there an etiquette for such an occasion? She felt awkward and unworldly and stiffened, her eyes screwed shut.

'Felicity. Look at me. Please.'

She did. Read the compassion in his eyes, but also the laughter that lurked in the background. Well, mayhap he was justified in finding her amusing.

'There is no need to be embarrassed. Not with me. What we have just done is natural. It is meant to be enjoyable. For us both.' He smiled, lines radiating out from the corners of his eyes. He kissed her on the forehead, then in one swift movement, he got out of the bed, and turned to tuck her back in. 'You sleep now. You must be exhausted. I will see you in the morning.'

The bed felt very big, and cold, and empty. Felicity wished he had stayed.

Chapter Sixteen

Felicity awoke with a start. It was early, judging by the light creeping around the edge of the curtains. She lay in bed and relived the day before, fingers twisting the gold band on the third finger of her left hand.

Married.

Well, and was that not what she wanted: a home of her own and a family? Richard was not quite what she had bargained for, but he was what she had. If she only thought of him as a means to an end, surely she could keep her heart safe?

She quivered with the memory of their lovemaking, and her hand crept between her thighs, where her flesh was still tender. Excitement flitted through her veins and her heart leapt at the thought of seeing Stanton…Richard…again.

Determinedly, she settled her thoughts, crushing the bud of happiness attempting to unfurl in her heart. This would never do.

Once she was with child he would continue

with his interests and leave her to hers. That was their bargain. She must protect her heart. If she could ensure that intimacies such as last night remained in the bedchamber...would that not suffice?

It would not be easy.

In need of distraction, she threw the covers back, tucked her feet into her slippers and wrapped her shawl around her. Her bedchamber was huge, with three tall windows spaced along the wall opposite the bed. She drew open the curtains to let the light spill in but did not linger at the window. She would explore the gardens of her new home later. Her home. It was strange, knowing she would be living here, yet knowing so little about the place or the people who lived here, not even her husband. A shiver spread across the surface of her skin and she hugged her arms around her body, pulling the shawl tight around her shoulders.

There was a light tap at the door, and it opened to admit a maid, carrying a wooden box.

'G'morning, milady; I'm sorry your fire wasn't lit ready for you.' She cast an anxious look at Felicity.

'Don't be troubled, I did wake very early. What is your name?'

'Tilly, milady.' The girl, round-faced and pink-cheeked, bobbed a curtsy.

'Well, Tilly, when you have finished here, could you send up some hot water, please? I should like to get dressed.'

'Of course, milady.'

Finally alone—fully dressed and ready to face her new life—Felicity paused with her hand on the door handle, butterflies dancing around inside. She turned back and drifted around the room, examining sundry objects, before stopping by the window. In the garden below, a man was raking leaves from the vast expanse of lawn. Beyond the grass, the contours of the land dipped to reveal a glimpse of blue. A lake. The butterflies settled. She could not skulk upstairs all day. A pleasant walk to the lake would be her reward for braving breakfast.

About to turn from the window, a movement caught her eye: Richard, dressed in riding clothes, was striding along the path towards the house. He glanced up, and Felicity jerked away from the window, her pulse skittering as her breath caught.

Stupid! Why dodge out of sight as though you've been caught in some wrongdoing?

She peered out of the window again, but Richard was no longer in sight. Hands clasped to her chest, Felicity gazed unseeingly at the view as she willed her heart rate to slow. If he had seen her, she must go downstairs. He would think her a complete ninny if she remained closeted up here. Still she dallied, until a peremptory knock forced her to open the door.

Richard stood outside. He brought with him the smell of outdoors, fresh and tangy. He was hatless, his dark brown curls windswept. His skin glowed and his eyes sparkled.

'Good morning, Felicity Joy. I trust you slept well and are fully refreshed?'

His rich baritone did strange things to her insides. She remembered the times she had sneaked a sip of brandy from her father's decanter after a cold ride. Richard's voice spread through her with a similar intoxicating warmth. Images of the night before flooded her brain and she felt her cheeks heat.

'Good morning, Lord St…Richard.' Her voice came out as a breathless squeak.

Richard grinned. 'I've just returned from my morning ride. Have you breakfasted yet?'

'No. I…I was just about to…to—'

'In that case, would you care to join me for breakfast in the parlour? Unless you prefer to take breakfast in your room, as my mother does?'

She straightened her back, striving for calm.

'Yes. Thank you. I should like to join you.'

Richard patted her hand as she took his arm to go downstairs. 'Don't worry; you will soon become accustomed to your new home.'

At least he seemed to understand how awkward she felt in this strange house. Not a guest, but not yet at home.

The food was laid out on a sideboard for them to serve themselves. Richard helped himself to thick rashers of bacon and eggs and placed it in front of the chair at the head of the table, big enough to seat eight. A second place was set at the opposite end, and Richard pulled the chair out for Felicity. 'Would you like coffee?'

'Yes, please.' Felicity set down her plate, with its slice of toast and boiled egg.

Richard poured them both coffee, sat down and began to eat.

'I always seem to eat twice as much when I'm down in the country,' he remarked. 'It is the fresh air and the exercise. I like to ride before breakfast as a rule, as long as the weather isn't too inclement.'

He paused, his eyes on Felicity. Heat erupted and her skin tingled. Would she ever become accustomed to him?

Richard watched his new wife surreptitiously as they breakfasted together. Her eyes glued to her plate, she picked half-heartedly at her food.

How little I know of her. Who is she, behind the mask? What are her interests? Her dreams? Her fears? Why was she so reluctant to accept me? Was it a ploy, to pique my interest, or was... is...there some deeper reason?

His jaw set. *Why plague yourself with such questions? Did you not merely require a wife who would fit in with your life? You have no need to know the whys and the wherefores.*

He focused on his bride. 'Do you ride, Felicity?'

Her amber eyes came alive. 'Oh, indeed I do. I love to ride. Do you have a lady's mount in your stables?'

'Not at present: my mother has not ridden for many years. Do you have a favourite animal at

Bath, or at Baverstock? I can send a groom for it, if it would please you?'

'Unfortunately, no. The mare I used to ride became permanently lame, and I was forced to retire her to Baverstock. Then my stepfather...' resentment soured Felicity's tone '...declined to meet the stabling costs for another horse. He believed hiring a job horse was sufficient should I wish to ride out with friends.'

It was something he could remedy very easily; something to make his new wife happy. 'I shall instruct Dalton to find you a suitable mount.'

'I'm sorry...Dalton?'

'My head groom.'

'I see. Thank you.'

Silence reigned once more.

'If you would like it, I will show you around the house and gardens today. It will help you find your bearings.'

What had happened to his intention to spend the morning with Elliott, inspecting the estate ledgers to ensure his bailiff had overseen estate affairs properly in Richard's all-too-frequent absences? One more day would not hurt, however, and it would be a worthwhile sacrifice to help Felicity settle into her new role and become accustomed to him. She had reacted like a startled fawn when he had entered her bathroom last night. Covering his eyes had been inspired; she had relaxed and responded, revealing her hidden passion. He would hate to have a wife who was indifferent to or—even worse—disliked the marital act.

'I do beg your pardon, my dear. I'm afraid I was wool-gathering.'

He had completely missed Felicity's response to his offer.

'I said "thank you but that will not be necessary". You no doubt have important duties. There is no need for you to trouble yourself—I shall ask Mrs Jakeway to give me a tour of the house and, as for the gardens and grounds, I shall be quite content to explore them on my own.'

Chapter Seventeen

Richard placed his knife and fork on to his empty plate, biting back an irritable retort.

'I have put the day aside especially for you, Felicity.' A touch inaccurate, perhaps, but at least he had made the gesture. Whereas *she*… 'I thought we would spend it together.'

A flick of her eyebrow spoke volumes. 'We have a marriage of convenience, Richard. There is no need for pretence.'

'Pretence? Is it so wrong to wish for a comfortable relationship?'

'Comfortable? Oh, no, of course it is not. But may we not be comfortable without living in one another's pockets?'

Why did those words chafe? The uncomfortable conclusion was that although he did not wish his marriage to change *his* way of life, he had—hypocritically—assumed he would be the centre of his wife's world.

'I have annoyed you. I am sorry. That was not

my intention. I wished to reassure you I will not
be a wife who expects or desires your constant
attention. That was not our bargain. I am accustomed to relying on my own resources for enter-
tainment.'

Bargain? Richard expelled his breath in an audible huff. 'The fault was mine. I made assump-
tions. I wish only to ensure we have a contented
marriage.'

'As do I. I promise I do not refuse your company out of churlishness. I simply wish to ensure
you do not spend time with me from a sense of
duty.'

How to respond? Their marriage had only
taken place because of his sense of duty. Had
that same sense of duty prompted his offer to
show her around Fernley?

In his mind's eye he saw Felicity in her bath,
felt again her silky skin, heard her soft sighs.
His blood stirred. His new wife might not be
as buxom as his usual preference, but her pert,
springy breasts had excited him every bit as much
as fuller, pillowy mounds had ever done. And
those lean thighs…her taut belly…her enthusiastic responses…

He studied her face, animated with discussion,
her eyes shining with sincerity.

'I promise I will never do that,' he said. 'I will
summon Mrs Jakeway to show you the house.'

The morning sped by. To Felicity's reeling
senses, it seemed Mrs Jakeway left no corner of

the huge house unvisited and no history of the Durant family untold. Who would have thought touring one house could be so exhausting?

Mrs Jakeway opened a door leading off an up-stairs landing and ushered Felicity through into a long, narrow, portrait-lined room. 'The gallery— the family are all in here.'

Felicity bit back a sigh, anticipating a long story to accompany each portrait, but as they stopped before the very first painting, the door at the far end of the gallery opened.

'There you are.' Richard strode the length of the gallery towards them. Felicity fixed her atten-tion on the portrait, willing her fluttering pulse to steady. 'Thank you, Mrs Jakeway. You may return to your duties.'

'Yes, thank you, Mrs Jakeway. You have been most informative.' Felicity smiled at the house-keeper then said to Richard, 'It is a magnificent house, but I had no notion of how big it is. I feel as though I have walked miles.'

Richard laughed. 'You will be ready for some refreshment, then, to replenish your energy.' He held out his arm, and she took it with some re-lief. 'I am pleased you approve of your new home, Felicity Joy.'

She gritted her teeth against the tremor that sped through her at his deepening tone. *Felicity Joy*, indeed.

'Oh, I do,' she said. 'Your mother has the most exquisite taste; everything is beautifully deco-rated and furnished.'

'You must feel free to make any changes you wish, especially in your own chambers,' Richard said. 'Whatever you wish for, Felicity, you may have.'

Whatever I wish for...? Hmmph. 'You are most generous, but I have seen nothing yet I would care to change.'

They strolled along the dim gallery. Felicity cast around for a subject to break the silence.

'Your mother—'

'Will be moving to the Dower House in the very near future.'

That had not been what she was going to ask. 'You do not appear very...well, very close.'

A bitter laugh was quickly bitten off. 'You might say that. My mother has never hidden the fact she would have preferred my brother to succeed to the title.'

'Your brother?' Felicity searched her memory. 'I had forgotten. He was older than you, was he not?'

Richard indicated a portrait of a youth with a much younger boy. 'By eight years.' The youth was a serious-faced lad with the same brown, wavy hair as Richard. 'That is Adam and me as children. For a long time, my parents gave up hope of having more children. Then I came along. Adam was always the favourite. My parents were inconsolable when he died.'

'How could they be otherwise? He was their son.'

Richard shot her a dark look, then strode on.

Felicity trailed in his wake, her mind spinning. They had the death of a sibling in common then.

At the door leading from the gallery to the up-stairs landing, Richard paused. 'My father died four months after Adam. He lost all interest in life. I was barely seventeen when I inherited the title, a position I never expected. Nor desired.'

His knuckles shone white on the door handle. He started when Felicity tentatively touched his hand. 'You suffered two grievous losses in a cru-elly short time. I do understand. I lost my father when I was fourteen and then my sister, Emma, two years later. She was only eighteen.'

'Eighteen. So very young.' Richard lifted his hand to her cheek. 'You must miss her.'

'I do.' Felicity's throat tightened. 'It was…' She paused. She could not divulge Emma's disgrace, or her mother's culpability, or her own guilt at the anger she still harboured towards her mother. After Papa had died, her mother had been incon-solable. Following her year of mourning, however, she had launched into a round of gaiety and par-ties, with the excuse of Emma's come-out. But Mama had become too intent on her own needs and pleasures, and her naive and innocent daugh-ter had paid a heavy price.

Determinedly, Felicity buried those memories. 'It was a dreadful time, as it must have been for you and your poor mother after Adam and then your father died.'

'After the initial shock, my mother coped ad-mirably, as she always does. She did not allow…'

Richard fell silent. 'Well, that is of no import. Come. Let us go and eat and, afterwards, if you will allow, I should like to show you round the gardens.'

She choked back her instinct to refuse, mindful of that glimpse of pain when he spoke of his family. 'Thank you.'

He smiled, and Felicity's pulse quickened. She spun round and headed for the stairs. As they descended, Lady Stanton was crossing the marble-floored entrance hall. Glancing up, she stopped. Richard's features were set in grim lines and, eyeing the dowager's haughty demeanour as they neared the foot of the stairs, Felicity felt a moment of sadness for them both. Two people, bound by blood and by common grief, should find succour in one another. All she could read here was resentment, in Richard's case, and indifference in his mother's; although...there was a glimmer of fear in her mother-in-law's eyes whenever she looked at her son that Felicity could not understand. What did she fear?

A footman held the door, and they sat at the table where luncheon—a selection of cold meats, bread and butter, pickles, salads and fruit—was laid out.

The dowager helped herself to a slice of beef. 'Did you find the Countess's suite to your liking, Felicity?'

'Thank you, yes. It is most agreeable.'

'I moved out of there when Richard's father died, into my current bedchamber.' Her gaze flicked towards Richard. 'I have sent the servants over to the Lodge to prepare.'

'The Lodge?' Felicity looked from her mother-in-law to Richard and back again.

'Fernley Lodge is the Dower House. Mother will move there now we are married.'

'We shall have to discuss which servants I may take with me, or do you wish me to hire new people?'

'Not at all, Mother. You may take your pick. I shall hire any replacements I need.'

'You will be happier with familiar people around you, I am sure.' Felicity ignored her mother-in-law's haughtily lifted brow; she was part of this family now; she would not sit quietly when family—and household—matters were discussed.

'Speaking of servants,' the dowager said, switching her focus to Felicity, 'I must insist you hire a lady's maid without delay. It is completely unacceptable—'

'It is in hand, Mother,' Richard interrupted. 'I have sent a message to Truman in Winchester to find suitable candidates for me to interview.'

'I should prefer to select my own maid.' Felicity pretended she did not notice the outraged stare of the dowager or Richard's amusement at her interjection.

'Then so you shall,' he replied.

'Thank you.'

'You are most free with your opinions,' the dowager remarked.

Richard's eyes were fixed on her, a distinct challenge in them. She pressed her lips together. *Start as you mean to go on.*

'I apologize if you think I speak out of turn, Mother,' she said, 'but I am, am I not, the Countess of Stanton? I am mistress of this house now, and I therefore believe I am entitled to express my opinion.

'What do you say, my dear?' she added, directing a searching look at Richard, who laughed.

'I have no objection to you expressing your opinions, Wife,' he said, 'just as long as they concur with mine.' The twinkle in his eyes confirmed he was teasing.

'I shall try and bear that in mind, Husband,' she murmured, narrowing her eyes at him before focusing on her plate once more.

Chapter Eighteen

*T*his is what happens when you allow sympathy
to overthrow your good intentions.

Felicity sat in a secluded arbour overlooking
the lake, resentment scouring her brain. She had
discovered the spot on her solitary exploration of
the gardens and grounds. Her *husband* had been
so easily dissuaded from spending time in her
company, she could almost laugh. She had only
accepted his offer to show her the gardens because she felt sorry for him. Well, maybe she'd
been a *tiny* bit flattered he had confided in her
about his brother's death and—possibly—she had
been foolish enough to hope…but no! She was
deluded. This neighbour…some crony of Richard's—she was so cross she could not even recall
his name—had called on his way into Winchester,
and Richard had jumped at the opportunity to
accompany him, with no thought for her or for
his promise.

Why so angry? You refused his company only

*this morning. Surely you are not already infatu-
ated with him after only one night of passion?*

She resumed her march around the lake. It was
too cool to sit for long: dark grey clouds scudded across the sky, playing hide-and-seek with
the sun much as her anger flirted with images of
their lovemaking from the night before.

Richard had behaved in perfect accord with
their bargain. Was that not what she wanted from
their marriage? She should thank him for not en-
couraging her silly, missish longings.

She completed her circuit of the lake, and made
her way back, to explore the flower gardens.

But…if only he had not been so tender…so
loving…so—seemingly—*appreciative* last night.
Her thoughts, as she wandered, sparked a myriad
of unwelcome emotions. Surely this intensity…
such pleasure…such ecstasy…would not—*could
not*—last? In time, their lives would settle into
the humdrum. Their paths need not cross during
the day and, at night, Richard would visit her bed
and service her until they had produced enough
children to secure the earldom. He would then
leave her alone. Unromantic, maybe, but those
sentiments were exactly what she had planned
for her marriage and exactly what she needed to
bring her down to earth.

Why, then, did she feel so wretched?

She returned to the house to consult with Mrs
Jakeway. The sooner she occupied her mind with
the everyday matters of running of the household, the better.

* * *

'I've appointed a lady's maid for you. She arrives next week.'

Felicity froze in the act of setting a stitch. Slowly, she looked up at Richard, newly returned from Winchester, a satisfied smile on his lips.

'You agreed I might select my own maid.'

'Yvette comes highly recommended, Felicity. She will make you an excellent maid.'

Of all the high-handed... Felicity bit her lip and bent her head to continue with her embroidery.

'Truman told me—'

'Who is Truman?'

'He is my man of business in Winchester. I needed to consult him over additional staff for Fernley Lodge and I mentioned your need for a lady's maid.'

'I see.'

'I met the girl. She is in need of employment and her references are impeccable. Dalton will collect her on Tuesday. I am certain you will approve of her.'

Is she pretty? The words stole uninvited into Felicity's thoughts, her father's penchant for comely maidservants still fresh in her memory even after all these years. She concentrated fiercely on her stitching. 'I reserve the right to refuse her.'

She glanced up. Richard was frowning. 'Do you not trust my judgement, Felicity?'

Start as you mean to go on. 'I do not know you well enough to answer that. Staff appointments, however, are part of *my* jurisdiction and the matter of my personal maid is of particular importance to me, as you might imagine.'

'Very well. I ask only that you reserve judgement until you have met Yvette. I am certain you will like her.'

Richard watched Felicity push the food around her dinner plate with a distinct lack of enthusiasm. As far as he could tell, not a morsel had passed her lips. She had withdrawn into herself; was she fretting about the night to come? With his mother present, he could say nothing to ease her uncertainties.

'Is the food not up to your usual standards?'

Felicity's head jerked up at his mother's question.

'It is delicious, Mother, but I am afraid I am not very hungry. Please do pass my regrets to Cook,' Felicity added, directing her comment to Trick, who stood to one side of the room, 'I should not wish to cause any dismay in the kitchen. The fault is not with the food.'

'Well, really, Daughter. Why should kitchen servants care about your appetite, pray?'

'Mother.'

His mother ignored Richard's warning, her attention on Felicity, their gazes locked. A mental image arose of two fencers, each on the alert for any hint of vulnerability in their opponent. Richard sipped at his wine, settling back to await the victor.

'It may well be they would not be concerned about my lack of appetite,' Felicity said. 'But I, you see, *do* care that their work should not go unacknowledged. If I cannot express my thanks by eating the results of their labour, it costs me nothing to pass on a few words of reassurance.'

His mother stiffened. 'Well!'

Silence reigned. He could almost hear the wheels spinning in his mother's brain.

'I suppose there is no harm in it,' she eventually conceded. 'You are sending such a message only because it is your *wish* to do so, and not under any sense of obligation to the lower orders.'

First round to Felicity.

'I will move to Fernley Lodge as soon as the servants have made it ready,' Mother said, 'but I shall leave Trick and Jakeway here. You will need them to maintain the standards to be expected in a house such as Fernley Park.'

'That is most generous,' Felicity said. 'Do you not agree, Richard?'

'Richard? Why do you not use your husband's title? He has been Stanton since his father's death fifteen years ago.'

'Richard specifically requested that I call him such, Mother. And I know you will agree a wife should always obey her husband.'

Richard bit back a smile as his mother inclined her head, indicating her approval. He detected the mischievous glint in Felicity's eye and the laughter that warmed her voice, nuances that passed his mother by.

'I am sorry we will have so little time to become acquainted,' Felicity said.

'Fernley Lodge is barely half a mile distance, Daughter. You may walk over and visit me whenever you are at home.'

'And you, Mother, will be most welcome to visit us here at Fernley whenever you choose,' Felicity said promptly. 'Is that not so, Richard?'

'Indeed.'

Dare he hope to forge a better relationship with his mother, now he was wed? It was hard to remember the time—before Adam's death—when their bond had been warm and relaxed. He had tried to excuse her rejection but, over the years, his understanding had withered away, stunted time and time again by her condemnation of him.

'Besides,' he added, 'even if Mother were to remain longer at Fernley, we will not be here.'

'Will we not? Are we going away? You said nothing about a journey this morning.'

No, he had not, for he had only that very minute decided. He had racked his brains for ways to help Felicity adjust to her new life…to him. He recognized her skittishness around him, despite her efforts to conceal it. She appeared to believe that reducing the time they spent together—as per their bargain—was the answer. He begged to differ.

'It was to be a surprise,' he said smoothly.

It had occurred to him, as they talked about Fernley, that she would become more quickly accustomed to him—and to the idea of being his wife—in a more intimate establishment.

And he knew just the place.

'I have a small fishing lodge in the Welsh Marches. We will leave after Mother has moved to the Lodge,' he said. 'On our honeymoon,'

'*Honeymoon?*' Two bright patches of colour stained Felicity's cheeks.

'Honeymoon. The lodge is isolated, surrounded by beautiful countryside. It will give us time to get to know one another.'

There was a prolonged silence. Richard watched as various expressions swept Felicity's face.

She cleared her throat. 'If we are to go away, might I request we visit London instead?'

Chapter Nineteen

'*London?* For our honeymoon?' Any other bride would have been overjoyed at such a romantic setting as a fishing lodge on the River Wye.

'I…yes, if you please. I would welcome the opportunity to visit Westfield again.'

'Westfield? What is Westfield, pray?' the dowager interjected.

'It is an orphan asylum and a school for destitute children.'

'And you were involved with such a place as an unmarried woman? Shameful.'

Mutiny gleamed in Felicity's eye.

'It is hardly shameful, Mother, to help those less fortunate than ourselves,' Richard said. 'If it is your wish to go to London, Felicity, then we shall. I am interested to visit Westfield myself, and it will be an opportunity for you to have some new gowns made.'

'Thank you.' She flashed a smile in his direction. 'It is a very respectable establishment,

Mother, run by Mr Peter Whittaker and his wife, Jane. You must not fear I shall run the family name into disrepute.'

His mother rose to her feet. 'If you have finished your meal, Felicity, we shall retire to the salon and you may tell me more about this place. We shall leave Stanton to his port.'

Richard had no wish to remain there alone, but he acquiesced, as he so often did in response to his mother's edicts. She was his mother, after all, and he had no intention of quarrelling with her over what was, to her, an inviolable custom. Once she had removed to the Lodge, he would establish his own customs. He stood as the ladies left the room.

His mother's voice floated back through the still open door. 'Now, would that be the Hertfordshire Whittakers?'

Richard eyed the two women in his life with mounting frustration. Somehow, in the time he had taken to visit the kitchen and arrange for a few tempting morsels and some wine to be laid out in Felicity's bedchamber, his wife had persuaded his distant, disapproving mother into a genuine interest in her work with the orphans.

'Your mother,' Felicity had informed him with a sunny smile as he sauntered into the salon, ready to persuade her to retire early, 'made her début with Mr Peter Whittaker's mother. Is that not a coincidence?'

The tea tray came and went and still Felicity

lingered, seemingly oblivious to his hints. Did she genuinely not realize he was longing to take her to bed?

Finally, he stood up. 'If you will excuse us, Mother, I am very tired and wish to retire.' He held out his hand. 'Come, Felicity.'

His wife's flaming cheeks spoke volumes. He caught his mother's amused glance at Felicity and felt a jolt of disbelief.

Amusement? From his mother? How was she so relaxed in Felicity's company, yet so stiff in his own? She had only known Felicity one day. It was as though a guard had been lowered in Felicity's company and yet, in his, that guard was constantly and insurmountably in place. He dismissed his stir of resentment with impatience.

'It is time I retired too.' His mother rose to her feet. 'Goodnight, Felicity; Stanton.'

Richard grabbed Felicity's hand and tugged her to her feet as his mother left the room. He could feel her trembling.

'Look at me, Felicity.' She did, her amber eyes round, the gold flecks in her irises reflecting the candlelight. 'I thought you enjoyed our lovemaking last night? There is nothing to fear, and no need to be embarrassed.'

A spark of…something…flashed in her eyes and her chin tilted up. 'I am not afraid.' She leaned forward, coming up on to her toes, and pressed her lips to his. 'I am not afraid.'

He swept her into his arms, lifting her with ease, deepening the kiss. Slender arms wrapped around his neck as he nudged the door open with one foot. A footman on duty in the hallway stared stonily ahead as Richard mounted the stairs, Felicity still cradled in his arms, their lips fused together as their tongues entwined.

He kicked the door of the bedchamber shut behind them, having dismissed the waiting maid with a jerk of his thumb. His blood was up, heart hammering, as he deposited Felicity on the bed and ran his fingers up her leg, stroking past the bare skin of her thigh to the moist heat at her core as he tugged down her neckline, exposing one small, firm breast, and sucked her nipple deep into his mouth. A gasp, cut short, inflamed him further.

Slow down. He wrenched away, shrugging out of his coat and discarding his neckcloth before approaching the bed again.

Felicity remained as he had left her. Spread-eagled, skirts rucked up to reveal smooth, slender thighs. His eyes roamed her body, lingering over her tiny waist, her heaving breast, the peaked nipple still glistening, to her face. Eyes glinted through half-closed lids as a pink tongue tip slaked across parted lips.

Little minx. With a growl that vibrated through his entire body, he launched himself on to the bed.

'Do you hunt, Lady Stanton?'

Felicity eyed her questioner. Lady Rowling was the local squire's wife—a handsome brunette with dark flashing eyes. Felicity disliked her already, seething all through dinner as her hostess had monopolized Richard, seated to her right, and ignored the vicar on her left. The newlyweds, together with the dowager and some other neighbours, had been invited to dine with Sir Timothy and Lady Rowling.

'No. I love to ride, but the hunt is too fast and furious for me, I'm afraid.'

'Oh, I love to hunt. You do not know what you are missing. Why, we have had many a splendid run, have we not, Stanton?'

'We have indeed.' Richard had joined them, the gentlemen having returned to the ladies after the port. Felicity felt his hand settle at the small of her back, sending shivers dancing up her spine.

Lady Rowling sidled up to Richard. 'Do you recall that hedge, the last time we were out? The rest of the field queued for the gate, but we were not so cowardly, were we? Thor is such a fine animal—he flew that hedge, and my Duchess followed on his heels.' She laughed, showing—in Felicity's opinion—teeth reminiscent of a horse: long and yellowing. 'My Duchess would follow your Thor anywhere, I do believe.'

Felicity gritted her teeth at such blatant flirtation, but before she could think of a suitable riposte, they were joined by Sir Timothy and Richard's mother.

'Then I must urge you to exercise better control over her,' Sir Timothy said. 'She is a fine animal, but she does not have Thor's scope. He is magnificent, Stanton. I should like to see him pitted against my Brutus in a race across country.'

'Name the time and place,' Richard said promptly. 'Your Brutus won't see our heels for dust.'

The dowager swayed, the colour leaching from her skin, before she visibly rallied, saying, 'I do wish you would not, Stanton. Think of the danger…your responsibilities. You have your wife to consider.'

'Oh, I am certain Lady Stanton can spare her husband for so short a time,' Lady Rowling said. 'Why, you would not care to interfere with your husband's pleasures, would you, my dear lady?'

What could she say? She had no more wish to see Richard risk his neck than her mother-in-law, but neither could she stand against him publicly so soon after their marriage. The challenge in Lady Rowling's eyes settled her response.

'I have no wish to curtail my husband's activities,' she said.

The squeeze of Richard's hand at her waist almost made up for the daggers in her mother-in-law's eyes.

'Saturday?' Sir Timothy said. 'We'll do a circuit of the parish, starting and ending here.'

In the carriage on the way home, the dowager berated Richard. 'The animal is unpredictable. You'll be thrown and injured. Even killed. You never consider the risks…you will get yourself killed. Like your brother.'

'His name was Adam. Why can you never call him by his name?'

Felicity heard the faint hitch in the dowager's breath. She reached in the dark, and clasped her hand.

'Please, Richard. Your mother is upset.'

'Have you *seen* Thor, Daughter?'

'Why, no.' She had seen little of her husband during daylight hours. Following their bargain.

'He is so huge, so strong—'

'I can handle him, Mother. You need not fear I will die before I do my duty and provide for the estate.'

Bony fingers dug into Felicity's palm at those bitter words.

'I am sure Mother did not mean…'

The carriage had pulled up in front of Fernley Park. Felicity's words faded as Richard flung open the door and jumped out. As he handed her down, he hissed in her ear, 'You do not know what you are talking about. I have lived with this since my father and brother died. It is *all* she cares about—the succession.'

He turned to help his mother from the carriage and into the house. Felicity followed thoughtfully.

Chapter Twenty

The following Tuesday Felicity made her way to Richard's study, having been informed by Trick that his lordship wished to see her. She had woken late and breakfasted alone. Richard had, according to Trick, been up since the crack of dawn. How did he find the energy? She was exhausted after a night of the most… She felt her cheeks bloom and, conscious of passing servants, forced her thoughts away from the night before.

She hesitated outside the study door. Raised voices sounded from within.

'She is totally unsuitable.'

'We must agree to differ in this instance, Mother. Yvette is a most experienced lady's maid.'

'Yvette. And French, too,' the dowager added in tones of disgust. 'And her *appearance*—'

'The decision is for Felicity to make.'

'No lady would countenance such a creature in their employ. I am astonished Truman had the effrontery to present her.'

'I reviewed all the available candidates. She was the best by far.'

'You should spare Felicity the distress of meeting such a woman.'

Richard's voice grew clipped. 'Yvette possesses all the necessary skills for a superior lady's maid.'

Does she, indeed?

'She has excellent credentials.'

Hmmph. No doubt she has.

What was so special about this Frenchwoman that Richard was so very eager to employ her? She was no doubt beautiful and flirtatious, as Frenchwomen were known to be. Felicity determined to dislike her on sight, and to send her back to Winchester and ask for some good, solid English girls to be presented for her approval.

She squared her shoulders, rapped on the door and walked in.

'Ah, Felicity. Yvette has arrived, for the post of lady's maid. She is in the parlour, if you would care to come and meet her?'

Richard urged her to the door, his hand warm at the small of her back. A shiver danced across her skin at his touch, further annoying her. She had her righteous indignation to maintain, she had no wish to be distracted by memories of the night before.

'Stanton!' The dowager's peremptory command stopped them in their tracks. 'I insist you forewarn Felicity about—'

'There is no need. Felicity is not a child to be protected.'

His hand urged her onward. Suspicion swelled. Would he try to coerce her into accepting this Frenchwoman? He would find she was made of sterner stuff than he imagined if he thought she would meekly submit. At the parlour door, Richard cupped her chin and looked into her eyes.

'All I ask is that you employ an open mind, Felicity.'

Felicity held his gaze, staring into deep brown eyes as open and honest as she could wish for. Was he really so false? All guileless innocence on the surface whilst hatching plans to bring a doxy into the house under the guise of a servant?

She stalked into the room.

A woman stood by the fire, her back to the door. She wore a plain black dress, her hair tucked neatly out of sight under a straw bonnet; medium height with a narrow back and arms so thin the sleeves of her dress hung in folds. She turned, head high, as Felicity entered.

Felicity bit back her gasp, quickly schooling her expression. So this was Yvette, the French-woman she had mentally accused Richard of having designs upon. Her mind whirled as she rethought Richard's motives, shamed by her sus-picions. This would teach her to judge. Not an attempt to introduce a pretty maid into the house-hold—quite the opposite. Her husband climbed several notches in her estimation.

She studied Yvette's face as she crossed the

room to greet her. Two scars, one above the other,
marred her left cheek. The higher, longer one—
silvery pink—curved from her mouth—where it
puckered her top lip—to her temple, just missing the corner of her eye. The second, shorter
scar angled across her jaw. The effect was exaggerated by her cheekbones, stark above hollowed
cheeks. Dark shadows smudged her eyes, which
were green and watchful, a hint of defiance in
their depths. It was impossible to ascertain her
age—she might be five-and-twenty or she might
as easily be twenty years older. Those eyes certainly gave the impression of a long, eventful life.

'Good morning,' Felicity said, before Richard could perform any introductions. 'I am Lady
Stanton.'

The woman curtsied, bowing her head. 'Good
morning, my lady. I am Yvette Marchant.'

French accent. Not too strong. Well modulated.
Yvette looked up again at Felicity and then her
gaze flickered uncertainly towards Richard.

Poor thing. But pity was no reason to employ
someone. Richard was watching intently. Was this
a test? Is that why he hadn't warned her? To gauge
her reaction? To see if she reacted in horror, with
a scream, averting her eyes from Yvette's scars?
Mayhap that should infuriate her but it actually
intrigued.

Felicity smiled at Yvette, and gestured towards
a chair.

'Please, take a seat, Mademoiselle Marchant.
Will you tell me about yourself?'

The green eyes exuded pride and defiance. This was a woman who had been hurt and—evidenced by those hollow cheeks—she was a woman in dire straits. Was she as experienced as Richard had claimed? But he was no fool, to take on a maid with no skill to attend to his wife.

'Where are you from?'

'I was born in Paris, milady. I came to England when I was seventeen years old.'

'To escape the troubles?'

Yvette nodded. An *émigrée*, then. There had been many during those horrendous times in France.

'I see. Do you have experience as a lady's maid, *mademoiselle*?'

'But yes, or his lordship, why would he have brought me here to you? I was the lady's maid to Lady Ashcroft until the last year, when she died.'

Lady Ashcroft—a mental image of the baronet's wife arose: always immaculately dressed and *coiffured*, skin glowing, even at her advanced age.

'I have the reference.' Yvette held out a couple of sheets of paper. Her hand trembled. 'Milady wrote them for me when she was ill. Sir Humphrey, he gives me the letter, too. He has no need for lady's maid now. He lives now in the country all the time. He is, I think, not well either. He misses milady.'

Felicity took the papers. They were creased and smudged in places, as though they had been handled many times.

'Have you worked since Lady Ashcroft died?'

Yvette's shoulders dropped as a quiet huff of expelled air revealed she had been holding her breath. 'No. I have…this.' She gestured at her face. 'You do not say so, but you see it. No lady likes a maid they cannot look in the eye.' She stood, and held out her hand for her references.

'Wait. Please.' Felicity clasped Yvette's outstretched hand. 'I would never reject you merely on account of your looks but, equally, I would not employ you *because* of them either.' She was conscious of Richard's scrutiny, but he maintained his silence. The decision was hers. 'I wish for a maid with skill, *mademoiselle*. I knew Lady Ashcroft, although not well, but I recall she was ever beautifully turned out…oh!' She laughed. 'Now I have made her sound like a horse, have I not?' A muffled snort sounded from the vicinity of the door, where Richard stood. 'Please, *mademoiselle*, be seated again whilst I read your references.'

Yvette sat, and Felicity read both documents. As she suspected—for Richard would not have presented Yvette unless he was impressed—they were glowing.

She smiled at Yvette. 'Welcome to Fernley Park, *mademoiselle.*'

'You will call me Yvette,' the Frenchwoman pronounced, pure delight shining in her eyes, 'for that is my name.'

After Mrs Jakeway had taken charge of settling Yvette—for her worldly belongings were packed into a valise she had brought with her—Richard said, 'Am I forgiven for bringing only the one applicant for you to interview, Felicity?'

'Indeed you are, although I wonder whether Yvette might regret taking the position when she sees what unpromising material she has to work with.'

Richard frowned, then strode across the room, taking her by the shoulders.

'Do not belittle yourself. You are the Countess of Stanton. You have the correct number of arms and legs, eyes and ears, do you not? Your body works as you wish it to work, and you are unscarred, unlike poor Yvette. If you do not judge her by her appearance, why do you judge yourself? You have a good heart and a bright and enquiring mind. And...' his eyes bored into her '...you are an attractive, passionate, vital woman.'

As his head lowered, sick fear clutched Felicity even as her blood heated and her treacherous lips parted, ready for his kiss. This was not their bargain. Lust was urging him to kiss her. Nothing more. She felt it too, that lust. But already her heart skipped a beat whenever she saw him, or heard his voice. She must confine their intimacies to the bedchamber, where they belonged, or she would be lost. During the day, all she required was polite co-existence.

About to claim her lips, Richard hesitated. His eyes searched hers. 'What is it? What is wrong?'

Felicity tore from his grasp. Oh, she wanted him. But how would she survive when—as was inevitable—he turned his attentions elsewhere? Her bed would feel deserted and cold enough but if she had become accustomed to his attentions during the day as well, that would be too much to bear. She dragged in a breath, hardening her heart even as she stretched her mouth into a smile, holding her courage against his stormy expression.

'Nothing is wrong, Richard. You are right, I should hold myself in higher esteem. You do not need to kiss me to bolster my confidence. Your words were more than adequate. Thank you.'

She hurried from the room, willing her legs to stop shaking.

Chapter Twenty-One

Two days later

Richard grabbed Felicity's hand as she reached for the door handle.

'Why?'

'Why what?' Felicity tugged her hand free.

Richard paced the library, hot anger surging through his veins. He came to a halt in front of his wife. 'Did I wed twins? You are a different woman by night and by day. I cannot fathom you.'

He had come into the library, and Felicity had been seated by the window, reading. He had smiled; made small talk; invited her to walk with him by the lake. She had been cool, monosyllabic, polite as she had rebuffed his every overture. Then he had reached to stroke her hair and she had flinched from him. *Flinched*. What did she imagine he might do?

She had stood up. He had taken her in his arms,

but she had ducked, evading him, and made for the door. Which is when he had grabbed her.

He studied her expression. 'What are you afraid of?'

'Nothing. I am not afraid. We have a bargain.'

'And my part of that bargain is to leave you entirely to your own devices all day every day?'

She nodded.

His teeth clenched so hard he feared they might crack. 'Very well. There is no need for you to go. I shall leave you in peace.'

He stormed into his study and strode to the window where he stared unseeingly at the view, his temper still simmering. His bride was an enigma. They had been wed a week and, by night, she was passionate, willing and generous: all soft gasps and breathy screams. But, by day, she held him at arm's length, shunning intimacy and shunning, it seemed, friendship and companionship too. Was it merely lust she felt for him? But, if so, where did that lust disappear to as the sun rose every morning?

Her confidence in her appearance was low—thanks to her mother—but she discouraged any attempt to bolster her self-esteem. Was he too impatient? Expecting her to change overnight, when she had spent many years seeing herself through her mother's eyes?

Women! Who could understand them?

Exasperated by his circling thoughts, Richard strode for the door. He was in dire need of fresh

air and physical exercise and he needed to keep
Thor fit for the race on Saturday.

Felicity sat in the library, her restless fingers
drumming a tattoo on the arm of the chair as
her equally restless mind pondered her marriage.
What was she to do? It would be so easy to accept
Richard's attentions and intimacies, but it would
be all too easy to become accustomed to them.
They had no meaning to him, despite his anger—
they were empty words and empty gestures cal-
culated to smooth the path of their marriage of
convenience. He was being kind. Nothing more.

She had only to remember her mother, and
poor Emma, to know what pain and despair lay
ahead if she failed to protect her heart. It would
be easier once in London, with more distractions.
If she could just hold her nerve until she was
with child, mayhap she could survive with her
heart intact.

The telltale bustle of arrival in the hall roused
her from her brooding. Visitors—just the thing
to take her mind off the conundrum of her marriage. It was not long before a knock at the door
announced Trick.

'My lady, his lordship's cousin, Mr Durant, has
arrived. I have shown him into the salon.'

Richard's cousin? She had no recollection of
meeting a Mr Durant during her rare forays into
society.

'Thank you, Trick. Where is Lady Stanton?'

'She is in her sitting room, my lady. I have sent Peter to inform her.'

'And do you know where his lordship is?'

'He went out riding a little over an hour ago.'

'Thank you, Trick.'

No doubt out on Thor again. She had now seen for herself the spirited stallion, and could understand her mother-in-law's fears for Richard's safety, but he seemed to delight in the challenge of mastering the animal.

When Felicity entered the salon, Mr Durant greeted her with a twinkle in his eye and a wide smile. 'I take it I have the pleasure of meeting the new Lady Stanton?'

'You do indeed, Mr Durant. I am pleased to welcome you to Fernley Park.'

He was around Richard's height—six foot—but there the resemblance ended, for Mr Durant was as slender as a whip, with blue eyes and fair, curly hair. He extended an exaggerated leg and bowed low.

'I am delighted to make your acquaintance, my lady.' He glanced past Felicity and his grin widened. 'And my dear aunt—you are well, I hope?'

The dowager swept past Felicity and Mr Durant and sat, ramrod straight, in her favourite chair by the fire. 'Good afternoon, Mr Durant. I do not believe we were expecting you, were we? To what do we owe the pleasure of your visit?

'Mr Durant is a *distant* cousin,' she added, looking at Felicity.

Uncomfortable with her mother-in-law's frosti-
ness, Felicity said, 'Welcome to Fernley Park, sir.
I look forward to becoming better acquainted.
Am I to understand you are a friend of Richard's
as well as his kinsman?'

'I like to think so and, as we are now cousins—
albeit *distant*—I beg you will call me Charles.'

'I have no objection,' Felicity said, warming to
him. 'And I would be pleased if you will recipro-
cate and call me Felicity.'

'Indeed I shall. I can see we shall get on fa-
mously, Felicity. My cousin is a fortunate man.'

Felicity sat on the sofa. Charles immediately
sat beside her.

'You were about to enlighten me as to the reason for your visit, Mr Durant,' the dowager said.

Charles appeared impervious to the dowager's
inhospitable tone. 'I was knocking around town
at a loose end, dear Aunt, and thought I'd pay my
favourite cousin a visit. Nothing whatsoever,' he
added, with a surreptitious wink at Felicity, 'to
do with my eagerness to inspect his new bride,
I do assure you.'

Felicity returned his infectious smile as two
maids entered the room carrying trays laden with
tea and cakes.

'I am sorry Richard is not here to welcome
you,' Felicity said to Charles. 'He is out riding,
but I expect him to return very soon.'

'Yes, so I was informed, on that crazy stallion
of his. And I hear he is racing it on Saturday.'

Felicity tried to ignore the squirm of apprehension in her belly at the thought of that race.

'I do wish you might do something to curb Stanton's penchant for taking risks, Felicity,' the dowager said, in a faint voice.

'I beg you not to fret, dear ladies,' Charles said. 'The stallion is highly strung, but Richard is an excellent horseman. I very much doubt he will come a cropper.'

'I am all gratitude for your unwavering faith in my abilities, Charles—' came a dry comment from the doorway '—but I fear neither my mother nor my wife are likely to be reassured by your words.'

Chapter Twenty-Two

Richard had tried to shake himself free of his unaccustomed fit of despondency with a fast and furious gallop on Thor but as soon as he turned for home his frustration with Felicity's inconsistent behaviour had resurfaced with a vengeance. She had been reluctant to wed him from the first and, despite the 'bargain' of their marriage, her rejection hurt.

He entered the salon, cheered by the news of Charles's arrival, only to hear his cousin inadvertently fuelling the fears of Mother and Felicity over that blasted race.

'Stan.' Charles leapt to his feet and hurried across the room to clasp Richard's hand. 'You must believe I had no intention of scaring the ladies… Oh, you know me, Coz—my mouth runs before my brain at times.'

'Worry not, Charles, they were both in a fret about it before ever you arrived. It is good to see you.'

'I am relieved to hear you say so. I did won-der…with your so recent nuptials…if I am in the way, you only have to say.'

'You are welcome, Charles. I see you have made Felicity's acquaintance.'

'I have, and we have been getting along fa-mously, is that not so, Felicity? Oh, do not take offence, dear fellow. I begged your lady's permis-sion before making free with her name.'

Richard glanced at Felicity, whose eyes were firmly fixed on Charles. His temper flared.

'My wife is nothing if not accommodating.'

Ah. Now he had her attention. Her amber eyes clung to his face, then travelled slowly down to linger on his clenched fists. Swearing silently, he loosened his fingers.

'I trust you enjoyed your ride, my dear?' Fe-licity turned to Charles before Richard could re-spond, continuing, 'A vigorous ride is so very soothing if one is feeling a trifle out of sorts, would you not agree, Charles? Oh, not that I am suggesting for one moment that Richard was in any way out of temper, of course.' Guileless amber eyes turned on Richard. 'It was merely an observation.'

'My ride was exactly how I expected it to be. I find consistency in all things so very essential. Do you not agree, my sweet?'

Felicity lifted her chin. 'I find consistency overrated, Husband. It can so easily result in *ennui*, don't you find?'

Richard felt his mouth twitch and his prickly temper slowly subsided.

'I am not certain I followed that exchange, Coz,' Charles said, in a peevish tone. 'No doubt I shall, in time, become accustomed to interpreting such pointed asides. Although why you married couples needs must talk in riddles quite escapes me, I am sure.'

'It does not escape me,' the dowager said, tight-lipped. 'Quarrelling within earshot of others is most unbecoming. I am surprised at you, Stanton. I suggest you apologize.'

'Oh, no, Mother, it is I who should apologize,' Felicity said quickly. 'I am afraid I provoked Richard beyond endurance earlier, and I am sorry.'

'And I too, my dear.'

'And now we are all friends again, might I ask what time dinner is served?' Charles asked. 'I'm famished.'

'Well, *really*.' Richard's mother rose. 'You too, Mr Durant, could do with a lesson in good manners. I shall rest in my bedchamber before dinner.'

'Well?' Charles looked from Richard to Felicity and back again. 'Do you intend to enlighten me about dinner, or must I beg?'

'*This* is an abomination, milady.'

The words jolted Felicity from her reverie. She stared at Yvette.

Abomination? 'I beg your pardon?'

'This, milady.' Yvette marched across the room

to the wardrobe and flung the door wide with a dramatic flourish. 'It is an abomination.'

Felicity sank on to a nearby chair. She had been preoccupied with Richard—it took her a few minutes to disengage her thoughts and concentrate on Yvette's words, and then a bubble of amusement lodged in her throat. She should be offended and take Yvette to task for her impertinence, or her lack of respect, or whatever else her mother-in-law would find to deplore in her maid's behaviour, but Felicity was, instead, diverted. The Frenchwoman was undoubtedly passionate and sincere.

'What, precisely, do you find to be an abomination, Yvette?'

'All of it.' Yvette flung a dismissive arm towards the open wardrobe. 'What are you to wear for dinner tonight, milady?' Yvette turned tragic eyes towards Felicity. 'There is a *guest*. And when we go to London? This?' She snatched out a white muslin dress and flung it on the bed. 'This?'

'Yvette!'

The maid stopped in the act of dragging another dress from the wardrobe.

'I am happy that you care about my appearance, but please understand that I have worn those same garments for some time now, and I have survived, have I not?'

'Ah, but, milady, then you did not have me. I have the reputation.'

Felicity bit back a smile. 'What are your objections to my clothes, might I ask?'

'The colours, they are *mal*. They make you—

how you say, sickly. Your lips, your cheeks, they go *bleu*. You need the strong, the jewel colours, to make your skin alive.'

'Well, in time, Yvette, I shall purchase new dresses, and I shall rely on your help. But, in the meantime, I am afraid I have no choice but to continue to wear my existing gowns.'

Yvette continued to grumble as she helped Felicity dress for dinner. She arranged her hair, brushing it thoroughly then twisting and pinning it up in a way that softened and framed her face rather than accentuating the sharpness of her features.

'I make the lotions for your skin, it will be soft and smell delicious, for your lord, and he will not be angry with the bills from the modiste. And your hair—with my own recipe I will make it glow with the health. You will see, milady. You will not regret employing Yvette.'

Her fingers suddenly stilled on Felicity's hair. 'I have the idea, milady. You will wait there.'

The maid flew from the room. As Felicity waited, her thoughts turned yet again to Richard and, as if the thought had conjured up the man, a soft knock at the door heralded his arrival.

'I thought to escort you down to dinner, Felicity,' he said, sauntering into the room, starkly handsome in his evening clothes, his brown eyes appraising her. He held out a jewellery case. 'By way of an apology for my behaviour, and a token of my esteem.'

He opened the lid, and Felicity gasped. Guilt

flooded her. She did not deserve gifts. She would try to find some middle ground in their everyday dealings.

'They are beautiful, Richard. Your mother—?'

'Never wears them.' He placed the case on the dressing table in front of Felicity. The ruby-and-diamond necklace and matching eardrops, cushioned on white velvet, glowed blood red and white-hot in the candlelight. 'They are part of the Stanton collection and, therefore, yours to wear whenever you please. If you wish to have any of the jewels reset, you need only to say. Some of the styles are too old-fashioned for today—they would swamp your delicate neck.'

Tingles raced through her as long fingers feathered the side of her neck.

One black-clad arm reached over her shoulder and lifted the necklace from the box. 'Allow me.'

The flesh between her thighs leapt in response to his deepening tone. Her teeth sank into her lower lip.

He bent to fasten the catch.

The hairs on the back of her neck rose as his warm breath played across her skin and, in the looking glass, the quickening rise and fall of her chest was emphasized by the glowing jewels. His face appeared over her shoulder, reflected next to her own as he rubbed his freshly shaved cheek against hers.

'You smell lovely,' he murmured and a delicious sensual awareness washed over her skin.

His head tilted and a warm tongue trailed up

the side of her neck to her ear. Gentle teeth nibbled. Then he reached for the eardrops and hung one from her lobe. He nibbled his way around the nape of her neck to her other ear. Shivers raced up and down her arms and she trembled as her nipples grew hard and her bones turned soft.

'There.'

She could remain still no longer. She rose to her feet, and turned. Straight into his arms.

'It is dark outside, Felicity Joy,' he murmured, his lips inches from hers. 'It is our time.'

He claimed her lips with a deep-throated 'mmmm' that made her bones melt.

Chapter Twenty-Three

The door opened but, before he released her, Richard put his lips to Felicity's ear.

'Later…'

That seductive promise whispered across her skin and reverberated deep in her soul, setting her senses aflame. She clung to him, a moan escaping her lips. Strong hands steadied her. She sucked in a deep breath before turning to a beaming Yvette, who had returned carrying a deep red Chinese silk shawl.

'Tallis, she did not tell the untruth. She said the rubies.' Tallis was the dowager's personal maid.

Yvette bustled towards Felicity to wrap the shawl around her shoulders, oblivious to Richard's perplexed frown. Felicity ducked her knees to look in the mirror. She had never worn this colour before. Her skin in the candlelight looked warm and alive, her eyes sparkled back at her, her cheeks were becomingly flushed…or was that the result of Richard's kiss?

'What has Tallis to do—?'

'Milady needs the colour, milord. Her dresses, they are all…' Yvette hesitated, lips pursed. 'They are *pah*.'

'And I find I am none the wiser. Felicity…?'

'Yvette seems to think that my entire wardrobe is…unsuitable.'

Richard stepped back and perused Felicity, head to toe.

'I like you in that colour, Felicity Joy. But, still…Tallis?'

'I beg for her help,' Yvette said. 'I ask her for the coloured shawl to suit milady, and she tells me about the rubies. *Bon*. You will not disgrace me tonight, milady.'

'No, I will not, Yvette. Thank you.'

On their way to the dining room, the memory of their quarrel still weighing on her mind, Felicity searched for a neutral subject.

'Why does your mother so dislike Charles? I can see he might not be her idea of the perfect gentleman, but he *is* a family member, and a guest.'

'He is not merely a cousin, Felicity. He is, until our son is born, my heir. He is not, you may have surmised, the steadiest of fellows and I am afraid that goes for his attitude to money as well.'

'So her objection to him is *what* he is rather than *who* he is?'

'Indeed, although I could not with any honesty claim Charles is the sort of young man who would ever gain my mother's approval.'

* * *

Dinner was quiet, the dowager's brooding disapproval casting a shadow over the conversation, and the men subsequently lingered over their port. When they eventually joined the ladies in the salon, Felicity sat at the pianoforte and sang and a warm glow filled her at the heat in Richard's eyes as he watched her.

'Later...'

His promise echoed through her mind, a delicious tremor of anticipation snaking through her, as the dowager bade them goodnight and retired. Richard and Charles were sprawled on facing sofas, discussing hunting. Felicity, next to Charles and facing Richard, caught his eye as she stood.

'If you will excuse me, I am tired,' she said. 'I, too, will bid you goodnight.'

Both men stood, and Richard took her hands, pressing a kiss on her suddenly overheated skin.

'Goodnight, my dear.'

In bed, she waited. And waited. Finally, when the clock on the mantel read three o'clock, no longer able to keep her eyes open, Felicity snuffed out her candle and tried to sleep.

Richard buried his head under the bedclothes at the knock on his bedchamber door. His head thumped in rhythm with his heartbeat, which was entirely too loud for comfort.

'Come back later, Simson,' he gritted out.

Even talking was an effort. Why had he allowed Charles to keep him up drinking so late?

'It isn't Simson. It's me.'

The bed dipped on one side and the sheet was slowly pulled back. Richard screwed his eyes shut against the light and groaned.

'Here. Drink this. My father used to swear by it.'

He cranked open one eyelid. A glass, filled with some noxious-looking substance, wavered in front of his eyes. He levered himself up into a half-sitting position.

'What is it? It looks foul.'

'Oh, it is. But it will settle your stomach and help with your headache,' Felicity said in a far-too-cheerful voice.

'If I drink it, will you leave me in peace?' He reached for the glass, willing to try anything to ease his pounding head.

'Don't sip at it, swallow it in one,' Felicity warned as his lips found the rim of the glass.

He tipped his head back, braced himself, and gulped the thick substance down. 'Urrgggh.'

He glared at Felicity, perched on his bed neatly attired in a white muslin morning gown, her hair pinned up. 'What time...?' He peered at the clock. 'Twelve o'clock?' He groaned, dropping his head back to the pillow.

'Charles has been up these past two hours.'

'He is accustomed to late hours and an excess of brandy. I gave up that particular weakness some time ago.'

'How do you feel now?'

Richard took inner stock. 'Better.' His guts were no longer roiling and the drumroll in his head had softened. 'What was in that?'

'It is better you do not know.'

Richard fumbled for her hand. 'Thank you. I hope you did not stay awake waiting for me last night?'

'Oh, no. I was quite exhausted. I was asleep almost before my head touched the pillow.'

Had she not missed him at all? The uncertainties that had plagued him after her rejection yesterday reared their heads again. Well, if that was how she wanted their marriage to be, who was he to deny her?

By the time Richard was fit to face the day, both the dowager and Felicity had eaten luncheon and only Charles was in the dining room, his plate still piled high.

'I came back for a second helping, Coz. Talented cook, your Mrs Pratt. I can recommend the pork pie. Help yourself.'

'Thank you, Charles. You are most generous.'

'Oh, don't mind me, Coz,' Charles said, waving his fork airily, 'you know I ain't one to stand on ceremony.'

Richard selected a slice of bread and some ham. His stomach lurched as he contemplated the pie, and he decided to pass.

'I am, as ever, delighted to see you, Charles, but I should warn you that Felicity and I leave for

London very shortly. You are most welcome to stay longer, however, if there is a particular reason for you to be out of town?'

Charles laughed, quite unabashed. 'The duns aren't beating down my door quite yet, Coz, although a monkey wouldn't go amiss.'

'I paid off your debts last year, Charles. What happened?'

'Now, don't go all poker-faced on me, Stan. A fellow has to live.' Charles fell silent, eyeing Richard hopefully.

'One hundred, Charles, and no more.'

Charles grinned. 'Can't blame a fellow for trying. No, truth be told, I couldn't contain my curiosity any longer. You've set the *ton* on its ears with your marriage, don't you know? The gabble-mongers are in their element with the news the Elusive Earl has been leg-shackled at last and the air is rife with speculation about the speed of the wedding and the relative obscurity of the bride.'

Richard felt his forehead bunch and lower. 'It is no one else's business.'

'Couldn't agree more, dear chap,' Charles said, with a lift of his fair brows, 'but you must have been prepared for rumours to fly about.'

He had not.

'I should hate you to think I have come to spread gossip,' Charles continued, around a mouthful of pie, 'but I thought you should be aware of what is being said.' He lowered his voice, leaning closer. 'The latest *on dit* is that she entrapped you.'

'What the…!' Richard snapped his teeth against a curse. 'I am not in the habit of being forced to do anything against my inclination.'

'Oh, *I* know that, Coz. I believe the gossip is fuelled by your wife's age, and the fact she has been out for…*ahem*…several years. I'm ashamed to admit I could not quite bring the lady to mind, so I determined to come and see the truth for myself.'

Richard tensed as his pulse pounded. How dare *anyone* speculate about his wife in such a way?

'She is delightful,' Charles rattled on, 'but not…if I might venture…*quite* in your usual style. Love match, was it?'

His knowing tone and the mischief in his blue eyes goaded Richard, whose head was starting to hammer once more. 'Love? Love is for fools. Ours is a marriage of convenience. I have neither time nor inclination for more. Now, if you will excuse me, I have business to attend to.'

He strode from the room, Charles's amused, 'Didn't touch a nerve there, did I, Coz?' floating after him.

In the hall, Felicity was heading for the stairs.

'Felicity, wait.'

Richard searched her shuttered expression. Had she overheard his words to Charles? Did it matter? She had not overheard anything she did not already know.

On a whim, he said, 'Would you care for a turn around the garden?'

Her gaze slid from his. 'Not now, Richard. I

have promised to go through the linen stores with Mrs Jakeway. And don't you have business to attend to?'

So she had heard. He watched her disappear up the stairs. Why had he even bothered to try? Why should he care? Love was a game for fools. Felicity had the right idea—stay aloof. That way you couldn't get hurt.

Clamping his teeth shut against the headache-induced nausea that swelled, he spun on his heel and marched into his study.

Chapter Twenty-Four

The next day was Saturday, the day of the race between Richard on Thor and Sir Timothy Rowling on Brutus. The course had been agreed, stewards placed at strategic points along the parish boundary and all gates along the route opened. The riders must pass each steward, but could choose to jump any hedge rather than divert through the nearest gateway.

Felicity, who had prayed for rain, cursed the cloudless sky as Charles drove her to Rowling Manor in time for the start of the race. Charles had ridden the course with Richard the previous afternoon, and described the course in frightening detail as he drove. Already sick with nerves, Felicity's mood was not improved when the first person she saw when they arrived was Lady Rowling, clinging to Richard, who had ridden over that morning.

'Do not worry, dear Lady Stanton, I have taken

good care of your husband and ensured he is well nourished in preparation for his exertions.'

'Thank you.' *Why don't you concentrate on your own husband?* Her jealousy of the other woman appalled Felicity. If seeing him with Lady Rowling sparked such emotions, how would she cope in London, where he would be surrounded by women even more beautiful? Felicity frowned. It would seem her husband had already taken residence in her heart.

Richard extricated himself from Lady Rowling, grabbed Felicity's hand and drew her to one side. 'I am very pleased you came, Felicity. I know you do not approve, but there is no need to look so worried. I promise I shall return safe and sound. Thor is much fitter than Rowling's nag.'

'That is what concerns me,' Felicity said. 'You appear to believe you—and Thor—are invincible. What if—?'

'Stop! You have been paying too much attention to Mother.'

'She is distraught. I do not believe she will rest until this nonsense is over.'

'Nonsense? Did you expect me to reject the challenge? Trust me. I will return in one piece. You do not see Lady Rowling worrying over *her* husband's ability.'

No, indeed. She is too busy dancing attendance on you. 'I do not doubt your skills, Richard. I just do not understand why you needs must take such risks.'

'Now you *sound* like Mother. I'm a grown

man. I know my abilities and my limitations. You should trust me not to take unnecessary risks.'

The whole race is one unnecessary risk. But she had said as much as she dared. He was clearly not listening. She watched, heart in mouth, as Dalton legged Richard up on to Thor, who wheeled round, ears flat. Richard settled him with a few words but both horses remained on their toes, sensing the atmosphere.

'Once they're off, there's a viewpoint up the hill where we can see most of the course,' Charles said in Felicity's ear. 'We will go up there, and you will see what a fine horseman you married.'

From the hill, they watched the two horses gallop neck and neck across fields, down lanes and through woodlands. Felicity was proud of Richard's undoubted skill as he handled the powerful stallion but, every time they faced a hedge, her heart froze until they landed safely on the other side. Towards the end of the course, it was clear Brutus was tiring and, before the last hedge, Sir Timothy steadied him, trotting through the gateway and lifting his hand in a good-natured salute as Richard and Thor disappeared towards the Manor.

'Shall we go and congratulate the victor?' Charles handed her into the curricle.

They drove up to the Manor in time to see Lady Rowling congratulate Richard with a kiss.

Shafts of pure jealousy speared Felicity. 'Charles. If you do not mind, might we say "congratulations" and then leave? I should like to set Mother's mind at rest.'

'Of course, if that is what you want.' Charles raised his voice. 'Congratulations, Coz. I never doubted you could do it.'

Richard, still red-faced, hair sweat-dampened, rounded the curricle to Felicity's side, his eyes searching hers. 'You look as tired as I feel.' He lifted her gloved hand to his lips. 'I told you I would be safe.'

Felicity forced a smile, conscious of Lady Rowling watching. 'You did indeed. Well ridden. I will see you at home later.'

'You must not take such women to heart,' Charles said as they took the road home. 'Richard has more sense than to be entrapped by such as Lady Rowling, I assure you. She is determined to fling herself at him, but she only succeeds in making herself look foolish.'

What could she possibly say to that?

Charles did not seem at all put out by her silence. Instead, he rattled on, 'Stan's not known as the Elusive Earl for nothing.'

'Elusive Earl?'

'They name him such in the clubs because he is discreet to the point of secrecy. In fact, there is a wager in the Book at White's as to the identity of his current mistress.

'Hoi, steady there!' He switched his attention to the horses, jibbing at a fallen branch on the road ahead.

Felicity absorbed his revelation, breathing

deeply until she was sure she had her emotions on a tight rein. Fortunately, Charles was preoccupied with the horses until they settled once more into a steady trot.

'What was I saying? Oops, my wretched tongue running on again. I should not mention the Betting Book to a lady, should I?' He laughed. 'They'd drum me out if they knew. Men's business, don't you know. Do not, I beg of you, mention this to Stan.'

That she could promise.

Chapter Twenty-Five

Ten days later

Felicity gazed from the window as the carriage pulled up outside Stanton House, in Cavendish Square. Richard, dressed for riding, top boots polished, riding whip in hand, appeared at the door, having driven to town in his curricle, with Charles. Felicity had managed to mask her hurt at his choice. She liked Charles, but she resented the way he had monopolized Richard's time.

Richard's words rang again in her ears: *'Love? Love is for fools. Ours is a marriage of convenience. I have neither time nor inclination for more.'*

How true that observation. As soon as there was an alternative to her company, he had become the Elusive Earl again.

Can you blame him? You rejected his every overture, even before Charles arrived.

'Welcome to Stanton House, Felicity.'

Still that cool smile as he handed her from the carriage. Despite it being safer in every way for her heart, she could not but regret the polite distance between them.

'Your house is very imposing.'

'*Our* house. It will be more suited to a family home than to a bachelor's residence, that is certain.'

Family? Not only had Richard avoided Felicity during the day since Charles's arrival, neither had he visited her bed at night. She had contrived to keep busy, allowing little time to think, but at night the minutes and the hours had stretched, mocking her futile efforts to banish him from her thoughts.

'You are going out?' *Is he going to see* her?

'I'm sorry to rush away, but I am sure Mrs Carter, the housekeeper, will show you around. I have some pressing business to attend to.'

'There is no need to apologize.' Felicity swallowed painfully. 'I am sure I will have plenty to keep me occupied.'

Who is she? How might I find out?

Her stomach screwed into knots. There was little hope of Richard returning to her bed whilst they were in London,

'I am sure you will.'

Richard smiled as he surveyed the street, his eagerness tangible. Felicity battened down her emotions and pasted on a bright smile.

This is how my life is to be.

'Will you be home for dinner?' she asked.

She forced her imagination away from Richard's likely activities that afternoon and concentrated on her plan to visit Westfield tomorrow.

I wonder if Dominic is back in town.

'Of course. I will see you later.' Richard lifted her hand before she understood his intentions, stripped off her glove, and pressed warm lips to her skin. She fought not to snatch her hand from his grasp. 'I shall look forward to dining *à deux* with my wife. This is meant to be our honeymoon, after all, even though it has been delayed. I must confess, although Charles is good company in small doses, his constant rattle does weary one after a time.'

'You have not the excitement to be back in London, milady?'

Felicity started. She had pleaded a headache, postponing her tour of Stanton House with Mrs Carter, forgetting Yvette would be in her bedchamber, unpacking her trunk.

She put a hand to her forehead. 'I have the headache, Yvette. Could you finish that later? I wish to rest,' she said, even as her inner voice berated her for allowing Richard to overset her.

Other women accepted the realities of their husbands' hedonistic lives.

How many, though, are like Mama, hiding their distress and boredom behind bright smiles?

Felicity refused to descend into despondency. She had forged an interesting life before her marriage—despite the disapproval of some—and she would continue to do so. She was not—could not possibly be—in *love* with her husband. She enjoyed their lovemaking, and she had missed it over the past week or so, but that was not love.

Yvette folded down the bedcovers and waited to help Felicity disrobe. A glance at the maid's face gave Felicity pause. The Frenchwoman had not given up, despite her disadvantages. Felicity had learned something of the deprivations of Yvette's life since the death of her former employer. Shame niggled at her own self-pity when she enjoyed so many of the advantages and privileges of her class.

'My headache has eased,' she said to Yvette. She glanced at the ormolu clock on the mantelpiece. Four o'clock. 'Let us go for a walk in the park. The exercise will refresh us both after the journey.'

'You wish to be seen with *me*, my lady?' Doubt laced Yvette's tone.

'It is customary for a maid to accompany her mistress if she wishes to go out alone, is it not?'

Mutely, Yvette touched her cheek.

Felicity chose her words carefully. 'Yvette, *I* have no qualms, as long as you will not be uncomfortable. I should much prefer your company to that of a maidservant I do not know.'

Yvette huffed aloud, then bustled to the wardrobe. 'Me, I am uncomfortable only to be seen with the lady not dressed to her very best. This makes my skills look poor. You will wear the new walking gown.'

Their delayed departure from Hampshire had given Felicity the opportunity to have some new dresses made up in readiness for their visit to London. Yvette brought forth a round gown of sprigged-primrose muslin, a pomona-green spencer, and a matching bonnet and, studying the result in the mirror, Felicity blessed her new maid's unerring eye for colour and style. She was still no conventional beauty, but the colours gave her skin a healthy glow and, privately, she did believe she looked quite striking.

The first person she saw in the park was her husband, astride a dapple-grey gelding, beside a smartly dressed woman riding a stunning light grey. Behind them were Cousin Leo, Dominic and another woman. Jealousy flared.

So this is his pressing business—riding in the park. I suppose I should be grateful he can spare some of his precious time to dine with me tonight.

Felicity waited as Richard and Dominic peeled away from the group and trotted over to greet her.

Chapter Twenty-Six

'Felicity. I had no expectation of seeing you here. I made sure you would need to rest after the journey.'

He looks uncomfortable. Who is that woman? Is she his mistress? Is that why he has not introduced me? Or is he ashamed of me?

'I felt the need for fresh air.' Felicity's temples began to throb. She forced a smile for Dominic. 'I hoped I would find you in town, Dominic.'

Dominic leapt from his horse and pulled the reins over its head. 'It is good to see you, Fliss.' He slipped into using the name he had used since childhood as he offered her his arm to lean on. 'With your permission, Stan, I shall walk with your wife.'

Richard tipped his hat. 'With pleasure, Avon. I shall see you on the next circuit, my dear.' He wheeled his horse round and trotted off to catch up with the others.

'Who is that woman?'

'That? Oh, no one in particular. I'm pleased you are back in town, Fliss. I hope you mean to visit Westfield soon. There's a problem.'

He had definitely changed the subject. Felicity's stomach hollowed. Had her nightmare begun already?

'What is the problem?'

'It's Millie. Do you remember her?'

'Of course. She went to work in Viscount Radley's household, did she not? Is she ill?'

'Not ill. She has been turned off for loose morals.'

'Oh, no! Is she with child?'

Dominic nodded. 'She refuses to name the man. Thinks he loves her and will stand by her. It appears to have been one of Radley's intimates rather than one of the other servants though.'

Unrequited love. These poor, deluded girls who believe a man's attentions equated to love. Like Emma, although at least she had not been with child.

'Do you think he will provide for her and the child?'

Dominic halted, looking at her with raised brows. 'Do you?'

They walked on, Dominic's horse plodding behind them.

'There are places, I have heard.'

Dominic might be four years her junior, but he gave her a look reminiscent of his father, and his tone was disapproving. 'What have you heard?'

Felicity's involvement with Westfield had

opened her eyes to much of life outside the confines of high society. 'There are charity places, like Westfield. For unmarried mothers.'

'My lady?'

Felicity turned at Yvette's interjection. 'Yes, Yvette?'

'I interrupt, I apologize. But I know of such a place. There is a lady, she is a...how you say...a patron.'

'Who? Do you know her name?'

'I do not, but this house is in Cheapside. My friend went there. They were kind to her.'

'Dominic, would you escort me to Westfield tomorrow, please?'

'Of course. I'll call for you at two. Take care you are ready, mind, for I—'

'Yes, do not say it,' Felicity interrupted, laughing. '*Don't keep your cattle standing in the cold.*' How typical of Dominic to worry about his horses catching a chill if she should dare to keep him waiting. 'I shall be ready for you at two.'

Richard tapped at the door dividing his bed-chamber from Felicity's, and entered. She was already in bed—despite the earliness of the hour—her plaited hair draped over one shoulder. She closed her book, placing it on the bed-side cabinet. He could gain no clue of her feelings from her expression. Was she pleased to see him? Indifferent?

'You are quite recovered from the journey, I hope?'

'Thank you, yes. I am sorry I did not join you for dinner tonight. I dare say I would have been wise to rest this afternoon instead of walking in the park. I was quite done in when we returned.'

'It is of no matter. It is more important that you take care of your health. Did you manage to sleep?'

'I did. And Yvette brought me supper on a tray earlier, so I have eaten as well.' She looked him and up and down. The tip of her tongue moistened her lips. 'You look very smart, Richard. Are you going out?'

Was that a hint of disappointment in her tone? There was a gleam in those amber eyes of hers that stirred his blood. He sat on the edge of the bed.

'I am going to my club,' he said. It was the truth, if not the whole truth. 'I did not think you would mind, as you are indisposed.'

She bit into her lower lip. His pulse quickened. It had been a week…more…too long… He swayed closer. '*Do* you mind, Felicity Joy?' He lowered his head, aiming for her cheek.

She turned her head.

Their lips met.

She was all hot, writhing passion in his arms as their tongues duelled. Frantic fingers tugged at clothing, threaded through hair, sought out sensitive places, tweaking and caressing. His jacket was pushed from his shoulders, his immaculate neckcloth pulled loose and discarded.

Small hands splayed across his chest, drifting ever lower. He reached between them and pushed down the bedcovers, kicked them free, reached for her nightdress, tugged it to her waist. The smooth nakedness of her thighs inflamed him further, and he fumbled for the fall of his trousers, only to find her fingers there already, deftly unbuttoning, delving within to release him, stroking and squeezing.

He moved over her, feeling her moist readiness, revelling in the wanting in her half-lidded eyes as she captured his gaze.

'Now.'

This was no supplication. It was a demand. One he was happy to obey. Scented skin, warm and silky, filled his hands as he cupped peachy buttocks. She opened for him, clamping her legs around his hips. All he wanted, all he could think about, was to be inside her. Hot, wet, welcoming, he entered with no finesse, no delay, and she gasped her pleasure as she stretched to take him, and then clenched fiercely around him as he moved in urgent rhythm.

Fast and furious, they came together, her scream almost drowned out by his triumphal shout. He collapsed on her, chest heaving, sweat beading his brow and upper lip, his brain tumbling in an attempt to catch up. He had come to her bedchamber to make sure she was not ill, to say goodnight. Not to make frantic, passionate love with his wife. He had exhibited no more control than a callow youth. As his breathing slowed and his pulse steadied, he eased his weight from her.

She whimpered, wrapping her arms around him, pulling him down, kissing his ear, whispering, 'I have missed you, Husband.'

Chapter Twenty-Seven

'And I have missed you, too, Felicity Joy.'

Richard sought her sweet lips and kissed her, slowly and thoroughly, until she began to shift restlessly beneath him again.

He reached between her thighs, stroking and circling, until she arched beneath him, small cries of pleasure tearing from her lips. Pushing the neck of her nightgown aside, he sucked one nipple deep into his mouth, flicking the swollen bud with his tongue.

'Richaaaaard.' Her scream trailed into silence punctuated only by gasps as her body bowed, pushing her hips against his hand. Then one final drawn-out cry, followed by her sigh of pleasure.

He took her lips in a long, soothing kiss. She smiled sleepily, lids drooping, lips still moist from his kisses. He straightened her nightgown and tucked the covers round her shoulders. She roused.

'Are you still going out?'

'I am. It is too early for me to sleep. I'm meeting Leo at White's.'

The purse of her lips struck at his heart, and at his conscience. It would take little persuasion for him to stay, to take her in his arms and to drift off to sleep together. He had missed her and he, too, was weary. But he had a visit to make that could not be postponed.

'Sleep well, sweetheart.' He kissed her cheek.

Felicity turned over and snuggled down with a deep sigh. 'I wish you would stay.'

Her words were slurred with fatigue and Richard had to strain to catch them. The urge to stay hovered, tempting, but he banished it with a silent growl. He was in danger of falling under his own wife's spell, and that would never do. Too much dependence on another would end in pain. His parents had taught him that.

He stroked the damp tendrils from Felicity's face and bent to brush her cheek with his lips. He had not lied, other than by omission. He had every intention of going to White's first, to meet friends, to hear the latest political intrigues and to play a hand or two of cards. But he would not stay long, for he had another, more important, visit to make.

Harriet. As he tied a fresh neckcloth, casting an eye over the rest of his clothing for creases, he pondered his former mistress. He owed her an explanation, face to face, about his abrupt ending to their arrangement. She had been an ideal lover—totally discreet, good company, and a pleasure in bed—and he hoped they could part on good terms.

After a pleasant few hours at White's, Richard elected to walk the short distance to Harriet's house in Sackville Street.

'Good evening, Stevens,' he said as he entered the hallway and handed his hat, gloves and cane to Harriet's butler.

'Her ladyship is expecting you, my lord. She is in her private sitting room.'

Richard entered Harriet's sitting room—which adjoined her bedchamber and was the scene of many of their passionate encounters—wishing she had chosen a more neutral setting.

'Good evening, my dear.' He crossed the room to where she lounged on her green-and-cream-striped *chaise longue*, and kissed her outstretched hand. 'You are in good health, I trust?'

He selected a chair that provided some distance between them.

Harriet pouted her full, pink lips as she patted the upholstered seat by her side. 'Are you not going to sit here next to me, Stanton?' She paused; the silence stretched. Then she shrugged. 'I can see by your expression that you have not, after all, had a change of heart. This is truly the end of our *affaire*, then?'

'It is.'

Harriet's lids drooped, concealing her thoughts, but her firmed lips hinted at her disappointment.

'I am sorry for the manner in which I informed you of my marriage. I have come to explain in person.'

'There is little need for further explanation.' Harriet's tone and words held no hint of chagrin. 'You have wed and you do not wish to continue our arrangement—at least, for the time being.'

Richard frowned. 'Do not labour under any misapprehensions, Harry. I have no intentions of continuing with any arrangements outside my marriage, until…'

He hesitated. He could not voice his intentions because, all at once, he was no longer entirely certain what they were. At this moment, he had no thought of bedding any woman other than his wife. He felt his frown deepen. He had never delighted in bedding as many women as possible. He had always preferred to have a mistress: one woman to be faithful to, until the *affaire* ran its course and he was ready to move on.

He had not considered the years ahead when he had so blithely decided to wed. There would be no clean break in the future: if he became dissatisfied with Felicity—or she with him, he realized, with a lurch in his gut—there would be no moving on. He would remain married.

Dark-fringed, violet-hued eyes regarded him teasingly. 'Until…?'

Richard stood abruptly. 'I have something for you, Harry: a token of my appreciation.' He delved in his pocket, withdrawing a small square box. He had visited Rundell & Bridge that afternoon, and selected a pair of amethyst-and-diamond earrings for Harriet.

Harriet opened the box. 'Oh, Richard. They are beautiful.'

'I am pleased you like them.'

He had said all he wanted to say. There was no point in lingering.

Harriet looked up. 'I am sorry to lose you, Stanton. I hope we may still be friends?'

'I hope so too, Harriet. Goodnight.'

In the hall, Stevens handed him his hat, gloves and cane. Richard bid him goodnight and headed out into the night. He turned towards Cavendish Square, lighter-hearted now he had seen Harriet.

The sudden rush of feet alerted him.

He spun round, raising his cane. Two men, armed with clubs, were upon him. He jabbed the cane, two-handed, into the attacker to his left, who doubled over with a *whoosh* of breath. Switching the cane to his left hand, Richard bunched his right into a fist, watching as the second man swung his club. Richard dodged back, then leapt in close, aiming a short jab at the ruffian's nose. He felt the satisfying crunch and squelch of connection as a cry of *'Oi, there!'* reached his ears, followed by the welcome sound of a night-watchman's rattle.

The world went black.

Chapter Twenty-Eight

Felicity awoke and stretched luxuriously, still enveloped in the afterglow of their lovemaking. If only Richard was asleep next to her. That wave of lust…it had swept him along too. It had been more than she had dared to wish for. Seized with an urge to see him, banishing the doubts that threatened to overrule her heart, she leapt out of bed and ran barefoot to the adjoining door. Sudden shyness caused her to open the door quietly, and only just wide enough to pop her head through.

Richard's bedchamber was empty, the bed already made. She closed the door and rang for Yvette. Richard must be at breakfast. It was barely ten o'clock. Surely he would not have gone out already?

Barnes, the butler, materialized in the hall as Felicity walked downstairs.

'Is his lordship at breakfast, Barnes?'

'I do not believe his lordship has arisen yet, my lady.'

She fought to conceal her dismay. Had he not returned last night?

'I make no doubt he was out late and is now catching up with his sleep,' she said, lightly.

'Indeed, my lady.' Not by so much as a flicker did Barnes hint that he knew any different. 'Breakfast is laid out in the back parlour, if you would care to follow me?'

Various dishes—tantalizing aromas scenting the air—were displayed on the sideboard. The table was set for two. Neither place setting had been disturbed.

'There is no need to remain, Barnes. I will serve myself.'

Barnes bowed. 'Very well, my lady.'

Had Richard gone straight from her bed to that of his mistress? Sweat prickled Felicity's spine as she recalled asking him to stay. At least she hadn't begged. Had she? She had been half-asleep: a dangerous state, for was that not the time the truth was most likely to be revealed? When the weary brain did not censor the words spoken? Was she developing feelings for Richard, despite her avowal to keep her heart safe?

She bit half-heartedly into a slice of toast and butter. It tasted of sawdust. She pushed her plate aside, and drank her chocolate, then shoved her chair back. That was enough soul-searching. She would not become a victim of love. By the time she had changed and was ready to go out, shops would be opening their doors for business. She would browse the linen drapers with Yvette and, later, she would visit Westfield with Dominic. It promised to be a busy day: precisely what she needed. There were far worthier causes on which to expend her energies than an errant husband.

In her bedchamber, Felicity contemplated her reflection in the pier glass between the windows. Mayhap she was no beauty, but Yvette had helped her to see she could look better. She fingered the curls that framed her face. Her hair was already glossier, with the use of the honey rinse Yvette had concocted. And her skin almost glowed, the rosewater-and-almond-oil lotion Yvette mixed proving more effective than the Bloom of Ninon de L'Enclos her mother swore by. If her husband preferred the bed of his mistress, she would not become embittered. She would channel her energy into her own life and interests, and learn to merely co-exist with him.

The closed door between her bedchamber and Richard's taunted her. With a muttered curse, she flung across the room and threw it open. She froze on the threshold. The room was still, mockingly, empty. But the bed…was she going mad? The bed that had been so neat and smooth was now rumpled and crumpled, a head-shaped dip in the pillow.

At the knock on her bedchamber door, Felicity hastily shut the linking door, her head whirling. Had she imagined it? No, she knew she had not. And that could only mean that Richard had not slept here last night, and that his servants were protecting him.

'I shall wear the ivory walking dress with the rose pelisse,' she said to Yvette, in no mood for anyone to dictate anything to her. 'And when I have changed, please fetch your cloak and bonnet. We are going shopping.'

Felicity and Yvette, accompanied by Thomas the footman to help carry their purchases, spent a pleasant few hours strolling the length of first New Bond Street, and then Old, examining the variety of goods displayed in the shop windows. About to turn for home, Felicity was accosted by a familiar voice.

'Good morning, Lady Stanton, or should I say "afternoon" as it is, indeed, past noon.' Felicity turned to greet Charles Durant, who was bowing before her. 'Might I offer you my arm?'

'Good afternoon, Mr Durant. You may indeed. We are about to turn for home.'

'That is indeed fortunate, for I happen to be heading in that direction myself.' He crooked his arm for her. 'Is Stanton at home?'

'I cannot be certain, sir. I have been out these past two hours or more.'

'No matter. I can always wait. Or mayhap he is at his club again. I saw him there last night, but he did not linger. Two hands of cards is all, and then he needs must rush off. One can only assume he had a more pressing engagement at home,' he added teasingly.

Felicity swallowed the bile that flooded her mouth.

After a beat or two of silence, Charles said, 'I trust you have spent a pleasant morning?'

'I have indeed.' Felicity indicated Yvette and Thomas, both laden with packages. 'As you see, I have been thoroughly seduced by the contents of the shop windows.'

'They have served their purpose, then.'

Felicity raised a brow.

'The shop windows, of course: the shopkeepers display their wares in the hope of enticing pass-ers-by into their emporia to spend. And, lo and behold, you have obliged. One buys with one's eyes in the first instance. Payment soon follows.'

'That is most profound, Mr Durant.'

'Oh, please, call me Charles. You did so at Fernley.'

'Charles, then, though I must take care to revert to Mr Durant when in company.' They crossed into Cavendish Square from Henrietta Street. 'I have no wish to incur the censure of the *grande dames* of the *ton* so early in my marriage.'

'Have you not, Felicity Joy?' a deep voice said behind them. Felicity's heart leapt, as though it might beat its way free of the cage of her ribs. 'And what, might I ask, have you been up to, to risk such censure?'

Chapter Twenty-Nine

Richard had walked up Henrietta Street, unnoticed, behind Felicity and Charles, who were deep in conversation. Anger had flared, shocking him with its intensity. Why should the sight of Felicity on another man's arm cause such emotion?

Possessiveness. What's yours is yours. Hasn't it always been thus?

He forced a calming breath. Charles was his friend and his cousin. This was a new situation for him, and it had provoked unexpected feelings. In time, he would adjust to having a wife.

Before he could hail them, Felicity laughed at something Charles said, glancing up at him. Why could she not be so easy around him? Why was she so guarded?

Except in bed. Perhaps he should be thankful she left her inhibitions at the bedchamber door. His mind drifted back to the night before, to the willingness of her soft, yet lithe, body in his arms. What would she do—how might she react—if he were to seduce her in the middle of the day? The idea excited him, despite the dull ache at the back of his skull.

At the sound of his voice, Felicity had stiffened and her expression, when she faced him, was wary, in stark contrast to her easy manner with Charles.

'Good afternoon, Richard.'

She failed to meet his eyes, but tucked her hand willingly enough in the crook of his arm after he and Charles exchanged greetings. As they continued around the square, the thump in Richard's head grew more insistent. Perhaps it had been unwise to walk home from Harriet's house, where he had been taken after the attack last night. He had thought the fresh air might do him good.

Richard glanced down at Felicity. 'And where have you been this morning, Felicity Joy?'

'I came upon her in Bond Street,' Charles said, before Felicity could reply. He gestured to the two laden servants walking behind. 'Your lady wife has been busy spending your fortune by relieving the merchants of their wares.'

'I am pleased you have occupied your time in such a pleasant manner, my dear. I understand you are promised to Avon later today, to visit Westfield.'

'Yes, I am looking forward to it.'

'I thought I might come with you, if you do not object?'

'There is no need, Richard. It will no doubt

bore you beyond endurance, and I shall be quite safe with Dominic.'

'I am sure you will.' Richard hid his irritation behind his polite rejoinder. 'However, I am curious about the place. I hope, therefore, you will indulge me by allowing me to accompany you.'

'But of course, if that is your wish.'

Her reluctance grated.

'Thank you for your company, Charles,' Felicity said, as they arrived at Stanton House. 'Would you care for some light refreshments?'

'I would indeed. Now I come to think of it, I *am* peckish.'

Richard thrust aside his exasperation. It appeared Felicity would do almost anything to avoid spending time alone with him.

After having eaten their fill, they moved into the drawing room. Felicity was waylaid by Barnes in the hallway and Richard took the opportunity to tell Charles about the robbery the night before.

'I was hit with a grappling hook.'

Charles winced. 'Painful. Did they steal much?'

'Enough. They took last night's winnings. I was lucky the night watchman came around the corner when he did. He sounded the alarm and the cowards ran off. I was taken to a nearby house to recover.'

Harriet's house. He must pray Felicity never got wind of *that* particular fact.

'I've hired an investigator to make enquiries. He'll start down at the docks. It seems logical, given they used a grappling hook.' He heard a noise by the door. 'Hush, not a word to Felicity, mind. I do not want her troubled.'

'Coz! Soul of discretion, don't you know.'

Felicity entered the drawing room, a card in her hand. 'It is an invitation from Lord and Lady Plymstock,' she said. 'Their ball is tonight, and they beg our attendance.'

'It would be a feather in Lady Plymstock's hat if you made your first appearance as a married couple at her ball,' Charles said. 'Shall you go, do you think?'

'Yes,' Richard said.

'But—'

'The sooner we become old news, the better, Felicity. People will soon find something else to gossip about.'

'I shall hope to see you there,' Charles said, as he took his leave.

When he had gone, Felicity said, 'I must go and change my clothes, ready for our visit to Westfield.'

'Wait a moment, Felicity.' Richard followed her to the door.

She had opened it and he reached across her and pushed it shut. The scent of violets tantalized his senses. He moved closer, trapping her between his body and the door.

'What...? Richard...?'

Richard lifted her chin with his finger, forc-

ing her to meet his gaze. 'What is wrong, Felicity Joy?'

'Nothing…nothing is wrong…I just need to…'

He silenced her with his mouth, angling his
head, softening his lips. 'Mmmmmm. I have been
waiting to do that. Do you not like to kiss me,
Felicity Joy?'

'No. I mean, yes. I mean, not now. D…Domi-
nic will be here very soon. I must change.'

He nuzzled at her neck, mouthing at her soft
skin. 'You taste and smell delicious. I will help
you change your clothes. Go upstairs and send
Yvette away.'

A sharp intake of breath met his words and his
wife turned rigid in his arms. 'It is not appropri-
ate,' she said sharply. 'Not when a visitor is expected at any minute.'

Richard released her.

She looked up at him, hesitated, lifted one hand
to his cheek.

Then she was gone.

Chapter Thirty

A familiar tremor raced down Felicity's spine. Richard had settled one warm hand at the small of her back as they entered Peter Whittaker's study at Westfield, Dominic having disappeared into the schoolroom as soon as they arrived. Would she ever be able to control her reaction to such casual intimacies? The touch meant nothing more than common courtesy to him, but to her…every nerve in her body screamed its awareness of him, triggering a yearning deep inside her body, and her heart.

She wanted him.

Desperately.

She must resist.

A weary smile crossed Mr Whittaker's face as he rose to greet them. New lines had appeared on his face in the months since she had last seen him and his hair had noticeably thinned.

'Good afternoon, Mr Whittaker,' she said. 'It is good to see you again.'

He crossed the room, with hands outstretched. 'Good afternoon, Lady Stanton. I was exceedingly happy to hear the news of your marriage.' His gaze slipped sideways to Richard.

'Mr Peter Whittaker, this is my husband, Lord Stanton—my dear, Peter Whittaker.'

'I am honoured to meet you, my lord. I do hope you will not raise objections to Lady Stanton continuing her support of our school? I cannot tell you what a boon she has been to us these past few years.'

'I am interested to see what good works you do,' Richard replied.

He did not reassure Mr Whittaker, and Felicity realized anew how much power he held. He could prevent her further involvement with Westfield, if he chose, despite his reassurances on the night of their betrothal.

'Might I show you around our establishment, my lord? It is not large, but we do our utmost for the children in our care.'

Richard motioned for Mr Whittaker to lead the way.

'Where do you find the children?' he asked as they left the study.

'Sometimes the magistrates will recommend a child to our care, if they judge a child who comes before them to be capable of redemption. Sometimes they come from the Foundling Hospital. If we can bring them up to be useful members of society, able to earn their living, then we consider our duty done.'

'Finding such children is never a problem. The problem is in choosing which ones are in most urgent need,' Felicity said.

'I understand from my wife that you seek employment for these children, when they reach a suitable age?'

'We do, my lord; we apprentice them with local tradesmen, or we place them in households as kitchen maids and boot boys. It is then up to the individual child to work hard to better themselves. I do not believe we would place half the number of children without the invaluable help of her ladyship and Lord Avon, for they have contacts where I have few.

'Come.' He opened the door to the schoolroom and waved Felicity and Richard through. 'The children are at their lessons. They have an hour of reading and an hour of writing every day. We do not presume to make scholars of them, but I believe it is important for every man and woman to have the ability to read the Bible and to sign their name at the very least.'

'Most enlightened, I am sure.'

Richard's enigmatic comment gave Felicity no clue to his real thoughts. His subsequent silence unnerved her as he stood in the wood-panelled schoolroom, taking in the scene before him, attracting surreptitious glances from the children. Dominic crouched by a young boy's stool, pointing to his slate, murmuring in a low voice.

Jane Whittaker, smiling uncertainly, hurried over to be introduced.

'I never imagined the next time I saw you, you would be a married lady,' she said, eyes anxiously searching Felicity's. 'Are you happy?' she added in a whisper as her husband explained more of the workings of Westfield to Richard.

'Yes, of course.' Felicity had no wish to elaborate. 'Might I speak with Millie, Jane? Dominic has told me of her circumstances.'

'I shall bring her to the study.'

'If you will excuse me,' Felicity said to Richard and Mr Whittaker, 'I must talk to Millie.' She briefly explained Millie's situation to Richard. 'I know you cannot keep her here, Mr Whittaker,' she added, 'but rest assured I will find a place for her.'

'Thank you. It will be a weight off my mind. I should hate to see the poor girl forced into the seedy existence that awaits many of these silly creatures who cannot resist temptation.'

Felicity bit her tongue against a surge of fury. Why did everyone assume such events were the sole fault of the female? She knew how persuasive and silver-tongued men could be in order to get what they desired. And the gullible girls—like her beloved Emma—were left to pick up the pieces of their broken hearts.

Millie, pale and slightly built, was in the study with Jane.

'Will you not name the man responsible, Millie?' Felicity asked.

'He said I mustn't or he won't love me no more.'

Felicity closed her eyes, hearing Emma's voice, stubbornly voicing the exact same sentiments eight years before. 'Does he know you have been turned off?'

A tear trickled down the side of Millie's nose as she shook her head.

'You do know you cannot stay here, Millie?'

'But where will I go, milady? I got nowhere else to go.' Panicky hands clutched at Felicity.

'Hush.' Felicity put her arm around Millie. 'There is a house for girls like you and I shall try to place you there. But you must face facts, Millie—this man does not even know you are in trouble. And you need to understand he is unlikely to stand by his word even if he does find out.'

Sobs racked the girl's slight frame. 'Oh, milady, but I love him. He said he loved me.'

Of course he did.

'It is a harsh lesson you must learn, Millie. Men—*some* men—will say anything to get what they want. Come, dry your tears. We will not see you on the streets, whatever happens. But I would urge you to tell me this man's name.'

And what would you do then? He would laugh in your face. She's expendable: a servant, with no family.

Sheer frustration over Millie's plight churned inside Felicity. The girl would be judged a hussy and beyond redemption by most people. Looking at her blotched face and swollen eyes, Felicity silently swore not to abandon her. She would not allow Millie to sink to the same depths of despair as Emma.

Nausea choked her as the image of her sister's body, lying broken on the flagstones, filled her mind's eye. Emma had died without ever naming the man responsible for her ruin. Scandal had been averted, of course. Suicide was a criminal act as well as a sin against God. Her death had been declared a tragic accident. Felicity knew the truth, however—as did her mother. She dug into her heart for forgiveness for her mother, who had failed to protect Emma. Her foolish, selfish mother, who was now more than half-convinced that the story they had concocted about Emma's death was true.

'Well, Fliss?' Dominic demanded, once they were on their way back home. 'What will you do about Millie?'

'I shall visit the house Yvette told us about, and see if they have room for her.'

Richard, sitting next to Felicity, stirred. 'I will escort you; you are not to go there unaccompanied.'

'Thank you. I admit I should not like to go without a male escort. I had intended to ask Dominic if he might accompany me this afternoon, but I am sure he has more interesting pursuits planned.'

'It is rather late to go today, but I shall hold myself at your disposal tomorrow.' Richard's voice was weary. Glancing at him, Felicity saw him touch the back of his head, wincing as he did so.

'Do you have the headache, Richard?'

'No. The merest twinge, that is all.'

Why won't he meet my eyes? What is he hiding? Suspicions over his whereabouts last night churned her stomach.

'Well, I must say I'm grateful to you, Stan,' Dominic said. 'Helping the children is one thing, but I can't say I'm eager to get embroiled in this other business. Besides, you'll be better placed than me to curb Fliss's enthusiasm for lost causes.'

'Dominic!'

'Sorry, Fliss, but you know it's true. Especially after—' He stopped abruptly as Felicity glared at him. 'Well, you know what I mean.'

'I confess that *I* have no idea what you mean, Avon,' Richard said. 'Pray enlighten me.'

Felicity thought quickly. She was not ready to confide in Richard about Emma's disgrace.

'Dominic merely means I was determined to help at Westfield despite my family's objections.' It was no lie. She had been unwavering in her effort to find some purpose to her life. 'You heard for yourself how Mama and Farlowe feel about the subject.'

'I did indeed. An encounter I should not like to repeat in a hurry. Your forbearance in the face of such antagonism does you credit, my dear.'

Chapter Thirty-One

The Plymstocks' ball was a success. Meaning, Richard thought, with an exasperated sigh, that it was a crush. Since their arrival, he and Felicity had been the centre of attention, every guest wishing to congratulate him and to claim acquaintance with Felicity, who was in high spirits. Her peacock-blue silk evening gown shimmered in the candlelight and a matching ribbon threaded through the shining ringlets framing her smiling face

'You look lovely,' he had said, as he escorted her to their carriage earlier. 'I can hardly believe the change in you.'

She had laughed, sounding delighted. 'You should thank Yvette: she instinctively knows what will suit me. I bless the day you found her, Richard. Thank you.'

As they waited in line to be greeted by their hosts, however, she had gone quiet, clearly on edge.

'What is wrong?'

He'd had to stoop to hear her low reply. 'There is nothing wrong. I am perfectly happy, thank you.'

So subdued, of a sudden. He had noticed her eyeing the other ladies queuing alongside them. Was she still so unsure of her appearance? He had slipped his arm around her waist and squeezed, intending to reassure her. She'd jerked away. He'd felt the frown gather on his forehead. The ups and downs of her moods were a mystery to him, and he brooded over her behaviour, unable to find any logic for her mercurial changes.

Now, whatever had worried her on their arrival had been put aside. She was sparkling, her manner easy as she conversed with the people around her and it was his turn to be on edge as he battled his unexpected compulsion to thrust away every young buck eager to write his name on Felicity's dance card. A visceral reaction, deep in his gut.

What's mine is mine, he mocked himself silently.

He masked his dismay behind his customary urbanity. Inside, he was restless. He felt…vulnerable—a feeling as unaccustomed as it was unwelcome.

She did not want to marry you. It's better not to care. Keep your guard up.

'Greetings, Coz.' Richard started at the voice in his ear. 'Your wife is in fine form, I see.'

'She is indeed, Charles.'

'It makes one wonder why she shunned society for so long,' Charles murmured, *sotto voce*.

'Meaning?'

'She was telling me of her interest in that school. I cannot help but wonder if—' Charles stopped abruptly.

Richard felt the growl begin deep in his chest. 'You wonder if…?'

'Oh, nothing, Coz. Ignore me, I beg you. It was merely…her interest in children…pure speculation, and an atrocious gaffe on my part. Not for the world would I pay attention to such scandalous rumours and, if I hear any such, I shall be sure to put a halt to them, you can rely on it. Never fear, Coz. You have me to watch your back.'

Fists clenched, Richard battled to keep his hands off his cousin. He knew Charles was a rattle, and prone to 'slips of the tongue', although he had never been entirely certain if such slips were innocent, or a deliberate attempt to stir trouble.

'I should be obliged if you would do that, Charles. And you may rest assured: if I should hear any such scurrilous tittle-tattle attached to my wife's name, I shall have no hesitation in dealing with the culprit. Do I make myself clear?'

Charles grinned. 'Eminently, my dear fellow. Sentiments exactly as I would expect of a doting husband. I shall make sure I pass on…'

'Cha-a-arles.'

Charles's blue eyes widened. 'Was that a growl, Stan? I am merely assuring you of my support. No need to take offence with me, old chap.'

'You will not speak of this to anyone else, unless they mention the subject first. Is that clear enough? I will not have my wife's name bandied about. Under any circumstances.'

'Of course not, Coz; as if I would. Very fond of Felicity, I assure you. Now, with your permission, I shall go and make my bow.'

Richard glared through narrowed eyes as Charles sauntered through the group surrounding Felicity, and bowed. Felicity's face lit up, and she handed him her card. Charles scribbled his name. Richard strode forward to take his place by Felicity's side. The sparkle left her eyes, although her smile remained in place.

'They are forming the set for the first,' he said. 'You have not forgotten you are promised to me, my dear?'

'Of course I have not forgotten.'

The change was subtle. He doubted anyone else had noticed that hint of reticence in her manner. He stroked one finger down the stiff length of her spine, tracing tiny circles. He heard her sharp intake of breath, felt her relax.

That was better, though he still could not help but contrast her caution around him to her behaviour with others.

Chapter Thirty-Two

Felicity suppressed the desire that shivered through her at Richard's touch.

Is *she* here? Is she watching?

She skimmed the crowd as Richard led her to the dance floor. This growing obsession with the identity of his mistress was painful but she could not help it. He had already spent their first night in London with her. After bedding his wife for the first time in over a week he had slunk away like a…like a *thief.* Well, she would not allow him to steal her heart. Or her newfound and burgeoning self-respect. She was happiest when she was surrounded by others, and when she could forget her conjectures about Richard and his mistress—who might be here, smiling in Felicity's face whilst all the time… She thrust away her thoughts, cramming her speculations about *that woman* to the darkest recesses of her mind.

True, he had appeared to be the perfect, attentive new husband since their arrival at the ball but

she could *feel* his underlying tension. She conjured up a smile as the musicians struck up the
familiar strains of a Scottish reel. If Richard could
put on a mask for others, then so could she.

This is torture.

Felicity had danced the two first with Richard,
responding to his comments with light ripostes.
Her hand had then been claimed by a succession
of partners, with whom she had exchanged the
usual pleasantries even as her skin had prickled with the awareness of her husband's heavy-
lidded scrutiny from the side of the room. He had
danced with no other. Felicity was both relieved
and rattled by this. As she danced down the set,
she caught his eye. Her bones almost dissolved
at the heat in that glance.

'You are quiet, Felicity.' Charles was her current partner.

'It is Richard,' she whispered, as the steps of
the dance brought them together. 'He is not dancing. Do you think he is bored?'

'I am sure he is not bored. He did mention a
headache earlier today, but I am certain he is more
than content to be here with you.'

The dance parted them. Felicity glanced again
at Richard, still smouldering at the edge of the
floor, brushing off any attempt to engage him
in conversation. His attention was still focused
on her. Desire coiled deep within her, and she
missed her step.

'Steady.' Charles gripped her hand and tugged

her into the correct formation. 'Do not allow Richard to unsettle you. I'll wager he'll claim your hand as soon as you have a dance free.'

Felicity continued to dance by rote, options bouncing around inside her head. Her feelings for Richard were growing stronger. The thought of him with another woman hurt. Were her attempts to protect her heart in vain? Which path should she choose to follow? Should she continue to keep him at arm's length, and risk pushing him into *her* arms? Or should she fight? Try to win his love?

Even the thought of the latter seemed ridiculous and doomed to failure. But was the first option any better? After only three weeks of marriage she could finally empathize with her mother. She had found it was nigh on impossible to deny your heart.

You will not feel affection or love for this man.

She could almost laugh at her naivety. Unless the man in question was cruel or disgusting—a man one could never respect—it would be hard indeed to share the intimacies of the bedchamber and not feel some tenderness for him. And Richard was neither cruel nor disgusting. He was kind, and thoughtful, and strong, and capable. And the most handsome, the most utterly desirable man here tonight.

But he had a mistress. What chance did she, Felicity, have?

As much chance as any woman, if you will but believe in yourself.

She danced on. New partners came and went until, about to embark upon a country dance, a large hand grabbed hers.

'Excuse me, Cheriton. Might I borrow my wife?' The rich, velvety baritone slid like warm honey through every fibre of her being. She threw an apologetic smile over her shoulder at Cousin Leo, who stared after them, eyes creased with fans of laughter. Felicity felt her face flame as Richard led her from the dance floor and headed purposefully for the door. In the hall, he turned to her.

'You look tired, Felicity Joy.'

She searched his face, reading the strain around his eyes, the weary lines bracketing his mouth, the furrows on his brow.

'Is your head still aching, Richard? Charles said—'

'Charles says too much. No, I do not have a headache.'

'Then what *is* troubling you?'

'Nothing. I am merely concerned you are doing too much.'

His effort to smooth his expression was not lost on Felicity. He put his lips close to her ear. 'I cannot wait to bury myself inside you tonight.'

As a distraction, it worked. Her belly clenched and her bones turned pliable. She moved her head, so his lips brushed her cheek.

'I am—quite suddenly—exhausted,' she said, with a tremor of anticipation. 'Would you mind very much, my dear, if we go home?'

* * *

He dismissed Yvette as soon as they reached Felicity's bedchamber. As the door closed behind her, Richard framed Felicity's face, his kiss slow, sensual. She drifted dreamily as his fingers dealt with the row of buttons fastening her gown. She squirmed closer, pushing his jacket from his shoulders. In no time, his upper torso was bare and her corset had joined her gown in a pool by their feet. Felicity splayed her fingers against his warm, muscular chest then pressed her chemise-clad body hard against him, digging into his muscular shoulders as he stroked up her thigh.

He deepened the kiss as he grasped her buttocks and lifted her. She wrapped her legs around him, clinging tight. He tore his lips from hers and strode to the bed, lowering her to the mattress, and prised her arms from around his neck.

'Look at me, Felicity Joy.'

Felicity cranked open one eyelid, the heat of lust flooding her as he unbuttoned the fall of his evening breeches. He was magnificent. And she wanted him.

'Now.'

He laughed. 'Patience, my sweet.'

She reached for him, and he backed out of reach, shaking his head, a wicked glint in his eyes, a teasing smile on his lips. As she scrambled from the bed, he dodged around to the far side. He leant forward, his fisted hands propped on the mattress.

'Do you know what I want, Felicity Joy?'

Confused, Felicity shook her head. His lips stretched in a slow, sensual smile.

'I want to see you naked.'

Her heart stopped. Lurched. Then raced into a gallop. His hands had caressed every inch of her body, as had his lips. But for him to look at her…to *see* her…

Richard straightened, his naked body exposed: erect; enticing; edible.

She wrapped her arms around her waist, trembling as his eyes pinned her to the spot.

'There is nothing to fear. I know your body. I know its feel, its contours, its strength. I have taken pleasure in your body, as you have taken pleasure in mine.' He sat on the bed and beckoned. 'Come here. Please.'

Her feet obeyed before her mind could raise a protest. She rounded the bed and stood in front of him. He tugged her closer, between his knees. He lifted her chin with one finger until she was looking in his eyes again. She suppressed a quiver: it was as if he knew her deepest fears. Her darkest secrets.

'May I?' His hands were on the hem of her chemise. Brows raised, he awaited her reply.

She nodded, her eyes snapping shut as she felt the cool of the air caress the skin of her thighs, her buttocks, her back. She lifted her arms, and the chemise was gone. Her protection had vanished. Her screen—behind which she could fool herself and her husband she was a desirable woman with the abundant curves men desired—was no more. Time froze. Behind the blankness of her eyelids she waited for the axe to fall. The only sound, above the soft crackle of the fire, was Richard's breathing. Quickening. A quiet groan, and then a mouth closed around her nipple as gentle hands slid to either side of her waist and caressed her hips and bottom.

'So delicate,' he murmured as he nuzzled first one breast and then the other. 'You have no idea how desirable you are, sweetheart.' He lifted his head. 'Look at me, Felicity Joy.'

She did. His eyes were dark and hot, penetrating deep into her soul, firing her blood. Desire flared and licked along her veins as he stroked her thigh, down, around, and up…up… Felicity threw her arms around his neck as she pressed her mouth to his, flicking her tongue against his sensual lips. He lifted her, splaying her legs as he lowered her on to his lap, filling her. Lips caressed lips, tongue caressed tongue. Hands gripped at her waist, lifting and lowering, and she caught the rhythm, rolling her hips, stroking her aching nipples against his hair-roughened chest, taking control.

Then he lifted her, laid her back on to the bed and settled between her open thighs.

'Look at me, Felicity Joy.' The third time of asking. His whisper was hoarse. Almost a plea. She opened her eyes, and he captured her gaze as he slowly, slowly entered her again. 'I want you to see me; to know this is me, inside you.

'It will only ever be me.'

He began to move.

Chapter Thirty-Three

Felicity stood in the hall of Stanton House at ten o'clock the following morning, wondering what Richard was planning. In accordance with his instructions—relayed by Yvette—Felicity was dressed for riding. She wondered what her husband was up to.

Trick opened the front door. The faint sound of hooves from outside grew louder, and then stopped as Richard appeared from the direction of his study, smiling.

'Good morning, Felicity.' He urged her towards the open door with a hand at her waist.

She walked through into a bright, sunny morning and gasped in delight. Dalton stood in the road outside at the head of Richard's huge dapple-grey gelding, Gambit, and *the* most elegant light grey mare, complete with side-saddle. The mare whickered and pawed the ground. She shook her head, sending her silvery mane rippling over her neck.

'Oooohhhhhhh.' Felicity took a hesitant step towards the mare, who lifted her head and regarded Felicity with an intelligent eye.

'Felicity; meet Selene.'

'Selene?'

'You can change her name if you wish. Selene was the goddess of the moon in Greek mythology.'

'No. It is perfect for her. She is *beautiful*. Where did you find her?'

'Do you recall our meeting in the park on Monday?'

The day of their arrival in London. Felicity pictured the scene: Richard riding alongside a woman on a grey horse. She had barely noticed the animal, her suspicious glare on its rider. Shame began its slow ascent from the pit of her stomach.

'Dalton heard she was for sale and I had arranged to see her in the park that afternoon,' Richard continued. 'Do you like her?'

'I *love* her.' *I don't deserve her, after those horrid suspicions.* 'She is beautiful.'

Felicity held her hand out. Selene stretched her neck and snuffled at Felicity's palm. Felicity moved closer still and rubbed gently under her chin, then smoothed her hand down Selene's neck.

'Thank you. I could not have wished for a more perfect gift.'

Felicity glanced at Richard as they rode side by side through the park gates. Pride swelled: he was so handsome, and he sat Gambit as if he was born in the saddle. *'It will only ever be me.'* She quivered at the memory of those words. He still had not stayed the whole night in her bed, but last night he had fallen asleep in her arms, and she had lain awake, reluctant to miss the moment, watching him. She must have drifted off eventually, for she had no memory of him leaving but, waking in the early hours, she had reached out and felt only chilled linen.

She had risen from her warm nest and tiptoed across the room to peep into Richard's bedchamber, ignoring her stab of shame at snooping. The flood of relief when she saw him in his own bed—sprawled spread-eagled on his back, sound asleep—had been overwhelming, as had her urge to climb in beside him, and run her hands over that wide expanse of bare chest. Instead, she had crept back to her own lonely bed and spent the rest of the night dozing fitfully.

Last night had given her hope. Could he be persuaded to love her, or was she fooling herself?

'How does she feel?'

She reached to pat Selene's neck. 'Wonderful. Her mouth is beautifully soft and she is as responsive as I could wish for.'

'Let's try her paces.'

They eased into a trot and Felicity gasped. Selene's trot was as smooth as riding in a well-sprung carriage. 'It is like floating.'

'I am glad you like her: she looks superb.'

His eyes lingered a moment on Felicity. She knew she did not do Selene justice. Yvette had been brutally blunt—her old black riding habit drained her of all colour.

'The new riding habit I ordered has not yet been delivered.'

Richard reached across for Selene's rein, drawing both horses to a halt. 'Why did you say that?'

Felicity bit her lip. Could he not have let her remark pass without comment? She did not want to engage in this conversation.

'You jumped to the conclusion that I found you wanting, did you not? Did last night teach you nothing? I was actually thinking what a fine seat you have.'

'Oh.' Felicity forced herself to meet his eyes. 'I am sorry.' She widened her lips in a smile. 'Thank you for the compliment.'

He held her gaze, then shook his head. 'You hear the words I say, but you do not listen, do you? You listen to that nagging voice in your head that says you are not good enough: not worthy of my esteem, or my compliments.'

His esteem? Was that all?

That instinctive reaction solved her dilemma: she would fight for his love, for that was what she desired above all else.

Esteem was a start. Love was the goal.

The conversation had become too challenging for this early in the morning. Without volition, Felicity's fingers squeezed the reins as she nudged Selene up to the bit with her leg. With the smoothest of transitions, the mare launched into a canter from a standstill. Within seconds, Gambit was alongside. Richard grinned at her.

'You win, my dear. Lecture over. Let us enjoy our ride.'

As Richard shrugged into his coat of green superfine, he contemplated that afternoon's visit to the house for fallen women with grave doubts. At least he would be with Felicity to—as Avon so eloquently put it the day before—'curb her enthusiasm for lost causes'. And to keep her safe.

Why was she so determined to help Millie? The girl's plight had clearly touched a nerve. Charles's hint that Felicity had given birth to an illegitimate child popped into his mind…might others wonder the same? It mattered not—*he* knew Felicity had been a virgin when he bedded her.

Yvette sat on the box with the coachman, Chivers, to point the way as they drove to Cheapside. Their destination was a tall, narrow, unremarkable house in the middle of a row of identical tall, narrow houses, its front door opening directly on to the street, which was noticeably more run down than most of the surrounding streets. Richard looked around in distaste. The carriage had already attracted the attention of young lads and loiterers.

'Drive around the streets a few times, once

we are inside, Chivers, I doubt we shall remain above ten minutes.'

Richard rapped on the door, which was opened by a woman of around forty summers, greying wisps escaping her cap.

'Oh!' Her hands flew up, trying in vain to tidy her hair. 'I did not expect visitors.' She eyed them uncertainly.

'Good afternoon,' Richard said. 'I am Stanton, and this is my wife, Lady Stanton.'

The woman bobbed a curtsy. 'Mrs Tasker, milord, milady.'

'Might we come in, Mrs Tasker? There is a matter we should like to discuss with you.'

'Yes, of course.'

She stood back and indicated a door on the right of the dark hallway. Somewhere upstairs a baby wailed. They went through into a small but clean parlour. Felicity glanced at Richard, who gestured for her to continue.

'I shall come straight to the point, Mrs Tasker. I am a patron of the Westfield School and Orphan Asylum, which provides education and training for orphans and destitute children and then finds work for them when they are old enough.

'One of our former girls has found herself in… in…*difficulties.*' A blush stained Felicity's cheeks. 'I understand you provide a haven for girls in such circumstances. Is that correct?'

'Well, it is and it isn't, milady. You must understand that I take my orders from the lady who owns this house and provides the funding. We help girls who have fallen from grace under certain circumstances. We do not take in girls who have behaved immorally.'

Richard could not help but ask, 'By definition, have they not all behaved immorally?'

Mrs Tasker folded her arms. 'Some girls have no choice, if you take my meaning, milord. Some *gentlemen* think nothing of abusing their position of power over these girls.'

'Indeed, and they swear to a love they do not feel, in order to take advantage of unworldly girls,' Felicity said, with a bitterness that had Richard's eyebrows shooting skyward. So vehement over the circumstances of a girl she barely knew? There *must* be more to her interest than concern for one servant girl. 'And that is precisely the case poor Millie finds herself in. She was placed in the household of a gentleman and it appears a house guest persuaded her of his love. He, naturally, is long gone and she has been turned off because of her condition.'

Mrs Tasker frowned. 'It sounds like the type of case that will interest my employer,' she said, 'but I will need to speak to her first. If she agrees, we will find the room.'

'What is the name of your employer? Might we consult with her directly?' Richard glanced at Felicity as he spoke, and she nodded her approval.

'That is an excellent idea. Won't you give us her name please, Mrs Tasker?'

'It is Lady Brierley,' Mrs Tasker said. 'Do you know her?'

Chapter Thirty-Four

Richard had suffered plenty of blows to the gut whilst sparring in the ring, but never had he struggled so to draw breath. *Harriet?* This house was *Harriet's?* And now here was a tangle, with Felicity so keen to help Millie, she was bound to want to speak to Harriet. His mind reeled with the implications.

'I confess I am not acquainted with her ladyship,' Felicity said. 'Stanton?' She turned her enquiring amber gaze on him.

'We have been introduced.' His voice rasped. He coughed to clear his throat. 'With your leave, I shall call upon her and put Millie's case.'

'I shall accompany you,' Felicity declared. 'I am certain we will have much in common. I am interested in her work here, and I should like to see if I can help.'

Richard cursed silently. He stood up. 'Come, my dear. We must not delay this good lady any longer. Good day, Mrs Tasker, and thank you for your help.'

Once in the carriage, and under way, he said, 'I did not wish to say this in front of Mrs Tasker, but I should prefer you not to become involved with Lady Brierley and her charity, Felicity.'

'You raised no objections before.'

'I thought your intention was merely to find somewhere safe for Millie. You must consider your reputation. It is not acceptable for you to associate yourself with such women.'

'If it is good enough for Lady Brierley, I do not see why...'

'Lady Brierley is not a suitable...' He paused. He could not bring himself to lie by smearing Harriet's reputation. This was not her fault. 'Suffice it to say, I should prefer you not to pursue an acquaintance with Lady Brierley. I will deal with this matter myself.'

Felicity's lips thinned. 'I should prefer to pass my own judgement on Lady Brierley. She must possess some redeeming qualities if she is prepared to help those less fortunate than herself. There are many in society—and I should know, for I have come across much prejudice from them over the years—who consider themselves pious and good Christians, but their actions do not support that view.' Her amber eyes impaled him. 'Yes, they—you *all*—attend church services on a Sunday, but as to helping the poor and weak, as the Bible teaches...*well*.'

'We shall discuss this further at home, Felicity.'

Yvette was travelling inside the carriage for the journey home and he had no wish to argue with Felicity in front of her. He was unused to opposition—he was master of his life, of his world. Felicity, the compliant wife he had bargained for, was anything but. She had her own agenda, her own opinions, and she was unafraid to voice them.

Am I too autocratic? Do I really want a wife who meekly obeys my every whim and demand?

In this instance, he had no choice. He consulted his fob watch. Half-past three already. Time was stampeding away from him. He must mollify Felicity, and then he must visit Harriet. He must nip all this nonsense in the bud before it got out of hand.

Felicity stalked ahead of Richard into the front salon at Stanton House, stripping off her gloves. He closed the door behind them.

'I insist you yield to me in this matter, Felicity.'

'What, precisely, is your objection to Lady Brierley?'

'Is it not enough that I have voiced my opposition to the acquaintance?'

Felicity—her mouth already open to argue—hesitated. She bit at her lip, then crossed the room to stare from the window, which looked out on to the square.

'I have no wish to be perverse. Can you not at least give me a valid reason for your objection?'

Her tone was conciliatory. Surprised, Richard moved to stand behind her. He cupped her shoulders, relief warring with guilt in his heart. Although he was no longer involved with Harriet, the prospect of his new wife and his former mistress becoming friends—a distinct possibility—was unthinkable. Mayhap in time—when his marriage was more settled—it would not feel so *perilous*.

'I cannot. I am sorry, sweetheart, but I will not insult the lady other than to repeat my distaste for any social intercourse between you.'

Felicity had removed her bonnet on her way through the hall, and her pinned-up hair exposed the back of her neck: vulnerable, inviting. Without thought, he leaned towards her and pressed his mouth to her soft skin. Her tremor vibrated through his fingers and he slipped one arm around her waist, pulling her back against the full length of his body.

Even as he kissed her neck, he was braced for her rejection. But she did not stiffen, or pull away. Instead, her head tilted to the side, allowing him free access. She wrapped her arm over his, caressing his fingers as a quiet sigh escaped her. He explored her neck and ear as she leaned into him.

All too soon, however, she straightened, her head snapping upright. 'Oh, no!'

Richard followed her stare and bit back a curse. Despite the veil covering her face, the lady alighting from a carriage in the street outside was in-

stantly recognisable. A maid climbed out behind
her, and assisted the wilting figure of Lady Katherine Farlowe to the front door.

Felicity ran into the hallway.

'Mama. What is wrong? Where is Mr Farlowe?'

Lady Katherine sniffed, followed by a hic-
coughing sigh. Recognising the signs, Felicity
clutched her mother's arm and steered her towards
the salon.

'Barnes, would you fetch a glass of ratafia
for my mother, please? And ask Mrs Carter to
show Wilkins—' she indicated her mother's maid
'—to the Yellow Bedchamber.'

Footmen were already hauling trunks in
through the door. Felicity cast an anxious glance
at Richard. What would he make of this intrusion?
She wavered between regret at the interruption,
and profound relief. It was all very well deciding
she would fight for her husband's affections, but
the speed of events had given her no time to mull
over the consequences of that decision. One touch
of his lips, and she had melted. Would his affection—his love—be conditional upon her submis-
sion to his decree in all matters? She found it hard
to believe that would make for a contented marriage; at least, not for her. His edict about Lady
Brierley, for instance; such high-handedness was
untenable. He'd offered no reasonable explanation
for his disapproval.

As soon as the three of them were alone in the

salon Mama threw back her veil and flung herself into Felicity's arms, wailing. Felicity guided her to the sofa, murmuring soothing words. Barnes brought the ratafia in, and immediately withdrew. Richard had remained silent throughout, standing with one arm propped along the mantelshelf.

As Mama's sobs subsided, she allowed Felicity to coax her to sip her drink.

'Come, now, Mama,' Felicity said, patting her hands. 'I wish you will tell us what is wrong.'

'Oh, Felicity. My life is over. I am undone. How could he do such a thing? And with Verity Godalming, of all people. I thought she was my friend.'

'He? Do you mean Mr Farlowe?'

A fresh paroxysm greeted Felicity's words. Richard stirred from the fireplace. He wore the expression of a man wishing to be anywhere but there.

'If you will excuse me, my dear, it would appear you have much to discuss. I will be in my study if you have need of me.'

Felicity wished it was possible for her to beat such an elegant retreat, and then immediately castigated herself for her uncharitable thoughts. Her mother was in distress.

Yes, but she will not listen to your advice. She will end up making excuses and will accuse you of casting Farlowe as the villain.

Gradually, her mother related the whole story of her stepfather's *affaire*—'Quite blatant, Felic-

ity, I assure you. Everybody in Bath knows'—
with her mother's friend, Lady Godalming.

'I have left him, my dear. I left him a note, telling him I was coming to you and dear Stanton.
But he has not come.' Tragic eyes, brimming with
tears, turned to Felicity. 'I made sure he would
catch up with me on the road. I even instructed
John Coachman to drive slowly. But he did not
come.' Another sob burst forth and she pressed
a lace-edged handkerchief to her lips.

Felicity put her arm around her mother, resigned helplessness churning her insides. She
had done all she could to prevent their marriage,
but her mother—in the exhilarating throes of
early love—would not listen to reason. There
was nothing she could do now other than support Mama through the next few days—or weeks,
she thought, with an inner shudder—until Farlowe arrived. And arrive he would, of that she
was certain. Farlowe knew exactly where he was
best off. He would arrive, with sweet words and
whispered excuses and deep regrets, and Mama
would allow him to coax her round. And they
would return to Bath and their life together. Until
the next time.

Bile rose up to burn Felicity's throat. What
would happen…how might she react…if…
when…Richard? She could not finish the thought.
Richard was a better man that Farlowe, that was
undoubtable. But he had a man's urges, and their
marriage was one of convenience. They'd made
a bargain. There was no love on either side.

She had been on the brink of softening, but her mother's arrival revived all those reasons as to why she must continue to protect her heart.

Chapter Thirty-Five

Richard was standing at the window of his study when Felicity sought him out, having persuaded her mother to go to her bedchamber and rest.

'How is your mother?' He turned to face her but otherwise did not move.

'Resting. I'm sorry for her unannounced arrival. I hope you do not object, but I've told her she might stay until she is reconciled with Mr Farlowe.'

Felicity remained by the door, her hands behind her back, gripping the door handle. The room gaped like a chasm between them. A fleeting wish that he would come to her and take her in his arms was swiftly banished. That intimate moment between them in the salon might never have happened, their disagreement over Lady Brierley looming large again in her thoughts.

'Of course she must remain with us. She is your mother. Is it likely she will receive Farlowe when…if…he arrives?'

'Oh, I am certain of it.' She could not disguise her bitterness. 'And I have no doubt he will come for her. Eventually.'

Richard's eyes narrowed. 'And you, judging by your tone, disapprove. You would rather see your mother permanently estranged from her husband?'

'No, I cannot wish that. I do wish, however, she had never met him.'

'Because then you would not have been forced to marry me?'

Her heart contracted painfully. 'That is not what I meant.'

'But it is true, however.'

In three long strides, Richard was in front of her, lifting her chin, searching her eyes as his head lowered. She jerked her head aside before his lips could touch hers. Richard stilled before, very slowly, straightening.

'I am going out.' His voice was devoid of expression. 'You have not forgotten we are promised to the Davenports for dinner tonight? Or should I send our apologies?'

'No, there is no need to cancel. Mama has already requested a light supper in her room tonight. She fears she will not be fitting company and raised no objection when I explained we were dining away from home.'

After he had gone, Felicity sank into the chair at Richard's desk. The chasm she had sensed upon entering the study had remained as vast even when Richard was standing right in front of her. What would their future be?

She was jerked from her thoughts some time later by a knock at the door. Barnes entered. Surreptitiously, she swiped a tear from her cheek, castigating herself for being a ninny.

'Mr Durant has called, my lady. Are you at home?'

Charles—a friendly face to divert her, exactly the remedy she needed.

'Thank you, Barnes. Please inform him I shall be with him shortly, and ask the kitchen to send up a tea tray, but do pour a glass of Madeira for Mr Durant if he would prefer it.'

Alone again, Felicity smoothed her hair back and pinched at her cheeks to give them some colour. Several deep breaths later she was ready to face him.

Charles sprang to his feet as she entered the drawing room, his grin lighting up his face.

'Cousin Felicity, your very obedient servant.' He sketched a bow.

As she approached him, his smile faded to a frown. 'Is anything amiss?'

Felicity felt her lips quiver, and Charles blurred.

'No, nothing,' she said. What was wrong with her? She had never been a weepy sort of female. She felt a sob build in her chest, and hurriedly crossed to the sofa. 'Please, sit down.'

She indicated a chair by the fire, which Charles

ignored, sitting on the sofa by her side and taking her hand.

'Do not think you can fob me off with such a feeble denial, Felicity, for you are clearly upset. Is it Richard?'

Felicity snatched her hand from Charles's grasp as the door opened to admit a maid with the tea tray. After she had gone, Charles brewed the tea and poured a cup for Felicity. Her hand trembled, and the cup rattled loudly in its saucer. Her mind whirled.

'It is my mother,' she said, before sipping at her tea. 'She arrived today for a visit, and…' She hesitated. How could she explain why her mother's arrival had so beset her? She had backed herself into a corner.

'And Richard disapproves of this visit?'

'No. It is not that. He is… Oh, I do not know, Charles. I dare say my mother's arrival has unsettled me. And Richard and I…' She really should not discuss their disagreement with anyone, but this could be her opportunity to find out. 'Charles, are you acquainted with Lady Brierley?'

'I am. Why do you ask?'

'You remember I told you about Westfield, the school I am involved with?' Charles nodded, and Felicity went on to tell him about Millie, and about the house in Cheapside. '…and I need to understand why Richard is so against our meeting,' she concluded. 'Can you enlighten me?'

'She is a widow and is universally received,

to my knowledge. Might Richard simply have changed his mind about your involvement with this Millie?'

'Then why would he not say so, instead of raising suspicions about Lady Brierley's character? It makes no sense. Charles, will *you* introduce us? Please? I only wish to meet her and to discuss Millie. If Richard still disapproves, I shall not pursue the acquaintance.'

'Well, I'm loath to go behind Richard's back, but I really cannot see any reason why you should not be introduced. Are you invited out tonight?'

'Yes. We go to the Davenports' ball, and we dine with them beforehand.'

'I, too, have an invitation, although not to dine. I shall invite Lady Brierley to accompany me to the ball.'

'I hope you do not object to my confiding in you, Charles? I am not comfortable either, arranging this against Richard's wishes, but he was so…so…*intransigent* that I cannot believe he will change his mind and he would not give me *any* reason why he was acting in such a way.'

'It will be our little secret, Felicity.'

Richard dashed into Stanton House to find Felicity, dressed in amber silk, waiting in the hall.

'I am sorry I am late, my dear. I was delayed.'

He had been to see Harriet, to persuade her not to offer Millie a place at the house in Cheapside. A complete waste of time. First, Harriet had kept him kicking his heels in her salon for ages. And then she had flatly refused to comply with his wishes. Although he *should* acknowledge that, in his haste to persuade her, he might have sounded a touch dictatorial.

'Why do you imagine,' she had said, 'that *your* dislike of your wife and me becoming acquainted is of more importance to me than the future of a fourteen-year-old girl in such need?'

Put like that, he had no answer.

Then, to compound his problems, Harriet's butler announced Mr Durant's arrival, begging a word. He had been compelled to skulk in the salon until Charles had been shown into Harriet's parlour. Conscious of the lateness of the hour, he had then driven his curricle home at breakneck speed, causing Dalton to gasp aloud more than once.

Richard paused, one foot on the bottom stair, looking back at Felicity. 'I like that dress,' he said. 'It suits you very well.'

Felicity blushed and a sudden image surfaced from the night before, her slender body naked and flushed as she rode him. He stifled the urge to haul her upstairs there and then. Who would have thought when he contracted to wed Lady Felicity Weston that she would stir his blood quite so effortlessly? The nights, he could not deny, were sublime.

'Thank you,' Felicity said, 'but, truthfully, you should thank Yvette. She is very talented at making a silk purse out of—'

Richard strode back to confront her. 'Do not dare to finish what you were about to say,' he said through gritted teeth. 'We have had this conversation before. It is time you stopped denigrating yourself. Look at me, Felicity.' She tilted her head up, amber eyes dark and wary. 'You have beautiful eyes, wonderfully tempting lips…' he brushed them with his own, registering her sharp intake of breath. He lowered his voice and put his lips to her ear '…and the most seductive body I have ever known.'

Felicity jerked free. 'You should hurry,' she said. 'We will be late.'

Richard bit back his anger and took the stairs two at a time. Every effort to bind them closer together was rejected. It should not bother him. It was what he had wanted in his marriage—a wife who did not cling to him or interfere in his life. The sooner she got with child the better. Mayhap then she would settle down and become the compliant, agreeable wife he had bargained for. And he could return to his sporting pursuits without guilt.

Is that truly what you want? What about love?

Love? Where had that ridiculous notion sprung from?

He slammed into his bedchamber, where Simson was waiting to help him dress for dinner.

Love was for fools. You love someone, and you lose them. Adam…his father…even his mother… oh, she was still of this world, but she did not love him as she had loved his father and brother, that was abundantly clear. No, it was far safer not to love.

Chapter Thirty-Six

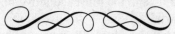

Later that evening, Richard wandered into the card room at the Davenports' house. He had danced the first with Felicity, and he had marked her card for the supper dance, but her card was now full and he had no desire to dance with anyone else. He perused the occupants of the room with little enthusiasm, selected the most promising of the tables, and sat down.

Two hands of loo later he excused himself and strolled back to the ballroom. He froze on the threshold, cursing silently at the sight of Felicity and Harriet, deep in conversation, on the far side of the room. *What the...?* Had he known Harriet was attending tonight he would have stayed to keep an eye on Felicity. To keep them apart. He strode across the dance floor, ignoring the exclamations and complaints of the dancers. As he reached the other side, two pairs of eyes—one wary yet defiant, the other apologetic—contemplated him.

'Richard.'

Did her voice tremble? Good. She should be worried. Did I not expressly forbid...?

His thoughts slammed to a halt. One thing he did understand about Felicity: she would do her duty, and what she believed to be right, even in the face of his disapproval. If he had given her a good reason why she should not meet Harriet, she might have accepted it. But he had not because he could not, and now it was too late.

'Charles was kind enough to introduce me to Lady Brierley,' Felicity said. 'I believe you already know her?'

Richard hauled in a deep breath. If he wasn't so furious, he would laugh. Could this be any more farcical? 'Yes. Indeed I do. Good evening, Lady Brierley. How do you do?'

'I have remained tolerably well since last we met, Lord Stanton. Felicity has been telling me about a young girl in need of help.'

Felicity?

'Yes, and Harriet has most generously said that Millie may move in tomorrow. Is that not splendid news?'

Harriet? They're already on first name terms? Richard's heart sank. Anything he tried to do now could only worsen matters.

Conscious of those two pairs of eyes watching, he cleared his throat. 'Splendid news indeed.'

'Evening, Fliss...I mean, Lady Stanton; Lady Brierley.' Dominic joined them, bowing to the ladies. 'I believe this is my dance?'

'Oh…yes, indeed, Dominic.' Felicity smiled at him and placed her hand in his. 'If you will excuse me?' She looked from Richard to Harriet, then back again.

'Of course.' Richard watched Felicity chatter happily with Dominic as they took their place on the dance floor. Would she *ever* be that relaxed with him?

'I like her, Stanton.' Harriet's soft-spoken words grabbed his attention.

'You must not pursue the acquaintance.'

'So you said this afternoon. And I shall give you the same answer I did then. I choose my own friends. You have nothing to fear—Felicity will never find out about us from me although, if you'll take my advice, you will tell her the truth.'

'Why would I do that?'

Harriet shrugged. 'It is my experience that truth will out in the end,' she said. 'It is your decision, however.'

'Indeed it is. Thank you for your advice, but I'm sure you will understand if I choose not to follow it. Tell me how you came to be involved with fallen women, Harriet.' He had not thought to ask when he saw her earlier. 'I believe it is not common knowledge?'

'No, it is not. And I have no wish for it to become so.'

'But why these particular women?'

'They are not just any fallen women. They are the poor souls who, by virtue of their need to work for a living, find themselves unable to reject the advances of their masters. And, if they are unfortunate, those same masters turn them away when they get with child.' Her violet eyes blazed. 'Such behaviour is despicable. I am appalled by the sheer numbers of girls soiled in that way. Including, I am ashamed to admit, two of my own maids when my husband was still alive.'

'Brierley seduced servant girls when he had you? I find that hard to believe.'

'He liked them young. They were not willing bed partners. I could not prevent him, but I could repair some of the damage he caused.'

Richard's opinion of Harriet climbed a notch.

'Would you care to dance?'

'I would love to. It will make a pleasant change to dance together without fear someone might guess our secret.'

'Indeed. You did not mention you were coming here tonight.'

'You did not ask. However, that was Mr Durant's purpose in calling upon me—to invite me to accompany him. If it will make you easier, I *did* try to dissuade him from introducing me to your wife when I realized his intention.'

'I thank you for that, and I am pleased we parted on good terms, Harry, but I should still prefer you not to become too friendly with Felicity.'

'It is a pity we cannot always achieve our heart's desire, is it not, Richard?'

Afterwards, Richard watched as Felicity danced with, and charmed, a succession of young men, and he pondered the discontent rumbling deep in his gut. Was it just possessiveness, or was his wife beginning to get under his skin? Whatever it was, it made him…tense.

Charles joined him. 'Surprised to see you dancing with the lovely Lady Brierley earlier, Stan.'

Richard stiffened. 'Why surprised?'

'I was given to understand you did not like the lady.'

'By whom, might I ask?'

'Your good lady wife. When she begged me to—'

'Begged you to what, Charles?'

Charles flushed, clamping his mouth shut.

'Now, let me guess. Did she, by chance, *beg* to be introduced to the lady in question?'

'Now, Stan…'

'And, despite knowing I disapproved, you went right ahead and contrived an introduction. Am I close?'

'I only meant to help.'

'Damn you for a meddling fool, Charles. Did it not occur to you I had a very good reason not to want the two of them to become acquainted?'

As soon as the words left his mouth, Richard could have bitten off his own tongue.

'Stan! No, do not tell me! Lady Brierley? You lucky, lucky dog! Stanton prevails where all others fail!'

Richard swore silently, viciously.

'I have no idea *what* you are bleating about, Charles.'

'You and Lady Brierley. Oh, this is priceless.'

Richard grabbed Charles by the arm and hauled him into the hall, currently deserted.

'Listen to me, Charles. I can see what idea you've got into your head, but it is *not true*. Do you understand? If you *ever* breathe a word of this to anyone, you will not only ruin the lady's reputation but you will upset me. Greatly. Do I make myself clear?'

Charles grinned. 'Eminently, my dear fellow, eminently. Never fear. I would not for the world upset either of you, you know that.'

Richard eyed him, unconvinced. Maybe Charles would not upset him deliberately, but Richard knew only too well how Charles often spoke without thinking. He could only hope his cousin would soon forget all about their conversation.

'What is so very urgent that it could not wait until the end of the ball?'

Felicity waited until the carriage was under way before challenging Richard. He had announced they were leaving immediately before supper. She had seen his anger when he spoke to Charles. Had he discovered she had inveigled an introduction to Harriet? She would not apologize for it. They had similar interests, and Felicity had relished every minute of their conversation, but it appeared their friendship was—for whatever reason—unacceptable to Richard. The tension in the carriage was palpable. His tension. He was like a wild animal on the prowl.

'I thought you did not care for society parties?' he said.

'That is no reason for such an abrupt exit.'

The carriage halted outside Stanton House. Once in the salon, a seated Felicity watched as Richard paced the room, occasionally thrusting his hand through his hair.

Attack is the best defence.

'Why do you not like Lady Brierley?'

He halted. His eyes narrowed. 'I do not dislike her.'

'Disapprove then. I noticed your *disapproval* did not preclude your dancing with her.'

'It would have been ungentlemanly to leave her standing there, after you went off with Avon.'

'You were angry with Charles for introducing us.'

'I'm angrier with you for persuading him to do it.'

'I had no choice. You would not offer a good reason why I should not meet her. I ask you again—why do you not like Lady Brierley?'

His jaw set, lips a thin line. Felicity felt her frown gather.

'What are you not telling me, Richard?' She held his gaze. Read his frustration as his brow lowered. It was clear he was unused to having his decisions questioned. Felicity was equally clear in her own mind, for the sake of their future together, that she was entitled to understand *why* his decisions were reached.

'This conversation is at an end. I am going out. Goodnight.'

No kiss. No kind word or softened glance before he strode from the room. Felicity's heart sank all the way to her toes. If she had thought she could cajole or even force her husband to take her into his confidence, she had been badly mistaken.

The distance between them gaped wider than ever.

Chapter Thirty-Seven

Felicity rounded on her mother. 'Please, Mama, tell me it is not true.'

Lady Katherine's mouth set in a mutinous line. 'Do not take that tone of voice with me, Felicity. Why should it not be true, pray? Mr Farlowe does not owe Miss Bean anything.'

'But you promised you would take care of Beanie.' Tears choked her voice as Felicity paced the room.

'Tsk. She is a servant. Anyway, I dare say she will be very content, living with her niece in Bristol.'

'A niece she barely knows, who has four children squeezed into a tiny cottage, and a husband who works in the shipyard. How did you suppose they would manage when an elderly, half-blind relative was delivered to their doorstep? Always assuming, of course, that you did not expect poor Beanie to travel to Bristol on the stagecoach?'

'Would someone care to enlighten me as to what is going on?'

Felicity spun round. Richard was at the drawing-room door, brows raised. Her first thought was how drawn he looked.

It was three weeks since Lady Katherine had arrived on their doorstep; three weeks since Felicity had met Harriet; three weeks in which their attempts at communication had grown more stilted by the day.

Mama's constant laments about Farlowe continued to fuel Felicity's fears for her own future and her friendship with Harriet was a festering wound between her and Richard, his disapproval turning any talk of Westfield or the house in Cheapside into an argument. He had spent more and more time away from home.

'It matters not, Richard. It was something and nothing.'

He directed a sceptical look at her.

'That is correct, Stanton. Felicity is always creating a drama out of humdrum events. There is nothing to be—'

'I believe I heard Beanie mentioned? She was your maid, I seem to remember, before we married.'

Felicity bit her lip and nodded.

Richard switched his attention to Mama, who returned his look with wide-eyed defiance. 'Miss Bean will be more comfortable with her own family than remaining with us.'

'And are those your sentiments, Lady Katherine, or those of your husband?'

Mama's cheeks blossomed pink.

'I recall a promise given by you to Felicity, on the day of our wedding—a promise to take care of Beanie.'

'It is not my fault. Miss Bean raised no objection.'

'How could she possibly object? How could she stand up to my stepfather? She is frail and half-blind. You were supposed to protect her from him.' *Like you were supposed to protect Emma.* A sob bubbled up her throat and escaped her lips. She clamped her hand over her mouth and turned to the window, desperate not to cry.

A hand touched her shoulder. 'Hush, Felicity.'

How long was it since he had called her 'Felicity Joy' in that special way…the deepening voice…the delicious shiver of anticipation it elicited? They were more than ever like two strangers, living in the same house.

Unrequited love.

'We will find Miss Bean,' Richard said. 'There is plenty of space at Fernley, or there is a vacant cottage in the village she can have, if she prefers. You can ensure her well-being for yourself.'

Relief flooded her. 'Truly? I can go and find her and bring her home?'

'No. *I* shall go and find her. After I have escorted you and your mother to Fernley Park.'

'But—'

A long finger tilted her chin. Dark brown eyes

drilled deep into her soul. A flutter of arousal reminded her how much she missed his nightly visits. Only once had he come to her since the Davenports' ball. He had not stayed afterwards: he had dressed again, and left the house, leaving her heartsore and suspicious and desperate. She longed to feel the comfort of his strong arms around her.

'No "buts", Felicity. You must be at Fernley to help Beanie settle in.'

'Of course.' She must write to Harriet, explaining the change of plans. Mayhap returning to Fernley would help mend some of the distance between her and Richard. And it would take him away from that harlot of a mistress; help to soothe the fearsome jealousy that seized Felicity whenever he deposited her at home after an evening out and went straight out again, leaving her to listen to her mother lament the fickle nature of men.

'Where does Miss Bean's niece live?' Richard asked Mama.

'Oh, in Bristol somewhere.' Lady Katherine waved a dismissive hand. 'John Coachman will know. He took her there. You see, Felicity. There is no harm done. Dear Stanton will ensure Miss Bean is taken care of.'

Felicity closed her eyes, willing the retort that battered at her lips to remain unsaid. Mama was…well, Mama. Felicity should have known that promise to take care of Beanie would last precisely as long as it took Farlowe to object to the arrangement. Mama's only aim in life was to agree with her husband in the vain hope she would become as essential to his happiness as he was to hers.

'It is not Richard's responsibility, Mama, but—' she smiled at him '—I thank you for making it so.'

'We will leave at ten tomorrow morning,' Richard said.

Richard stirred and stretched, easing his stiff muscles, as the carriage finally turned in at the gates of Fernley Park. He was alone in the carriage, Felicity having joined her mother for the second half of the journey, after they had stopped for refreshments at the White Hart in Bagshot.

He did not blame her. The atmosphere in their carriage had been thick with words unspoken. He gazed out of the window at his familiar home. Maybe here, without all the distractions of town life, he and Felicity might grow closer again. They had appeared on the verge of a new understanding, just before her mother had arrived and Felicity had met Harriet, but since then they had once more become strangers. He could not deny his share of the blame. He had thrown himself into his old way of life—visiting his club every day, boxing at Jackson's, fencing at Angelo's, shooting at Manton's—seeking any distraction so he did not have to address the complex swirl of emotions his wife provoked within him.

He alighted at the same time as Lady Katherine's carriage pulled up behind. A footman hurried to open the door, and Richard handed first Felicity and then her mother from the carriage. Felicity avoided looking at him, merely murmuring her thanks.

'Mama is not well,' she said as they entered the hall. 'If you do not object, I will see her settled and then I shall retire myself. I am very tired, and it is late.'

'I have no objection.'

He was tired too. There was a decanter of brandy in his study with his name on it. A couple of drinks and a good night's sleep was what he needed. He had another long day ahead of him tomorrow, travelling to Bristol to find Beanie.

Lady Katherine clutched at Richard's arm with urgent fingers. 'Stanton; you must instruct the servants to inform me *the minute* Farlowe arrives.'

Richard patted her hand. 'You may rest assured they will do so.'

Lady Katherine's maid helped her to the stairs, where Mrs Jakeway waited to show her to a guest room.

Felicity flicked a glance at Richard. 'Mama is concerned my stepfather will arrive at Stanton House and not know where she has gone when he finds the knocker removed from the door.'

'Barnes will tell him soon enough. Always supposing Farlowe has enough nous to enquire at the tradesmen's entrance.'

Was that a glimmer of a smile? It was gone in a flash, and he could not be sure.

'Goodnight, Richard.'

He watched her walk up the stairs, struck by the weariness of her movements.

'Welcome home, my lord. Is there anything you need?' Trick was at Richard's shoulder.

A compass capable of navigating a female's mind?

'No, thank you, Trick. It is good to be home.'

Richard went to his study and sat at his desk, but could summon no enthusiasm for the mound of correspondence awaiting his attention. Instead, he leaned back in his chair and pondered his wife and their marriage.

An image arose: Felicity, turning from him, rejecting his advances. She had been reluctant to wed him from the first. Was her pleasure in their coupling a cynical ruse? Once she got with child, would she turn from him as unequivocally in the bedchamber as she did the rest of the time?

Papa. Mother. Felicity. They have all rejected you. Stay strong. Don't weaken. It will only cause more pain.

He swallowed past the lump constricting his throat.

It was safer not to care.

Chapter Thirty-Eight

Three days later Felicity dropped her embroidery and rushed outside at the sound of Richard's return. She had missed him more than she would have thought possible, and not only because the effort of keeping the peace between his mother and hers had proved exhausting. For two ladies who disagreed on almost every issue, their insistence on exchanging daily visits was incomprehensible to Felicity.

She drank in her husband's tall, muscular frame as he climbed from the carriage, his brown hair tousled, his expression...she peered closer. Her spirits plummeted. He looked livid: his brows almost meeting across the bridge of his nose, his lips a tight line. Did he regret his impulsive offer to travel to Bristol for the sake of her old nurse?

When he saw her waiting, his scowl lifted. A fraction. 'Good afternoon, Felicity.'

His voice was a deep, reassuring rumble, enfolding her like a warm blanket. Felicity felt her own expression relax into a smile. Whatever had annoyed him, he did not blame her. Her resolution to heal the divide between them grew.

'I am pleased to see you, Richard.'

His brow twitched. 'Well, I am pleased that you are pleased,' he said, and smiled. 'And there is someone else here you will be pleased to see, no doubt.'

He leaned back into the carriage and Felicity could hear him murmuring. Then he straightened, and lifted a frail figure to the ground.

'Beanie…' Felicity wrapped her arms around the elderly lady '…I am so happy to see you. You must be tired after your journey. You will stay here for a few days to recover your strength, and then we shall decide where you would like to live permanently.'

'Oh, my lamb.' Wrinkled hands cupped Felicity's cheeks. 'I am so pleased to see you.' She lowered her voice. 'You have a good man there, my dear. Not like your poor mama.'

She half turned towards the carriage as she spoke. Movement caught Felicity's eye as Quentin Farlowe's tall, rangy form sprang from the vehicle. One glance at Richard confirmed the cause of his bad mood.

'I say, this is an impressive pile, Stanton. No wonder you can offer pensioners homes for life. Good afternoon, Felicity.'

'Farlowe! My darling, you have come for me at last.' Lady Katherine tumbled from the house and launched herself at her husband. 'Oh, I have missed you so. Come. You must be exhausted. I shall instruct Jakeway to make up the room next to mine.' She turned to Richard. 'It is most fortuitous you had to go to the West Country, Stanton, for now all has been resolved most satisfactorily, has it not?'

Felicity watched her mother and Farlowe disappear inside the house, then glanced at Richard's frowning face. 'I will talk to Mama, and ensure they leave tomorrow.' She hesitated, suddenly shy. 'Thank you for fetching Beanie. I must go and settle her, but I am *very* pleased to see you.'

The following morning Felicity sat in her private sitting room, staring from the window at the overcast sky as she twisted her handkerchief in her hands. What was wrong with her? She was constantly weepy, with no energy or enthusiasm for anything—as grey and dull as the weather outside.

Her pleasure at Richard's return had been short-lived. Between keeping the peace between her mother and the dowager—who had been invited to dine with them—and between Richard and Farlowe, she had been exhausted by bedtime. As she climbed the stairs, she had tripped and, had Richard not been behind her, might have fallen. He had swept her into his arms and carried her upstairs, placing her gently on the bed.

'You look exhausted. Get some rest. I will see you in the morning,' he had said, before leaving her to Yvette's care. How she had longed for him to return. To take her in his arms and hold her; to reassure her that they would resolve their problems.

At a tap on the door, she straightened and swiped at her eyes.

'I wondered where you were hiding, my lamb. I hope you do not mind me coming in?'

Beanie hobbled towards Felicity, a small brown book in her hands.

'Of course not, Beanie. Did you sleep well?'

'Oh, yes. Like a babe in arms. Such a comfortable bed, after...' Beanie pursed her lips, shaking her head. 'No, I will not complain. Jeannie was so kind to me. It is not her fault they have so little room.'

'No, indeed.' A tide of shame washed over Felicity. What right did she have to sit there moping, when there were women like Jeannie, struggling their way through life? 'Sit down, won't you, Beanie?' She patted the sofa next to her.

'Thank you, my dove, but I only came to give you this.' She held out the book.

Felicity eyed it. 'What is it?'

'Emma's diary.'

'Her *diary*? I did not know she kept a diary. Where did you find it? How long have you had it?'

'I saved it for you. Your mama, she told me to burn it, when we found it.'

Felicity's hand trembled as she reached for the diary. 'What does it say? Have you read it?'

'You know I cannot read well enough for that,

my lamb, and your mama… It upset her too much to finish it but she told me it was about *that* summer. That is when I decided I must save it for you. I thought *someone* should know Emma's innermost thoughts.'

'You did the right thing.' Memories flooded back. Desperate, heart-wrenching memories. Felicity's throat ached and the book blurred as she stroked the fine-grained leather cover.

'Why did you not show me this before?'

'I could not. Your mama said it was *detailed*, and you were so young and innocent. I hid it away and I forgot about it, until I packed my things to go to Bristol.' Beanie laid her hand briefly on Felicity's head. 'I hope I have done the right thing by giving it to you now. I know I should not like to relive that time, but I thought it important for you to read it.'

After Beanie had gone, Felicity read Emma's diary, stopping frequently to mop her eyes and blow her nose. Her sister's words brought her to life in a way no mere memory ever could, and Felicity suffered the pain of losing her all over again.

She was staring numbly out of the window, the diary clasped in her arms, tight to her chest, when Richard walked in.

'Felicity, there you are. It is time…' In two strides, he was by her side, kneeling down, clasping her hands. 'What is it? What is wrong? Are you unwell? Shall I send for the doctor?'

Felicity gulped, then forced a laugh. A doctor

could not cure what ailed her. Part of her wanted to curl into a ball and never think about Emma and the agony of her loss again; another part of her...*that* part raged and fought and rattled the bars of the cage around her heart. It longed to break free: to talk about Emma—her disgrace and her death—and to try to make sense of it all.

'I am upset. Not unwell.'

'Is it Farlowe? Tell me, for—stepfather or no stepfather—it would give me the greatest pleasure to plant him a facer before they go.'

How could she tell him? But how could she not? Her emotions swirled and whirled, dizzily fast. She must talk to someone. Her mother? Impossible. Beanie? It would be unfair to resurrect such painful memories. Could she trust Richard? His face swam before her: concerned, kind. He had never been anything but kind.

Her husband. They were bound together, were they not? Surely he would not sully Emma's name by revealing her scandal and her sin to the world?

Chapter Thirty-Nine

'Felicity, if you do not tell me what is amiss, I shall send for the doctor.'

Felicity took an audible breath. 'Beanie gave me this.' He noticed for the first time the book she clutched. 'I did not even know it existed.' She sounded dazed.

Richard took the book, turned it over in his hands, opened it.

'It's a diary. Whose is it?'

'My sister, Emma's.'

Emma. All he knew of Felicity's sister was that she had died after her first Season.

'What did she write to upset you so?' He read the first entry. It began with a date in March 1802. He flicked through the pages, all written in the same neat, feminine hand. It was three-quarters full, ending in the December of the same year.

He sensed Felicity's eyes on him. 'Read it. That last entry.'

Some of the words were faded by tears that had

been shed as they were written. There were fresh splodges on the page. Still damp.

> *I cannot go on. There is no hope left. He will never return to me now. He is gone. All the light and the colour have gone from my world. I pray to God to forgive me and to watch over my beloved family. I am sorry.*

'She killed herself?'

Felicity nodded. 'Herself…and her baby.'

'She was with child?'

Felicity moaned as fresh tears poured down her face. 'I didn't know. She didn't tell me. She went up to the roof and…and…' Her voice trembled. 'I…I found her… Oh, dear God!'

Her hands flew to hide her face. Richard gathered her into his arms, rocking her and stroking her hair as scalding tears soaked his shirt. Suddenly, she stiffened and pushed away.

What now? Am I now not allowed to comfort her when she is in distress?

'Urrrgh.' Hand clapped to her mouth, Felicity shot up from the sofa and through the door into her bedchamber.

Richard followed. She was leaning over the basin on the washstand, heaving. His arm around her waist, Richard supported her until she finally stopped retching, then dipped a cloth into the jug of water on the stand and wiped her face. A glance into the basin revealed no solids.

'Have you not eaten this morning?' He picked her up and laid her on the bed, hitching his hip to sit on the mattress facing her, stroking her hair back from her ashen face.

'I could not face breakfast.'

'Have you been sick before?'

'I was sick yesterday, after breakfast.' Her eyes rounded. 'Do you think…?'

He pinched her chin, smiling at her incredulous expression. 'Do you not know? When were your last courses?'

Her face fired red. 'Not since before we left for London. Oh! How wonderful, if we are to have a baby already.'

Wonderful? Yes, but… Richard studied Felicity. *Will she now withdraw completely? At night as well as during the day?*

Her eyes darkened. 'I do not want to tell anyone. Not yet, until we are certain. And not my mother… Not now. Not so soon after reading Emma's diary…it brought it all back, so vividly.'

'We will say nothing before they leave. You can write and tell her your news when you are ready.'

'I tried so hard not to blame her for failing Emma. If only she had chaperoned her, as she should have done.'

And yet, despite Lady Katherine's neglect and Felicity's anger, there was still love in their relationship.

Regret wormed its way into Richard's thoughts.

Neither Adam's death nor his father's had been his mother's fault but, somehow, there was this awkward gulf between them. Words left unsaid; emotions left unexplored.

Suicide.

The word revived all the horror and pain of Papa's death. A sin and a crime. To be hushed up at all costs, and never spoken of again.

'My father also committed suicide.' He had not intended to blurt it out, but the words were out there now, tainting the air. He studied his hands, clenched in his lap. 'He could not bear to live, after Adam died. I always regret...' He paused. His innermost fear. Could he reveal it?

'You regret...?' Soft-spoken words; delicate hands—warm—covering his.

His thoughts spilled in a rush. 'He lost one son. But he had another. And I could not make up for his loss. I was not good enough for my father to want to live.'

The words were out there, in the open, screaming of his failure as a son. He had let his father down. Voicing that failure had exposed his vulnerability. He was a man. How could he be so weak?

'Oh, Richard.' The mattress dipped as she knelt up. Her arms enfolded him, comforting, and her soft cheek rubbed against his. 'I'm sure that is not true. People...in grief...they sometimes behave...they do things they would not do if their minds were not overset. Like Emma. Another day, maybe even another hour of that day, and she would not have jumped. But, in that split second…it was the only way she knew to be free of the pain.'

Richard scrubbed his hands over his face, then wrapped his arms around his wife.

'Thank you.' He mulled over what Felicity had said. He was comforted by her support but she did not know the whole. It was not only his father, but his mother too. The way she had withdrawn from him. No matter what he did, he had never been good enough for her. But that was his cross to bear. He would not burden Felicity.

'Will it distress you to tell me more about Emma? In her diary, she writes of a man. How did she meet him? Who was he?'

Felicity drew a shaky breath. 'Until today, all I knew was she had fallen in love with a man who seduced her with promises and lies and then deserted her. She says in her diary that she wrote to tell him she was with child, believing he would return to her. He never replied.

'So young, so foolish, so blindly *trusting*. Believing the strength of her love would conquer all. Just like Mama. Stupid! Stupid!' A fresh wave of tears shook her. 'And now…the diary…*still* she is protecting him. She does not name him. Not once. "M" she calls him.'

'Where did she meet him?'

'At a house party, the summer after her first Season.'

'How on earth did he get close enough to a young innocent to seduce her? What was your mother doing? I presume she was chaperoning Emma?'

'She was meant to be. Mama does not always show good judgement of others.' Her voice hitched. He could feel the effort it took for her not to break down again. 'Poor Emma. I never knew she was with child. I thought she killed herself because he broke her heart.'

'Your poor sister.'

'She was not a bad girl.' Felicity wriggled free of his embrace, anxiously scanning his face.

'I do not condemn her,' Richard said. 'Your mother, however—'

'I have tried so hard not to blame her but, deep down, I do. I always have done. And then I feel guilty, for thinking of my own mother in such a way. Oh, I do not expect you to understand.'

But he understood only too well. He had tried to be a good son, but the pain of knowing his mother could never love him as much as she'd loved Adam had driven them apart. And if his own mother could not love him…

A tap at the door, and Yvette came in, her eyes apologetic. 'Beg pardon, milady—' She got no further.

'There you are, Felicity.' Lady Katherine brushed past Yvette with a barely concealed grimace of distaste. 'I do declare you are the most thoughtless girl alive when it comes to your family. We have been waiting this age to leave. Dear Farlowe has come all this way to take me home, and you needs must leave him kicking his heels

awaiting your convenience. And you, Stanton…'
she wagged her finger at Richard. His temper
simmered '…I thought you came to fetch Felicity and here you are, making love to your wife
instead of attending to the needs of your guests.'

'We are coming now, Mama,' Felicity said.

How did she remain so calm in the face of
such provocation? Renewed respect for his wife's
strength of character warred against his longing
for Felicity to stand up to her mother's tyranny.
For that is what it was. What child could withstand the mental onslaught of a disparaging parent without starting to believe that criticism? That
Felicity had grown into such a kind, thoughtful
and caring young woman gave witness to the
goodness of her heart.

He held out his arm for Felicity and they followed her mother down the stairs.

Chapter Forty

It was a relief to wave goodbye to Mama and Mr Farlowe as their carriage rumbled down the drive of Fernley Park. And a *profound* relief that she had not voiced the rage burning inside.

Richard's incredulity had eased Felicity's guilt for that rage, and had allowed her to view the full extent of her mother's failure in her duty to protect Emma, whose beauty had inevitably attracted male attention of the worst kind. She had been flattered into falling in love and, with no one to stand sentinel, she must have been as vulnerable—and as innocently unaware—as a newborn fawn circled by hungry wolves.

'Come…' Richard's arm wrapped around her waist, and she leaned into his embrace '…let us go indoors. You must be cold.

'Trick?'

'Yes, milord?'

'Please bring some tea and something to eat to the salon. Her ladyship is hungry.'

Felicity opened her mouth to protest, but remained silent as Richard's arm tightened on her waist. When Trick was out of earshot, he murmured, 'It is possible you have two mouths to feed now, Felicity. You will oblige me by not starving yourself. If you are unable to face large meals, at least promise you will try to eat little and often, to keep up your strength.'

A few weeks later, Richard's insistence on cosseting Felicity to an almost excessive degree was driving her to distraction. He had even sent for the family's London physician, despite it being too early for Sir Roger to be able to fully establish that Felicity was with child. Her symptoms were, however, consistent with that condition.

'I will be perfectly safe on Selene,' she protested, when he came upon her in the stables, about to ride to the village to visit Beanie in her new cottage.

'I will order the carriage. Sir Roger—'

'*Sir Roger* advised me to take light exercise and to get plenty of fresh air. He *said* it would help my appetite.'

'That is a low blow, Felicity Joy, knowing I worry about how little you eat.'

Felicity Joy. Her heart leapt. It was a long time since he had called her that. Longer even than he had remained absent from her bed. Did he believe he would somehow damage the baby if he lay with her, or was there another reason for his lack of interest? Felicity had, with much blushing, asked Sir Roger if the baby would be hurt, and he had been most reassuring. But she had not yet plucked up courage to tell Richard.

And now, he appeared to want to ban her from riding Selene until after the baby was born.

'Do you not trust my common sense enough to believe I would never put myself or our baby in jeopardy?'

'If you should fall—'

'I will *not* fall. Have you so little faith in my ability as a horsewoman?'

His brow remained furrowed. 'I cannot spare the time to escort you. What if—?'

'I do not need your escort, Richard. Selene is completely trustworthy and I shall have a groom with me. I promise the most I shall risk is a slow canter—no galloping and no jumping. I am as concerned as you are for the baby's welfare, but I cannot stay cooped up for the next seven and a half months.'

'I shall teach you to drive,' he said, his frown clearing. 'Then you will not feel so penned in.'

'Well…I cannot deny it is a skill I should like to learn, for I have never driven anything apart from Boxer, our old cob, before…but that is a separate issue. I enjoy the exercise I get on horseback, so I should like to continue riding until it becomes uncomfortable.'

'Very well.' Richard heaved a poor, put-upon male sigh. 'But *please* promise you will take care. You, Harry…' the groom straightened from tightening Selene's girth '…are you accompanying your mistress to the village?' Harry nodded. 'Woe betide you if any harm befalls her, then.'

Harry grinned. 'She'll be safe with me, milord.'

'She had better be. Hold the mare steady, will you?'

Harry moved to stand at Selene's right shoulder, holding the reins with one hand and steadying the saddle with the other.

Strong hands settled at Felicity's waist. She had barely thickened, but she gratefully dispensed with her corset whenever possible. His intake of breath and the widening spread of his fingers suggested Richard had just discovered that fact. She looked up to see almost-black eyes boring into hers. She gasped when he pulled her closer, his thumbs brushing the underside of her breasts. Under her habit her nipples tightened into hard buds and arousal fluttered deep inside. Then, before she quite knew what was happening, she was in mid-air, being swung into the saddle.

Harry went to fetch his own mount, and Richard held the mare as Felicity hooked her right leg between the pommel and the second horn of the side-saddle, and found the slipper stirrup with her left foot. Selene fidgeted and fussed beneath her until she gathered the reins and settled her.

'Ride carefully, my dear. You carry a precious cargo.'

How can I forget? She watched Richard stride away from her, down the path towards the house. The width of his shoulders strained at the centre seam of his jacket and accentuated his narrow hips as his long, muscled legs, sheathed in tight breeches and gleaming topboots, covered a yard or more of ground with each pace. She swallowed a sigh as she arranged the skirts of her new olive-green riding habit.

Her husband hardly seemed to notice her presence these days, unless it was concerning the baby. Their days had settled into a humdrum existence of running the household for her and overseeing the estate for him. At least, if he did teach her to drive, they would spend more time together. Always supposing he did not delegate that chore to Dalton or one of the other grooms.

She had hoped their shared confidences about Emma and Richard's father might draw them closer, but it appeared to have had the opposite effect on Richard. He had grown more distant, not less, much to Felicity's frustration. He had flatly refused to discuss his father's suicide, or his feelings about it, and he had become adept at avoiding her company. Except, she thought, with an inner *hmmph*, when he deemed her in danger of risking her health, or that of the baby.

Cast around as she might for a solution, the only one to come to her was one she was unwilling to take. The thought of taking the initiative and visiting him in his own bedchamber brought her out in a cold sweat.

What if she took the risk, and he still did not want her? What if her fears were proved correct and, now he had got her with child, he had no further use for her until his heir was born? There was no longer any need for him to fabricate any interest in her or any pleasure in her company. Cold dread settled in the pit of her stomach. Was she doomed to follow in her mother's footsteps after all?

As soon as Harry was mounted, Felicity nudged Selene into a trot and they clattered out of the yard. She could do little about her feelings for Richard—whatever they proved to be—but she determined then and there never to sink into despondency.

Mayhap the promised driving lessons would bring them closer together?

Felicity's mouth set in an uncompromising line.

'What is wrong?' Richard indicated the pony and gig standing patiently in the yard. 'George is very docile. He—'

'When you offered to teach me to drive, I assumed it would be a pair. I already possess the skill—if that is what it is—to drive a pony and gig.' Narrowed amber eyes glared at him. 'I expected a challenge.'

'But you are—'

'*If* you say—once more—"but you are with child, my dear", I swear I shall scream.'

Dalton, at George's head, was studying the sky, whistling through his teeth. Richard took Felicity by the arm and marched her out of the stableyard to a nearby bench.

'Sit!'

She did, averting her head and sticking her nose in the air, two bright spots of colour staining her cheeks.

He hovered a moment, then sat beside her. A little too close, their upper arms touching. He could not risk shifting away. It would be too blatant. But to be touching her, so close he could smell her violet fragrance and, beneath that, her own unique, woman scent... He gritted his teeth.

'How often have you driven, Felicity? And how recently?'

She stilled, holding her breath. Then slumped. Glanced at him through her lashes. 'Not often. Not recently.'

A grudging admission as delicate fingers plucked at her skirts. Richard tamped down the urge to take her hand, the old uncertainties plaguing his gut. Ever since he had confided in Felicity about his father, and exposed his deepest fear that he was not good enough for his father to want to live, the old wounds of vulnerability and inadequacy—wounds he had believed long healed—had reopened. A single crack in his outer shell of strength and confidence, a crack that was raw and bloody, and deeper than he had ever realized.

'It is not like you, to fly up into the boughs so readily.'

'No. I'm sorry. I...' She paused. 'No, you're right. I'm sorry.'

What had she been going to say? He wished she had not stopped. He studied her, head bowed. He hated this awkwardness...the things unsaid between them. What was she thinking? Why could he not take the risk, and talk to her of the things that mattered? She was a good woman. She would not reject him, like his parents.

Would she?

She rejected you before. Many times. She only married you because she had no choice. The devil riding his shoulder, on constant alert, raked him with its spurs. It ensured he never forgot; never weakened.

He loathed this indecisiveness, this cowardice. It was not like him. Why did he feel so vulnerable with Felicity? He buried any urge to expose himself further. Risking another rejection was a risk too far.

'*If* you had allowed me to explain,' he said, cringing inside at the pomposity of words that revealed nothing of the doubts plaguing him, 'you would know that George is merely the starting point. We will progress to a pair, you have my word.'

He knew what he wanted.

She was his wife. She would be the mother of his children. But that was no longer enough. He also wanted her as his friend and his companion. As his lover. He wanted her on his side. No...he wanted them to be on the same side. Partners.

The question was: what did she want?

Chapter Forty-One

When the winter weather permitted, Felicity's lessons continued, and she began to cherish the time she spent with Richard. They chatted about the weather, the scenery, the estate, mutual acquaintances…any subject, in fact, that could not be construed as personal.

After a few days of driving the placid George, Felicity walked into the yard to find a large bay gelding harnessed to the gig. She received an inkling of the test to come as she manoeuvred horse and gig out of the yard gate.

'Get over, Trusty.' The horse seemed intent on scraping the gig against the gatepost. Thankfully, they exited the gate without damage to either gig or post.

'Well done.'

A sideways glance revealed Richard's fists relaxing.

Felicity drove Trusty down the lane at a spanking trot, whip ready in her left hand as the horse revealed a tendency to drift towards the near-side. 'Whoever named him Trusty has a sense of humour,' she said. 'Is that why I am driving him today? To see if I can cope with a less obliging animal than dear old George?'

'Indeed. For if you cannot control a wilful sort like Trusty, how will you cope with two?'

'So you intend to send me out with *two* wilful animals in the future? You do surprise me.'

Richard laughed. 'Not deliberately. But you know what flighty animals horses can be. If one imagines he sees a monster in the hedgerow, his mate will almost certainly see two. If you can anticipate Trusty and his tricks, then we will take a pair out tomorrow.'

At last. If I prove I can handle Trusty, then I can drive a pair.

Felicity started to get Trusty's measure as they bowled along the lane through the estate. She checked him as they approached the gateway leading to the track through the woods that would bring them out on to the Whitchurch road, where the traffic provided a better challenge.

'Steady, now, lad,' she called as Trusty, true to form, fought to cut the corner. She breathed a silent sigh of relief as they drove through the centre of the narrow gateway without mishap.

'Oh, well handled.'

She glowed at Richard's praise and sent Trusty along the track with a flick of the whip. Suddenly, a pheasant flew from the undergrowth with a clatter of wings and a raucous cry and Trusty jerked his head into the air. His powerful hindquarters bunched, then propelled him forward.

Bracing her feet against the front of the gig, Felicity struggled to regain control. Richard threw his right arm round her, pulling her into the side of his rock-hard body as he reached across with his left hand to take the reins.

'No! Let me…do…it.'

The hand withdrew. Surprised, she risked a sideways glance. One brow lifted as Richard caught her eye. 'He's…all yours…Felicity.' His voice jerked in rhythm with the rocking gig.

Trusty, ears flat to his head, charged blindly on. Felicity was conscious of Richard, next to her, poised to take over if necessary but if she did not prove herself now he might never let her drive again.

She fought to stay calm until Trusty's wild pace slackened and she could bring him to a halt. Richard tied the reins off, jumped down and held his arms out for Felicity. As her feet touched the ground, her knees buckled and she was only saved from landing in an ungainly heap by Richard's strong arms around her. He clasped her tight, his chin resting on her head. She leaned into him, inhaling his familiar, masculine scent: comforting and yet arousing.

All was still; all quiet now save for their harsh breathing, and the thunder of Richard's heart in her ear. Somewhere, a thrush sang, rousing Felicity. She wriggled to loosen Richard's embrace.

'Thank you.' She leant back to study him, hands braced against the solid wall of his chest. He was pale. A vertical slash divided his brows whilst his lips were so tightly compressed they were barely visible.

'What are you thanking me for?'

'For trusting me.'

'Trusting you with Trusty, eh? You did well. Are you all right?'

'Yes. And you?'

'Yes. No thanks to…' His head swivelled and he stared back along the path. 'Wretched pheasant.'

'No wonder poor Trusty bolted. It startled me too.'

'Poor Trusty?'

With a single quirk of his brow, Richard indicated his opinion of the horse. Then he stilled. He cupped Felicity's chin. Desire licked through her veins as she stared up into his darkening eyes. His head lowered. He hesitated, searching her face, his mouth scant inches from hers. With an impatient inner huff, Felicity slid her fingers through his hair and crushed her lips to his. She wanted him. She was weary of tiptoeing around him, fearing he did not desire her. His eyes revealed the truth: at this moment in time, he wanted her. She would deal with any regret later.

Richard's arms slid beneath her cloak, enfolding her as the kiss deepened and she pressed against him, the evidence of his arousal hard against her belly. As their tongues tangled, his hands slid around her waist and up the sides of her ribs. He tore his lips from hers to murmur huskily, 'No corset, Felicity Joy?' before reclaiming her mouth. Pure lust sizzled through her as he unbuttoned her jacket and caressed her breast through her linen shirt. She reached between them, unfastened his breeches and closed her hand around him: hot, silky skin sliding over engorged flesh. She stroked and he growled, deep in his throat, pulling her skirts up, and up again to her waist, exposing her.

A long finger slid between her aching, swollen folds and she pushed against it, frantic for more, her cry of pleasure swallowed by his kiss.

Then she was in the air, her legs tightening around his hips as he entered her. Still coupled, he turned to trap her against a tree. He was quick, hard, demanding. She urged him on, meeting each thrust, clenching around him. Frantic for release, she wound tighter and tighter until she shattered, throwing her head back, her cry echoing in the still December air, drowning his deep cry as he pumped his seed into her.

His forehead rested against hers as they stilled, panting. Felicity closed her eyes. He was still inside her, softer now, her legs still tight around his hips. Warm lips caressed her lids, trailed down her nose to kiss its tip.

'Why have you stayed away from me?' The words were out before she could stop them. She kept her eyes tight shut.

'I…when?'

'At night.'

Silence. She peeked through her lashes. He studied her, frowning. Her courage faltered. If only she could unsay those words.

'You must be uncomfortable.'

He supported her as he stepped back from the tree and slowly lowered her to the ground. She did not meet his eyes as she rearranged her clothing.

'Felicity?'

Reluctantly, she looked at him; took heart at the hint of vulnerability in his expression.

'Do you mean…that is, I thought, now you are with child, you—' He spun round and strode over to a nearby sapling which shook as he thumped it. His shoulders rose and his back broadened as he sucked in an audible breath. 'I have been trying to respect your wishes.' He strode back to face her. 'You seemed unhappy with my attentions, other than in bed, and I thought you only welcomed those as you were keen to get with child.' Deep brown eyes bored into hers. 'Was I wrong?'

She tamped down her embarrassment at discussing such intimate details. He was her husband, if she could not discuss such matters with him, then with whom?

'Yes. I would like it if we could still…' Her face burned. 'That is, I would like it if you would continue to visit me at night.'

He lifted her chin. 'Only at night, Felicity Joy?'

No. I want you to love me. Always.

An image of her mother, hopelessly yearning after her father and, now, her stepfather, swept into her mind, followed by Emma, in despair over a man she had trusted, who had heartlessly abandoned her. They would go back to London in February. He would go back to his mistress. She hardened her heart. 'I think it is for the best.'

'Why?' His eyes seared into her, scrambling her thoughts. 'What are you afraid of? Is it because of your sister?'

'It is not only her.'

He gripped her shoulders. 'Not only Emma? Who else? Why does this barrier between us feel insurmountable? Your mother? Is it her?'

Felicity wrenched away from him. 'It is how I feel. It is what I want.' Every nerve in her body was strung tight, every muscle rigid.

The silence hummed with tension. She refused to look at him, staring fixedly down the track, back the way they had come.

'Very well, if that is how you feel, I shall not ask again.'

Richard strode over to the gig. 'It is time we went back,' he said, and waited to help Felicity aboard. What else could she have said? She had no words to explain. Her feet dragged as she walked towards the gig.

'Richard?'

'Felicity?'

'I am sorry. I—'

He almost threw her up into the vehicle and leapt in after her, gathering the reins.

'Get up, Trusty.' He slapped the reins on Trusty's broad back, his lips tight as he glowered at the track ahead.

Chapter Forty-Two

Mid-January, 1812

As Richard crossed the hall, he glanced up at the staircase. Felicity, dressed in a woollen walking dress that clung provocatively, was walking down the stairs. His breath caught at the tantalizing sight. He never tired of caressing the gradual changes to her body—her ripening breasts and the gentle swell of her belly. Her condition was not yet obvious, except to him, who knew and revelled in every inch of her.

'Are you going out for a walk, my dear? I should be happy to provide an arm to lean on,' he said, as she had reached the foot of the stairs.

'Thank you, Richard, but I am to call upon your mother. I am persuaded you will find it tedious beyond measure and, as you see, Yvette is to accompany me.' She gestured behind her to where her maid had followed her down. 'Besides, I see you are dressed for riding and I make no doubt you will enjoy such exercise far more than walking at my slow pace.'

His wife was consistent, he would give her that. She had said she would not welcome his attentions during the day, and she had kept to her word. Despite his efforts to convince himself it was for the best, the terms of their marriage were eating away at him. Angry words, he knew, would get him nowhere.

He bowed. 'Enjoy your outing, dear. I shall see you later.'

Ten minutes later, Richard waited, tapping his whip against his boot, as Dalton saddled Thor.

'You'll be wanting someone to accompany you, milord.' Dalton voiced it as a statement, not a question.

'No. I shall ride alone.'

Dalton paused in his task. 'He's very fresh, milord. Mebbe—'

'Are you suggesting I cannot handle my own horse, Dalton?'

The groom stiffened before buckling the throat lash.

'Forgive me, Dalton, I should not have snapped at you. I am in no mood for company. There is no need to worry about my safety.'

'Very well, milord.' Richard closed his mind to the doubt in the groom's tone.

Dalton held the stallion as Richard mounted and Thor threw his head up in reaction to the weight on his back. As the horse's muscles bunched beneath him Richard grinned in anticipation of the ride to come. It would take all of his concentration to settle the horse—exactly what he needed. He rode Thor out of the yard, using seat and legs to drive him up to the bit and encourage him to drop his head.

The strains of the day drained from Richard as they trotted along the track leading from the stables down to the river meadows a mile away. Once down in those broad, flat fields—through which the River Fern flowed—he would give Thor his head and shake the fidgets out of them both with a long gallop. Despite his intention to focus his full attention on Thor, Richard's mind continued to meander, his body reacting instinctively to the stallion's antics as he boggled at rustles in the hedgerows and shied around puddles.

Why was he so restless? Why did he feel as though something constantly hovered beyond the reach of his understanding?

He should be content: his mother was now settled at the Lodge and Felicity was with child, yet she continued to welcome him to her bed. A tremor shuddered through him at the thought of the spine-tingling satisfaction he found in his wife's arms night after night. She oversaw his household in a calm and uncomplaining manner and she *appeared* content with her life, yet… No amount of teasing or probing by him had yet uncovered any chink in her outer shell. He hated that Felicity would not confide in him.

Trust. He longed for his wife to trust him. He

wanted…*needed* to be the centre of her world, the most important person in her life.

They reached the gate at the end of the track, and he stretched down to unlatch it. As it swung open, Thor bounced into the meadow, snatching at the bit.

Richard laughed, his spirits lifting. 'You know what's coming, don't you, old fellow?'

This had been a favourite ride since his boyhood, when he and Adam would race their horses, jumping over the numerous ditches that drained the fields above into the river, then riding home, happy and exhausted, through Fernley woods. Despite the age gap, they had been close. Until… His spirits dived again, like a swallow in flight.

He nudged Thor until he breasted the gate shut, then reached down to latch it. He felt those powerful haunches bunch under him as Thor tried to wheel round, anticipating the gallop. Richard sat deep, holding the stallion between hand and leg, heading for the river at a slow, collected canter. The decision to gallop would be his, and his alone.

As they reached the bank, lined with trees, he reined to a halt to admire the sun glinting on the river and the sound of the river rushing past. He sat and watched for several minutes, enjoying the moment, aware of half a ton of quivering horseflesh between his thighs. Then he turned Thor and pointed him downstream. The big horse needed no further encouragement, catapulting into a gallop, the ground a blur beneath his pounding hooves. Richard felt his lips stretch into a wide smile as they flew over familiar ditches, the wind in his face blowing his troubles away.

At the far end of the meadows they slowed to a canter, a trot and, finally, a walk, both heaving for breath. Here, a tributary joined the river. It was too wide to jump and the sloping banks were too high and unstable to negotiate, so a footbridge— around fifteen feet long and strong enough for a horse and rider—had been constructed. Once over the bridge, there was a quiet lane to cross into Fernley woods, towering majestically up a steep slope before levelling out.

The way home.

Thor jibbed at setting foot on the bridge.

'Come on, lad. I know you don't care for it, but you've done it before.'

After some urging, including firm encouragement from Richard's heels and a tap with the whip, Thor ventured on to the narrow bridge, ears flat to his head. He jibbed again at the halfway point and an inkling of danger struck Richard.

Too late.

The wooden structure sagged and tilted with an ominous crack. Frantic hooves scrabbled for purchase on the wet boards as Richard kicked Thor on, hoping they might, by some miracle, reach the opposite bank before the bridge gave way. The stallion made a valiant attempt to respond, lurching forward, his front hooves almost home even as his hind legs slipped over the side of the bridge. He hung there for a few seconds, giving Richard precious time to kick his feet free of the stirrups and throw himself clear of the falling horse. He landed with a thump, on his back, in the freezing water.

Remorse needled Felicity as she took tea with her mother-in-law. It had been so very hard to resist the heat in Richard's eyes as he watched her come down the stairs, but she had forced herself to deny his company.

She was a coward. She did not want their marriage to continue like this but, whenever she was on the verge of relenting, the thought of his mistress stopped her. Her dread was all too real that, once back in London, Richard would forget her and once again plunge back into his old life. She must not become reliant on him or his presence.

Other than their continuing driving lessons— she had by now graduated to driving a pair—she had become adept at avoiding any but the most fleeting of interactions with Richard.

Except at night.

A tug of anticipation deep inside recalled the passion and ecstasy she experienced night after night at his skilful touch.

A gentle cough returned her with a jolt to the present, and to her mother-in-law's cool appraisal.

'Oh.' Felicity felt her blush build up once more. 'I am sorry.'

The dowager patted her on the knee. 'Ladies in your condition are known to be prone to a little absentmindedness.'

The dowager had been delighted with the news

of Felicity's pregnancy, and she and Felicity had become ever closer over the past weeks. Richard's relationship with his mother, however, had continued to be fraught.

'It will be dark shortly,' Felicity said eventually. 'I should—'

A sudden flurry of activity in the hall—raised voices and running footsteps—prevented her from finishing her sentence. A glance at the dowager revealed a face leached of colour.

'Wait there, Mother. I will see what is amiss.'

Richard—skin whiter than the neckcloth swathing his head, his clothes soaking wet—sat on a chair in the hall whilst a footman tugged at his boots. The butler and various other servants hovered nearby.

'I am perfectly well, I tell you, Davis,' Richard said to the butler. 'There is no need for the doctor. Send for Dalton immediately, will you? Thor is in need—'

'Never mind your horse.' Felicity dropped to her knees beside him. His hand was freezing. 'What on earth happened?' She reached to the cloth wrapped around his head, and he flinched. Then she saw the blood and her stomach roiled. 'Davis,' she said. 'Send someone for the doctor. Immediately.'

'Yes, my lady.'

'Hold hard there, Davis.' Richard glared at Felicity. 'What do you mean by—?'

'You have an injury to your head. I cannot be

certain you are capable of making rational decisions, so I have done it for you.'

Their gazes clashed, a storm brewing in Richard's brown eyes.

Chapter Forty-Three

Felicity held her breath, determined to stand firm. Richard held her gaze for what seemed like an age until, suddenly, he smiled. It was like the sun appearing from behind thunderclouds.

'Very well, Felicity Joy. Davis?'

'Milord?'

'Tell Dalton to come here first, before he sees the horse.'

'Dalton? But he's a groom.'

'He's patched me up many times, Felicity. I'll not have that quack from the village anywhere near me, and anyone else is too far away.'

'Very well.' Dalton was a man of sense, he would very soon say if he thought Richard in need of a doctor. Felicity touched his cheek. 'What happened? Were you thrown?' She was always apprehensive when Richard rode the lively stallion.

'*Thrown?*' Disgust coloured his tone. 'No, I was not *thrown*. The bridge gave way as we crossed. We landed in the stream and had to wade along the river until the bank was low enough to climb out.'

Felicity's imagination embroidered his spare tale with horrific images. 'You were fortunate Thor did not...' Her blood ran cold. She probed Richard's ribs as she scanned him for injuries. At his bellow of pain, she snatched her hands away. '*Did* he land on you? Were you crushed?'

Richard hacked out a laugh, which merged into a cough which, in turn, merged into a groan. Felicity sat on her heels, hardly daring to touch him in case she caused any damage. Eventually, he gasped, 'Do I...look crushed? I rolled...clear... pleased to say. Ribs...damnably sore. This was... nearest place.'

'I am so glad I was still here. Here, let me help, can you stand?' Felicity slid her hand under his arm, then hesitated before she tried to help him to his feet. He had begun to shiver violently, and she did not like the sudden greyish cast to his skin, or the roll of his eyes.

She beckoned to two male servants. 'Help his lordship upstairs immediately. He needs to be dried and kept warm.' Davis came hurrying back along the hall. 'I think a measure of brandy would be welcome, Davis, if you have such a thing. And you,' she addressed one of the maids, 'go to the kitchen and ask Cook to send up hot water and a tea tray, please.'

Richard's arms were draped over the servants' shoulders, and their arms linked together around his back. Felicity could see the effort he made to take some of his weight on his own legs, which alternately buckled and straightened.

'I will go ahead of you and—'

A moan caught Felicity's attention. The dowager had emerged from the drawing room and stood, visibly trembling, her eyes riveted on her son.

'No, you go ahead. I will be with you shortly.' Felicity scanned the hall, and spied the worried-looking housekeeper hurrying from the rear of the house. 'Mrs Norton—' she called, as the men began their slow climb up the stairs, half carrying Richard, whose head lolled alarmingly '—her ladyship is taken ill. Please ask Cook to prepare another tea tray for the drawing room and ask Tallis to attend us there.'

Anxiety clawed at her as she hurried to the dowager's side. As she put her arm around her Felicity registered, for the first time, her physical frailty. Her erect stance and unyielding manner gave the impression of strength but, in reality, there was little flesh covering her bones.

She settled the dowager in a chair by the fire then drew up a footstool, sat on it, and chafed her bony hands, which were as chilled as Richard's. Thinking of her husband triggered an urge to be with him, but she could not leave her mother-in-law until Tallis—her maid—arrived.

'Richard will be all right, Mother.'

Those dazed eyes settled on Felicity's face. 'I could not bear to lose him, too,' she whispered.

'You won't. He is strong; he will recover in no time, you'll see.'

She believed it—she *had* to believe it.

What would I do...? What if...? No. He is strong. He managed to walk this far. He is bruised and exhausted.

'We will *not* lose him, Mother.'

'The Stanton men, they all die before their time.' The dowager shuddered, grabbing Felicity's hand, nails cutting into her flesh. 'I thought him improved...you have been good for him. He has always been like his father...and his brother... worse, even...seeking out excitement...getting involved in anything and everything dangerous... oblivious to the risks...' She moaned, rocking back and forth. 'If anything...if he should—'

'He will not—'

'I should have told him.' Tears tracked down the dowager's pale cheeks, dampened her bloodless lips. 'Now it is too late...'

'What should you have told him? It is not too late, Mother. Please, try to stay calm. Richard will not die.'

Please, God. Oh, where is Tallis? I need to see him...to take care of him.

'I only did it to protect his memories of his papa—'

'Milady?' Tallis rushed into the room, followed by a kitchen maid carrying a tea tray.

The dowager released her grip. 'Go to Richard, Daughter. He has need of you.'

Richard? That was the first time Felicity had

heard his mother call Richard anything other than Stanton.

'Take good care of him, please. And let me know…let me know…'

'I will let you know how he is as soon as I can.'

The dowager smiled, although her lips trembled. 'Thank you, dear.' She straightened in her chair with a visible effort. 'I pray you will forgive my moment of weakness. It was the shock. Tallis, you may sit with me while I drink my tea, and then I shall go to bed.'

Felicity pondered her mother-in-law's disjointed words as she climbed the stairs. What had she not told Richard? He already knew his father had shot himself—what could be worse than that? Of one thing Felicity was certain: Richard was wrong to believe his mother wished he, and not Adam, had died. Her mother-in-law cared very much for her second son, despite her constant criticism. And she was terrified of losing him.

Her trepidation as she entered the bedchamber was unfounded. Richard sat in a comfortable armchair by the fire, a blanket tucked around his legs, as Davis dabbed gingerly at the blood in his hair. As Felicity entered, Richard's head snapped round, knocking Davis's hand aside. She crossed the room and peered at his scalp where the gash—a good three inches long—continued to ooze blood.

'Felicity, where have you been? Can you *please* stop this imbecile from fiddling with my head? It stings like the…that is, it's very sore.'

Davis cast a reproachful look at Richard.

'He is only trying to help,' Felicity said. 'But I do not think you can achieve much more, Davis— you have done an excellent job of cleansing the wound. If you have a clean pad to cover it, Dalton will soon tell us if any stitches are required.'

She bit back a smile at Richard's barely audible *hmmph*.

A tea tray was on a nearby table. 'Have you had a cup of tea?'

'I've had some brandy.'

'Then I shall pour some tea for you, and sweeten it well, for it is said to be beneficial in cases of shock.'

'I am not in shock. I am angry. I could have lost Thor.'

Felicity opened the tea caddy and spooned some leaves into the teapot, then poured in hot water to allow the leaves to steep.

'As I said before, you were fortunate Thor did not crush you.' She stirred the pot as she willed her voice not to tremble. 'Is he injured?'

'Not seriously, thank goodness. Bruised and scratched, but nothing broken. I need to examine that bridge tomorrow and find out why it gave way.' Richard sipped at his tea and Felicity was relieved to see his colour improve. 'I am sure I recall an entry in the ledgers showing it was repaired last spring. I need to speak to Elliott.'

'You are unlikely to be fit enough to ride tomorrow,' Felicity said. 'It is possible you have broken your ribs.'

Richard glowered at her. She smiled in return. It would be what it would be, and no amount of willing it otherwise would change it.

'Where were you?' he asked. 'I thought you were behind us but you disappeared.'

Felicity glanced round. Davis was occupied on the far side of the room. 'I was with your mother. She was very disturbed, so I waited with her until her maid could attend.'

'Hah. No doubt petrified I'd die before we have our heir.'

'That is unfair. She was much shaken. She cares about you, more than you realize.'

'I do not—'

'Hush.' Felicity laid her fingers against his lips. 'Trust me. She cares.'

Their gazes fused. His tongue flicked against her fingertips and her pulse stuttered. At the sound of a knock, she snatched her hand away just as Dalton walked in.

After examining Richard, Dalton stitched his scalp and strapped his ribs. 'It don't appear no worse'n a bump, far as I c'n tell, milady.'

'You may address me, Dalton,' Richard said irritably. 'I am perfectly rational, you know.'

'Nor do the ribs look to be broken,' Dalton continued, 'but I reckons a couple're mebbe cracked. They're like to be sore awhile. You'll need to rest up a few days, milord.'

'I shall return home in the morning,' Richard said. 'I've things to attend to, and I need to inspect that bridge.'

Dalton raised his brows. 'You know best, milord, I'm sure. All I know is cracked ribs is very painful an' takes time to mend. They'll be a sight worse by morning, you mark my words. I'll take a look at the bridge tomorrow and report back.

'Now then, Simson's on his way and he's bringing arnica for your bruises. If that's all, I'll go and see to Thor.'

After seeing Richard settled in bed with Simson to watch over him, and reassuring her mother-in-law that Richard was not lying at death's door, Felicity ate a solitary supper before retiring. After Yvette left, she tossed and turned, sleep evading her as she relived those terrible moments when the dowager's fears had awoken the possibility she might lose Richard.

She clasped her belly protectively. What would the future hold? She saw now, with absolute clarity, that her life was in danger of becoming a self-fulfilling prophecy. If she continued to push Richard away, the result would be the kind of life she feared above all else.

But their lives at Fernley Park were one thing, London was quite another. What would happen when they returned in February as planned? What of Richard's mistress?

Chapter Forty-Four

Next morning, Richard roused sleepily, began to turn over, and catapulted awake.

'Aaaaargh.'

The pain in his side spiked before easing to a throb. Memories of his fall flooded back: the split-second realization that Thor might crush him, his frantic efforts to scramble clear; the terrible certainty that Thor was dead, until his legs began to thrash about. Tentatively, Richard probed the clipped area at the back of his head, the stitches scratching at his fingertips. He massaged his temples.

'How do you feel?'

The delicious scent of violets surrounded him as Felicity leaned over him, forehead puckered in enquiry, plait dangling, a shawl wrapped around her shoulders. Her hands clutched the shawl below her breasts, doing little to cover the burgeoning mounds revealed above the lace-trimmed neckline of her nightgown. He forced his attention to her face. Her lids were heavy as she stifled a yawn.

'How long have you been here, Felicity Joy?'

Her eyes skittered from his scrutiny as she perched on the side of the bed. 'I couldn't sleep.'

'How long?'

'A few hours. I wanted to be here in case you needed anything.'

'Simson was here. There was no need for you—'

'I sent him to bed. There was no need for us both to stay.' She paused. 'I wanted to be with you.'

Warmth flooded his body. 'Did you miss me, Felicity Joy?'

A blush spread from her neck to her cheeks but she held his gaze and nodded. 'I was afraid... that is, there was a moment, yesterday, when I thought...' Her chest heaved, his eyes drawn to her breasts as a bee to nectar. She was still small breasted, but pregnancy had added to their lushness. Saliva flooded his mouth, and he swallowed, silently cursing his sore ribs.

'You thought...?'

She pleated and repleated the fabric of her nightgown. 'It forced me to consider how I might feel if anything should happen to you.'

Moving carefully Richard reached to cover her hands with his. They stilled.

'And how might you feel?'

Tears sheened her eyes. 'I could not bear it. I realized...how very glad I am that I married you.'

'Come here.' He gave a little tug and she moved closer.

He stroked her soft cheek then hooked his fingers around her nape. She leaned down willingly, bracing her hands on the pillow either side of his head, lips—soft, pink, alluring—parting. She hesitated, and then brushed his mouth in a sweet kiss before sitting back again.

'More.'

She laughed down at him. 'You will not thank me if I get carried away and bump your ribs. I can think of nothing more likely to cool your ardour. We can wait.' Her amber eyes darkened as she swept his lower lip with her thumb. 'We have our whole lives ahead of us.

'Are you hungry? Would you like breakfast sent up?'

'No.' Richard winced as he sat up and eased the covers down. 'That is, I am hungry, but I wish to get up and eat breakfast downstairs. Will you ring for Simson?'

'Do you think you should…?'

He was already on his feet. 'You *are* a little worrier. It was only a tumble. I promise I will be sensible about resting. Ah, Simson, that was quick. Thank you. I am going downstairs for breakfast. Will you help me on with my banyan?'

As they ate breakfast, Tallis came in. 'Begging your pardon, my lord, but her ladyship wishes you to attend her in her sitting room when you have finished your breakfast.'

Richard lowered his forkful of eggs as Tallis left the room. 'I've been summoned. No doubt to hear a lecture on how—yet again—my penchant for risk-taking might have cleared the path for Charles to inherit Fernley and throw my mother to the wolves.'

Felicity frowned. 'That is unfair. Your mother was distraught: her only concern was for you. I do not believe any thought of the succession crossed her mind.'

A knot of resentment lodged in his chest. What did Felicity know? She'd not had to live all these years with the knowledge that his mother would rather it was he—Richard—who had died. He had barely existed in her eyes after his brother's death.

'Besides,' Felicity continued, 'as I am with child, Charles will not necessarily inherit Fernley.'

'And I can assure you I intend to live a long, healthy and—hopefully—happy life with you and our children.'

Felicity's smile wobbled. He pushed back his chair and beckoned.

'Come. We will go and hear what my mother has to say.'

'Me? Oh, I don't think your mother would expect me—'

'*I* expect you to be privy to our conversation, Felicity. You are my wife. I should like you to understand why my relationship with my mother is so troubled.'

His mother sat staring into the fire, her lips

pinched and pale. When she looked round, Richard's lungs seized. She looked old, and grey, and…shrunken, somehow. How had that happened without him noticing? She lifted her hand to Felicity, who clasped it and stooped to kiss her cheek.

They have become so close. Why can neither of them be as relaxed with me?

Or me with them? He thrust that thought aside.

'Thank you for coming,' Mother said. '*Both* of you.'

A peculiar sensation of watching from outside himself settled over Richard as they sat down. This felt different to Mother's usual rant about needlessly courting danger. *Is she ill? Seriously ill? Am I going to lose her?* His throat thickened. He coughed, then dragged in a calming breath.

'How are you this morning, Richard?'

About to utter a dismissive, 'I am perfectly well', Richard paused. It was time for honesty. 'My ribs hurt abominably and I am bruised, but I will recover.'

'Good.' Mother stared pensively into the flames. 'I have to tell you something I should perhaps have told you many years ago. I make no excuses, although I did have good reason. But I promised God—when I prayed for your recovery—that I would tell you the truth. About Adam.'

In the sixteen years since his brother's death, Richard could probably count on the fingers of one hand the number of times his mother had spoken Adam's name aloud.

What truth? I already know everything.

'Richard was away at school when it happened.' Mother glanced at Felicity before returning her attention to the fire. 'It was a lovely autumn, and Richard's father and Adam went shooting.'

Richard shifted on the sofa. He knew what was coming. It had been an accident. Adam had been careless.

'They ran to tell me,' Mother continued. 'Oh, my dear, but I hope you never have to endure such agony.' She paused, her knuckles white as she visibly composed herself. Felicity slid from the sofa to kneel by the chair and hold her hand. 'Adam was already dead by the time I reached them. Shot in the back.'

'What?' Richard surged to his feet, barely noticing the agonising pain that shot through his torso. 'The *back*? Who—?'

'Your father.'

That stark reply hit him with the force of a knockout punch. The air left his lungs with a *whoosh* and he fought for breath.

Papa shot Adam? No! It cannot be true.

'No.' The word came out a croak. 'No.' He shook his head, trying to rid himself of the words, the image they evoked.

'It was an accident. Your father *pleaded* with me not to tell you the truth and I promised I would not. You idolized Adam, and Papa could not bear that you might grow to despise him.'

Richard scrubbed his hands over his face,

struggling for composure. 'It was an accident. Why would I despise my father? He did not shoot Adam deliberately. Why did you not tell me the truth after Papa died?'

Mother sighed. 'I vowed to tell you the whole truth, and I shall. If it had not been for me, I believe your father would eventually have told you the truth. It was *I* who despised *him*, in those first months. In my grief, I blamed him for taking my child, my son, my firstborn.

'It is *my* fault Papa killed himself. If only I had supported him through his own guilt and grief. But, no.' She paused, and when she spoke again, her tone was bitter. 'No, I could barely bring myself to be civil to him. It was easier to withdraw completely and leave him to drown in his own misery whilst I drowned in mine.'

'You were mad with grief,' Felicity said. 'No one could blame you for reacting—'

'I blame myself. And what I didn't see, until it was too late, was that not only had I cut myself off from my husband, but also from Richard. By the time I realized, it was impossible to bridge the gulf between us.'

She struggled to her feet and went to Richard. Every muscle in his body was rigid as his brain tried to make sense of his mother's words.

'I was a coward, and I am so very sorry. Every time I thought to tell you the truth, I became petrified you would blame me for the loss of your father the way I blamed him for the loss of Adam. All I could do was try to protect you and keep you safe. You were all I had left, but the more I tried to curb your activities the more you resented me and so the gulf widened.'

'I believed…' Richard closed his eyes, sorting his thoughts. *Should I say this? Is now the right time?* A rational decision eluded him, but if he did not admit what he had held to be true these past fifteen years, it would continue to eat at him and the rift between them might never be healed. 'All these years, I believed my father killed himself because I was not a good enough replacement for Adam; that he did not love me enough to want to live.'

'Oh, no! My darling son…' Her voice caught on a sob. 'I have been blind. And foolish. To think you believed that, all this time. Your father *never* thought that. He loved you both. Equally. We both did. But Papa could not live with his guilt.'

He felt her hands cup his face and he forced his eyes open. 'Yesterday, you looked so weak and pale. I have never seen you like that. I suddenly understood that if my worst fears ever came to pass, you might die and I would never have the chance to tell you the truth. I saw what I must do—what I should have done years ago. Can you ever forgive me?'

He pulled away and strode to the window. Angry clouds scudded across the sky, mirroring the thoughts charging around his brain. Trees bowed before the strengthening wind, their top branches whipping back and forth and, as the first raindrops spat against the glass, Richard turned to face his mother.

He was tempted—oh, so tempted—to vent his anger on to her: anger for deceiving him for all these years.

It is hardly her fault you believed what you did. You could have simply asked her.

I was a child!

Not so much a child at seventeen. And you have long been a man.

Even as he turned, he wasn't certain what words would come out of his mouth: angry words to lash out and hurt, or conciliatory words to heal?

And there was Felicity, in his path, amber eyes anxious and searching, hands on his chest.

'Think.'

The word was whispered so softly he barely heard it, but it was powerful enough to stay him for that split second whilst his rational mind fought with his gut emotions. Rationality won. He crossed the room and, in the end, no words were needed as he wrapped his arms around his mother and held her, feeling the sobs that shook her frail frame and blinking back the moisture in his own eyes.

Chapter Forty-Five

Early February 1812

They arrived in London on a grey February afternoon. Their visit would be brief, because of Felicity's condition.

'I confess I am disappointed we shall miss most of the Season,' Felicity said to Richard, lounging on the seat next to her, booted feet propped on the opposite seat. 'I had hoped to attend Olivia's coming-out ball.'

'Maybe we will still be here. Knowing Leo, he will ensure his daughter's ball is one of the first, and the best. Then he will sit back and enjoy watching the rest of the *ton* in their attempts to emulate his opulence.'

Felicity laughed. 'I can just see him "coming the duke", as Papa used to say.'

'You have changed, Felicity.' Richard lowered his feet to the floor and swivelled sideways to face her. Her pulse leapt, as it always did when he turned those velvety brown eyes on her. 'Five months ago, you would not have given a fig that you might miss the ball of the Season. Now...' he studied her '...now you have become a stylish society lady.'

'Thanks to Yvette.'

Richard cocked a brow. 'You give Yvette too much credit. You have developed confidence I never thought to see in you, but I believe you would have changed anyway. I hesitate to criticize your mother, but since you ceased to be influenced by her shallow perception of what is important in life, you have bloomed.' Gentle fingers drifted down her cheek, and she leaned into his touch. 'You are as lovely on the outside as you always have been on the inside.'

Rendered awkward by his praise, Felicity stared out of the window.

'Do not blush and turn aside, Felicity. Hold your head high. Be proud of who you are and what you have achieved.'

'Achieved? I have achieved nothing.'

'What about the difference you have made to all those children at Westfield? How many young women in your position concern themselves in the plight of orphans? To my shame, I never thought of such people either, until I met you. So you have changed my attitude too.'

He took her hand and raised it to his lips. Even through the fine kid of her glove, she could feel the heat of his mouth and, before she could think better of it, she leaned over and kissed him. In an instant, he clasped her to his chest and took possession of her mouth, his lips working their magic until she was lying prone on the seat, panting, with Richard atop her, his arousal pressed against her thigh.

'That,' he said, chest heaving, 'was most scandalous behaviour from a society lady, if I might say so, Lady Stanton. Mayhap I should rethink my appraisal of your character to that of an abandoned hussy.' He kissed her soundly. 'You once told me you were glad you married me. I shall return the compliment, and say I am very glad I married you. I think we suit very well.'

He sat up and rearranged his neckcloth, gazing out at the passing sights.

Still no words of love. Felicity tamped down her disappointment.

Since the dowager's confession, Richard and his mother had grown closer, step by faltering step. Felicity had found it hard to believe two people could drift so far apart over words they dared not say. She had vowed not to let unspoken words strangle her relationship with Richard in the same way. But it was easy to make that vow, much harder to put it into practice as, night after night, Richard made love to her and then left her bed.

The words 'I love you' died unspoken on her lips many times.

Was it so very important he should love her? He had said he was glad he had married her. Was that not enough?

She knew the answer before she finished formulating the question. No. It was not enough. She must live with it, but she would never stop hoping for more. Fear and doubt still gnawed at her confidence. What if he grew bored? She was under no illusions: she would be left to her own devices whilst he pursued his many other interests.

Loneliness loomed.

'What brings you to town this early, Stan?' Leo hailed Richard from a chair by the window of White's the following day.

'I might ask you the same, Duke,' Richard replied as they shook hands.

'Cecily *insisted* Olivia needs a hundred fittings before her ball,' Leo said, with barely concealed disgust. 'We've only been in town a couple of days and I've already had my fill of it. What's a man to do?'

'Hide in his club and leave the women to it?'

'Now why did I not think of that? And you?'

'Oh, Felicity was keen to visit that school of hers, and I need to visit Barker's. I've ordered a phaeton for Felicity from them and I want to inspect it before it's delivered. I'm also looking for a well-schooled pair, if you should hear of any. She's become quite skilled with the ribbons.'

'I'll keep an ear open. How is Felicity, by the by?'

Richard felt a wide smile split his face. Leo raised a brow.

'We weren't going to tell anyone yet but, as you

were there at the conception of our marriage, I think it only right—'

'Hold hard, Stan. There are some things a man has to draw the line at. I point-blank refuse to be present at the conception of your heir.'

Richard stared, momentarily taken aback, then guffawed.

Leo beamed. 'I take it congratulations are in order? Felicity is well?'

'She's very well, but she tires easily so we won't stay in town long. Besides, I cannot be away from Fernley for too long. I've had to dismiss my bailiff.' Richard told Leo about his accident on the bridge and his subsequent discovery that Elliott had been siphoning funds from the estate by putting forged invoices through the accounts. 'I believed Elliott to be trustworthy—he's been with me years—but I won't make the same mistake with the new man.'

Felicity, meanwhile, had penned a note to Lady Brierley, informing her of their arrival in town. The footman sent to deliver the note returned with an invitation to take tea that afternoon. Harriet was her usual charming self, entertaining Felicity with the latest gossip. They arranged to visit Westfield together the following day.

The tea tray had been removed, and Felicity rose to her feet, saying, 'I fear I am monopolizing your time, dear Harriet. I must...'

The walls appeared to bulge and then recede,

and Harriet's voice came as though from a great distance: 'Felicity? What is wrong?'

'I…I…' Felicity's legs turned to jelly. A hand gripped her elbow and she was eased back on to the sofa. She hauled in a deep breath, and the room steadied before her eyes. 'Oh, goodness, I am so sorry, Harriet. Might I take a few moments to compose myself?'

Harriet chafed Felicity's hand. 'You may take as long as you like, my dear. There, you have some colour back in your cheeks. Did you feel faint?'

Harriet skimmed Felicity's body. 'Ah,' she said.

Felicity sighed at the speculation embodied in that simple utterance. 'I stood up too quickly. It happens from time to time. Please promise me you will not tell anyone.'

'That you are with child?'

Felicity nodded. 'Richard and I agreed to keep the news secret until we return to Fernley. I long to attend Lady Olivia Beauchamp's come-out ball—the duke was my guardian, you know, and I have known Olivia all her life—but I cannot bear being an object of scrutiny. The sticklers would be alert for the merest hint that I should already be retired from society.'

'Your secret is safe, dear. Please, stay until you are completely recovered. Now, tell me all about your first winter at Fernley Park.'

One story led to another and, eventually, Felicity found herself telling Harriet about Beanie, and how Richard had gone to Bristol to find her, and bring her home. Her voice faltered as she recalled Emma's diary and, before she knew what she was doing, she had confided in Harriet about Emma, her seduction, and her suicide. Instinct told her she could trust the other woman, and it was a great relief to share her past with another female.

'I remember your sister—such a beautiful young woman. We attended several of the same house parties in the summer of…let me see…was it '02? Or '03?'

''02,' Felicity said. 'She was eighteen and was presented that spring.'

'Such a tragic story. Forgive me, but I thought at the time that some of those gatherings were unsuitable for such an innocent. In a way, I cannot be surprised at such an unhappy ending. Do you know who the scoundrel was?'

'No. She referred to him in her diary as "M". They first met at a house party in Hertfordshire but it seems they met at other parties too. I did not know she was with child until I read her diary. I always believed she had been driven to suicide by grief because her lover abandoned her.'

I have allowed that belief to overshadow so much of my life.

'I must go, Harriet.'

It is time to make amends to Richard for my suspicions and my stubbornness.

Richard was kind, attentive and the most wonderful lover she could ever have imagined. She was in love with him, but did he love her in return? Or was their marriage still a novelty, to hold his attention until another woman caught his eye?

Unrequited love.

It was time to take the risk. It was time to say those words.

I love you.

Chapter Forty-Six

'What do you say, Stan? Can you bear to leave Felicity to fend for herself for a week or so?'

Richard leaned forward and topped up Leo's wine glass. The duke had called round with the news of a driving pair for sale by a neighbour of his cousin, who lived in Buckinghamshire.

'They should be perfect for Felicity; Rockbeare's cattle are always beautifully schooled.'

'It sounds too good an opportunity to miss,' Richard said.

'And the hunting in the area is excellent,' Leo added persuasively.

Richard sat back, considering the implications of being out of town for several days. The purchase was to be a surprise for Felicity, hence the cover of going hunting. He pictured her amber eyes lighting up and her joyous smile at having her own phaeton and pair. He would miss her, though.

'Why the hesitation?' Leo said. 'Can't stomach leaving Felicity for so long? I never thought to see you so in thrall, Stan. I thought you and I were as cynical as each other about love and matters of the heart.'

Richard forced a laugh. He had always believed that too. Lately, though...

'Love? I merely wish to keep Felicity happy and contented for the baby's sake.'

Disingenuous, perhaps, but he was in no mood to become embroiled in a discussion about love.

'Good afternoon, your Grace. You are well, I hope?'

Both men leapt to their feet at Felicity's words, Richard's stomach hollowing. *Did she overhear?* Her expression revealed nothing other than pleasure as she greeted Leo.

'I am very well, my dear,' Leo said as he sauntered over to Felicity and kissed her cheek. 'As are you, I hear.'

'I hope you do not object, sweetheart, but I told Leo our news yesterday.'

'Of course not.' Felicity smiled at Leo.

'Have you had a pleasant afternoon?' Richard asked as Felicity settled on the sofa and he and Leo returned to their chairs.

'Most enjoyable, thank you. I took tea with Lady Brierley, and we have arranged to visit Westfield tomorrow.'

Harriet? Richard could only hope she remained discreet. It would seem his wife and his former mistress were fast becoming friends. There was nothing to be gained now from trying to keep them apart. Why had he not admitted the truth to Felicity right from the start, as Harriet had advised? But at least no one else was aware of their connection. Leo, who knew most goings-on, had not batted an eye when Felicity spoke of Harriet.

'I am glad you will have some company whilst I am out of town.' At Felicity's look of enquiry, he continued: 'I'm going into Buckinghamshire, hunting, with Leo and one or two others.'

'Oh.' Felicity hid her disappointment well, but there was a definite tinge of it in her tone. 'Well, I shall miss you, of course, but you will enjoy the change, I make no doubt. Will your ribs—?'

'They will be fine.' An image arose of Felicity riding him the night before, after ministering to him with skilful fingers and lips. He had not protested. She had become quite the seductress whilst his ribs had been mending, and he had thoroughly enjoyed her attentions. A scorching glance from those amber eyes, and a pinkish tinge to her cheeks, told him that she was thinking the same. He would make it up to her tonight. His loins tightened at the thought and he propped one ankle on the opposite knee to conceal his arousal.

'I am pleased to hear it,' Felicity replied, dropping her eyes demurely to her lap as the tip of her tongue stroked her upper lip.

Little minx!

'Ahem.' Leo rose smoothly to his feet, voice bubbling with amusement. 'This is not the level of deference a duke expects from his associates,

my dears. I am feeling decidedly *de trop*. I shall
say my *adieux*, and I will see you first thing in
the morning, Stan. Don't be late.'

As Leo left the room, Felicity said, '*Are* your
ribs completely healed, Richard?'

'I should hardly arrange to go hunting if they
were not.'

Such an innocent tone. Felicity narrowed her
eyes at him. 'Last night?' He had claimed the
soreness had returned, blaming the journey to
town.

He shrugged. 'You seemed to be enjoying
yourself.' His voice quivered as he bit back his
grin, his brown eyes brimming with laughter. 'I
had no wish to spoil—'

'Oh, you…you…'

He cocked a brow. 'Yes? Are you struggling to
articulate your thoughts, my sweet?'

Felicity relaxed into the sofa, draping one arm
along the back. 'Come here, Husband.'

Richard sucked in one cheek. 'I detect some
sorcery at work but…is it retribution on her
mind…or seduction? Hmmmm, only one way
to find out.'

He rose with the lithe grace of a big cat, and
prowled towards the sofa, taking his time. Her
heart leapt at the intent in his dark, hooded eyes,
then lurched into a mad gallop. Heavens, what
had she started?

'The servants!'

Richard swerved to the door. He opened it,

stuck his head out and said, 'No one, under any circumstances, is to disturb us.' He shut the door and turned to face Felicity. 'Now—' his voice was at its silkiest '—where were we?'

His breeches revealed the extent of his arousal and Felicity's breath all but seized at the sight of her powerful, handsome husband.

Mine! At least... No! She batted the unhelpful and unwelcome doubt away as she rose to meet him and took him in her arms, tilting her face as his lips lowered to take hers.

Sometime later, sprawled on the sofa, cosily wrapped in Richard's arms as he dozed, her treacherous mind bombarded her again with doubts. She had heard Cousin Leo's comment about love and matters of the heart earlier, and she had paused to hear Richard's reaction. His words had stung, particularly after her earlier resolve. How could she say those words to him now?

Carefully, she moved her head and she studied his face: at peace with his world, dark lashes feathering his cheeks, brown hair dishevelled, sensual lips relaxed and slightly apart as his breath huffed in the quiet of the room.

Had he spoken the truth of what was in his heart? Was it likely he would have admitted he loved her when the duke's unwavering cynicism about love was common knowledge?

No. She did not believe he would, but still she did not quite have the courage to open her heart to him.

* * *

The following day, Felicity and Harriet visited Westfield. Felicity's childhood friend Jane Whittaker greeted them warmly, and they spent a pleasant afternoon helping the children with their lessons, discussing ideas both to raise money and to encourage more employers to take apprentices.

On the journey home, Felicity reflected on how pleasant it was to have a friend such as Harriet. Most other ladies of her acquaintance thought her eccentric for even bothering with the orphans. Jane also liked Harriet and the feeling appeared mutual. For the first time in her adult life, Felicity began to feel like she belonged.

'Are you and Lord Stanton going out tonight?' Harriet asked.

'No. I did not tell you, did I? He has gone out of town for a few days, with the duke. They are staying with the duke's cousin, in Buckinghamshire.'

'In that case, would you care to dine with me this evening, if you are not too weary? And, if you should care to join me, I intend to go to Cheapside tomorrow afternoon.'

'Thank you, Harriet. I am delighted to accept *both* invitations.'

The note, clearly scribbled in haste, was delivered to Felicity at breakfast the following morning.

Dearest Felicity
I regret to inform you that I must leave
London for a few days to attend to some ur-

*gent business. I am sorry to cancel our visit
to Cheapside, but I shall contact you upon
my return to rearrange the outing.*
    Your friend
    Harriet

Felicity read it again. What had happened
between when she had left Harriet's house last
evening and this morning? Self-pity loomed, but
Felicity thrust it away, impatient with such self-
ishness. Rather she should feel sympathy for her
friend, for good news rarely forced such an abrupt
change of plans. She hoped it was not *very* bad
news, for Harriet's sake.

Stanton House was too large and, somehow,
less colourful without Richard's presence, and the
days stretched dully before her. She called upon
Cousin Cecily and Olivia, Cousin Leo's daughter, and the few other acquaintances in town this
early, but was aware she was merely passing the
time until Richard came home. He wrote to her
once, and she broke the seal, hope burgeoning.
She scanned the contents, praying for news of
his return, only to subside at his words. After the
first few days of indifferent scent, he wrote, the
weather had improved and the hounds were running sweetly, so they had decided to stay a day or
two longer. He hoped she would forgive him, and
that she missed him as much as he missed her.

Irritated to have become so dependent upon
him, Felicity forced herself to keep going out. She

had heard nothing more from Harriet and could only hope she was all right.

'When is my cousin due to return?' Charles enquired one day, just over a week after Richard had gone away, as he escorted Felicity to Hookham's Circulating Library to exchange some books.

'I know no more than I did yesterday when you asked.' Felicity was immediately riven with guilt for snapping.

'I merely asked,' Charles said, with a lift of his fair brows and a touch of affront in his tone, 'because I understood you to say he went with Cheriton.'

'He did. Why do you ask?'

'Is that not the duke in his carriage over there?'

Charles indicated a carriage, bearing the Cheriton coat of arms, at the head of a line of vehicles trailing behind a slow-moving coal wagon.

'Yes, but…' Felicity peered closer. Charles was right. She recognized Leo's profile. 'Oh!'

'You will tell him I need to see him urgently as soon as he gets home?'

'I will,' Felicity promised, although she knew it would not be for a few days. She had only received Richard's letter the day before.

Suspicion reared its head. If Leo was back in London, where on earth was Richard?

Chapter Forty-Seven

Four days later, Richard finally arrived home. He sent Dalton ahead to instruct Felicity to be at the front door at three o'clock sharp. Dalton waited with her on the front step and, as the longcase clock in the hall struck the hour, a gleaming phaeton, drawn by a pair of chestnut high-steppers, swung around the square and came to a halt in front of Stanton House.

Felicity's interest, however, was reserved exclusively for the driver. Richard grinned down at her: rich chocolate eyes creased at the corners, lips parted to allow a glimpse of white teeth.

'Well, Wife?' he said, removing his hat before leaping to the ground with the grace of a cat. With a deep laugh, he swung her into his arms and kissed her soundly on the lips.

'*Richard.*' Felicity struggled to free her arms to push him away although, secretly, she was delighted with his show of affection, her heart full to bursting. 'What will people think?'

'That I am a most fortunate fellow, to be welcomed home with a kiss from my lovely wife,' Richard responded, with an aplomb that made Felicity giggle. He tugged her around so they were both facing the phaeton and pair. 'Well? What do you think?'

Felicity studied the phaeton—midnight blue with gold-painted trim—and the beautifully matched ponies. They were glossy chestnut geldings with eye-catching flaxen manes and tails, identical white blazes, and four white socks apiece.

'They are exceedingly handsome,' she said.

'A bit like your husband?'

'*Exactly* like my husband. What are their names?' She felt Richard's eyes on her as she spoke, and she glanced up at him. 'Oh, how I have missed you, my love.' The words burst from her lips before she could think what she was saying.

'And I have missed you too, Felicity Joy. And their names are Nutmeg and Spice, although you may wish to change them.'

'Oh, no. It's unlucky, and I think their names are perfect.'

'And so, my sweet, are you. Come, let us go indoors. Dalton, will you take care of these two, please?'

'Can I not drive them?'

'Not now, my sweet. I am weary, and I make no doubt they are too; we have been on the road since yesterday. I did not wish to hurry them. Besides, Dalton will be keen to settle them into their new homes. We will take them to the park tomorrow morning, I promise. Tomorrow morning, eleven o'clock.'

'Lord Stanton!' A man, dressed in an ill-fitting brown suit, hurried across the road towards them.

'Turner, any news?'

'Yes, milord.'

'At last. You'd better come inside.' In the hall, Richard said, 'I shall join you in the drawing room shortly, my dear. This should not take long.'

Felicity hid her irritation at being dismissed. This Turner had clearly brought news important to Richard and, therefore, it was important to Felicity. She paced the floor.

Before fifteen minutes had passed, Richard came in.

'You look pleased, Richard. I must presume Mr Turner brought good news. Might I be allowed to share in it?'

Richard gathered her into his arms and nuzzled her neck. 'I should rather share something else with you, sweetheart.'

She wrapped her arms around his neck as her insides swooped but, despite the involuntary responses of her body, her mind still fretted over Turner and his errand. Why would Richard not tell her? His reaction had suggested news of some importance. She pulled away, tilting her head to study his expression.

'Is it a secret?'

A crease appeared between his brows, then relaxed as he huffed out a sigh. 'You are not going to let the subject drop, are you, Felicity Joy?'

'Should I? It sounded important, and you seem pleased. I admit I am curious, and I do not like feeling something is being kept from me.'

'Very well.' Richard led her to the sofa. 'It was…well, not quite a secret, but I did not want you to worry about it. I was set upon by…'

Set upon? The rest of his sentence was drowned out by the panicked clamour in Felicity's brain. 'Are you all right?' She twisted to face him, cupping his face between her hands. 'Are you injured? What about your ribs?'

Richard grasped her wrists and pulled her hands away from his laughing face. 'Calm down. It happened last time we came up to town.'

'Where? When?'

'I was attacked and robbed by three men in Sackville Street on our very first night in London in October. I hired Turner to investigate. He tells me there have been several similar attacks since. Evidently one of the waiters at White's has been passing information to the gang, telling them who had won at the tables, so they knew who was likely to have a heavy purse.'

'I wish you had told me.' Felicity stroked Richard's hair back from his brow.

'And what would you have done, Felicity Joy? Worried on my behalf? Now, tell me how you have been spending your time whilst I have been away.'

'Oh, the usual round of morning visits and

walks in the park,' Felicity said. 'And...oh, I nearly forgot. Charles is very anxious to see you. He asked me to tell you *most particularly.*'

'I will speak to him tomorrow. I am going nowhere tonight. It is good to be home.' Richard cupped Felicity's face, brushing his thumbs gently under her eyes. 'You look tired, my love.' Heat swirled in the depths of his darkened eyes. 'I prescribe bed rest before dinner.'

Pulse quickening, Felicity leaned into his touch. 'I am not so very tired, Husband, but I think a lie-down might help restore my spirits.'

'Your spirits?'

'Mmmm.' She raised her lips to his. 'They have been feeling neglected.'

'Are your spirits the only part of you suffering from neglect?'

Long fingers trailed down her neck to play with her neckline. Her pulse pounded as their lips met. She relaxed into Richard's strength, his masculine scent pervading every cell of her body: comforting, enticing, exciting.

He took his mouth from hers. 'I missed you too, Wife,' he murmured, before claiming her lips again.

That night, Richard came to Felicity again, took her in his arms and made love to her with such intensity she could barely catch her breath. His lips and his hands caressed every inch of her skin, his body moved over her and inside her with such tenderness she had to blink back tears for fear they might be misconstrued.

When she reached for him—to show her love for him the way she always had, with her body—he pinned her hands above her head and slowly, relentlessly, brought her to the brink of ecstasy once more, driving her until she shattered into a thousand million stars, and flew free, scattered into the infinity of the night sky.

'Richard…I love you!'

Richard rose up on his forearms, sweat glistening on his forehead. 'I love you, too, Felicity Joy.'

His deep voice reverberated through her as the tremors racking her body subsided and she drifted off to sleep in his arms, secure and content and loved.

Felicity awoke the following morning to the sun filtering through the curtains, still clasped in Richard's embrace, and felt her heart would burst with happiness.

He had become her whole world. Within her heart, her soul, her mind, there was only him. He fulfilled her, he completed her. He had become an intrinsic part of her, and she could not imagine how her life could be better.

Chapter Forty-Eight

'I'm sorry, Felicity, but we must postpone our drive until this afternoon,' Richard said as he came out of his study at eleven o'clock that morning and found her waiting in the hall. 'I have to go out on urgent business.' There was a letter in his hand.

'I am sure it cannot be helped, Richard,' Felicity said. She was disappointed, but it would not hurt to wait a little longer to drive Nutmeg and Spice. Nothing could spoil her mood today; she felt as though she could fly if she wanted to. She suppressed a smile. She had certainly flown last night.

After Richard had gone out, Felicity sent for Yvette, to go shopping in Bond Street.

As they left the house, a familiar figure approached.

'Good morning, Charles. What a pleasant surprise. I am just on my way out, as you can see.'

Charles tipped his hat and flashed a brief smile

at Felicity before his gaze slid past her, to the front door.

'Good morning, Felicity. I hear my cousin returned yesterday. Is he in?'

Taken aback by his abruptness, Felicity said, 'I'm afraid he was called out on urgent business. I did tell him you wish to see him. Can I not help?'

'No. Yes. Oh, I don't know.' Charles swept the hat from his head and raked his fingers through his already dishevelled curls before replacing it again. He glanced at Yvette. 'Might I have a word in private?'

'Why, yes, of course, Charles. Shall we go back inside?'

'No. Thank you. This will be easier if we walk and talk at the same time. That way, I shall not have to read the disdain in your eyes.'

'Disdain? Oh, no, Charles. Why should I look at you with disdain?' His blue eyes were filled with worry. 'Please walk on ahead, Yvette. We shall be right behind you.'

'Thank you.'

Felicity took Charles's arm. His tension was tangible.

'Will you not tell me what troubles you? If I can help, you must know that I will.'

'I should not discuss such matters with a lady,' Charles muttered. 'Stan would have my guts if he knew, but I can wait no longer.' He fell silent, and Felicity waited. Eventually, he drew in a ragged breath. 'It's these debts. I don't quite expect you to understand, but I have borrowed against…against…'

'Against the expectation of the earldom, and all that goes with it?'

A sidelong glance revealed a flush on Charles's cheeks as he fixed his gaze on the pavement ahead of them. 'Put like that—so baldly—it sounds so very heartless.' He spun on the spot, clutching Felicity's hands. 'I have to…I am sorry to ask, but could you lend me some money? I wouldn't ask,' he added hurriedly, 'but there are some unpleasant coves after me for a debt, and I must pay them *something*.'

'Money?'

They began to walk again, crossing Oxford Street into New Bond Street.

'I wouldn't ask if I wasn't desperate. Richard refused last time I came down to Fernley. It was a blow, I don't mind telling you. He'd barely notice such a paltry sum.'

'Lend? Have you *ever* repaid anything you have borrowed?'

Charles huffed a short laugh. 'No. I take your point. And I have changed, I promise you. I've been careful, I swear. This particular debt…it is of long standing. Truth be told, I had forgotten about it, until the duns came knocking.'

'How much do you need?'

'Five hundred guineas should be enough.'

'I'm sorry, Charles, but I do not have that much at my disposal.'

'Will you talk to Richard? Please? Tell him this will be the last time, I promise.'

'You invest too much faith in my powers of persuasion, I fear, but I will…oh, *look*, there is Harriet. I did not know she had returned. Come, I should like to speak to her.' She called to Yvette, 'Please wait there, we will be back very soon.'

Felicity urged Charles across the road. A sweeping boy hurried to clear their path, and Charles tossed him a coin.

'That is most obliging of you, Charles, as you are so short of money yourself.'

'Oh, it was only a farthing. That barely counts as money, does it?'

And therein lies much of your problem.

'Harriet turned down here,' Felicity said, as they turned the corner of Brook Street. Time appeared to slow as Felicity's lungs seized. Harriet had stopped next to a waiting carriage, its door standing open. Richard stood close to her, gazing down into her face as she spoke earnestly, her hand on his lapel. As Felicity watched, Richard took Harriet's hand, lifted it to his lips, then handed her into the carriage. He climbed in behind her and slammed the door.

'What the…!' Charles trapped Felicity's hand in his elbow and towed her back around the corner.

She couldn't summon the strength to resist. *Richard?* And *Harriet?* The intimacy of the scene scorched her brain.

'Come, my dear.' They paused to wait for a

break in the traffic to cross back to Yvette, waiting on the opposite side. 'I am sure there is a perfectly…they *are* old friends, after all.'

Old friends? Then why has neither of them ever said? Aware she was clutching Charles's sleeve, Felicity loosened her grip.

'Old friends?' she asked lightly.

'Oh, yes,' Charles continued airily. 'Don't worry. I'm certain Richard must have ended their *friendship* as soon as he married you.'

Harriet was Richard's *mistress*? All Felicity's old doubts and suspicions charged to the fore. 'Urgent business,' he had said. That letter…from *Harriet*? Stomach churning, nausea crowding her throat, Felicity fought to keep control. What a complete and utter fool, to be taken in by their lies. She cringed when she remembered how she had confided in Harriet. Her husband's mistress.

When had Harriet returned to London? Had she been out of town with Richard? Felicity herself had told the scheming hussy where he had gone. Is that what he had been doing after Leo came back to town?

Oh, dear God…

'Steady on, Felicity. You almost fell then. I say, you don't look… Hoi! Girl! Drat it, what the blazes is that girl called?'

'Yvette,' Felicity whispered. She dredged up a memory. The attack he had told her about. In Sackville Street. Harriet's street. That was the night he had not come home, and the servants had lied to cover his absence. He had gone to visit Harriet. No wonder he had objected to Felicity becoming involved with the house in Cheapside.

Pain knifed through her, and she gasped, suddenly terrified for the baby.

'Yvette!'

Heads turned to see who was shouting. Charles's grip on Felicity's arm was painful, and she could feel his panic, but it helped clear her head. As the pain subsided, she forced her head high, gritting her teeth. She refused to provide fodder for the gossipmongers. The pain had not struck her womb, but higher. Her heart. Five months ago she would have scoffed at such a fanciful notion, but not now. Her heart was shattered. Every beat was agony.

Yvette hurried to join them.

'Quick, girl, your mistress is taken ill. I think she should—' he waved urgently at a hackney coach '—return home forthwith.' He handed Felicity up into the coach. 'Should I come with you?'

She shook her head. 'No. Thank you. Yvette will look after me. Charles?'

'Yes?'

'Please, not a word, about…about…'

He pressed her hand. 'I shall be the soul of discretion. Never fear.'

'Thank you. Oh, and Charles? About that other matter? Give me a few days, and I will see what I can do to help.'

'You, my dear, are an angel. Please, do not fret about…that.' He waved a hand in the general direction of Brook Street. 'I am certain there must be—'

'Yes! Thank you, Charles. Please ask the driver to drive on.'

'Milady?' A hand touched her shoulder, then stroked across her back.

Felicity pushed against the mattress, shuffling around into a sitting position.

'Is it the baby, milady?'

Felicity shook her head, not trusting her voice not to wobble and to set off a fresh bout of tears.

'Then it is, milord,' Yvette said. 'Tsk. If what you think, it is the truth, then he is not worth your tears. But, it is possible, *bien sûr*, that you have jumped to the conclusion, is it not?'

Yvette's words lingered in the air. If only last night hadn't been so perfect. She had been so happy, finally feeling secure in Richard's love. Now, not only had her husband and her best friend lied about knowing each other but, to discover they had shared a secret liaison out of town…so many emotions pounded at her heart and her brain that she barely knew what to think. One minute she wished she could die—*Oh, Emma*, now *I understand your agony*—and the next, murderous impulses charged through her mind and body until she had to restrain herself from racing to confront the lying, cheating, despicable pair.

How ironic, that this is the exact situation that made Mama leave Farlowe.

I *will not run.*

It had been her first instinct: to pack her bags and to leave, never to see Richard again. The very thought brought more tears to blur her vision.

How can I bear to face him?

You have faced worse, and survived. This, too, will pass. Protect your heart. Protect your baby.

She caressed her belly. Oh, yes, she would protect her baby.

Galvanized into action, she swung her legs off the bed. 'Yvette?'

'Milady?'

'Please help me to make myself presentable. I must go downstairs.' She would not skulk in her bedchamber. When Richard returned home, it would not be to a wet rag of a woman, but to a proud and strong lady who would never reveal her heartache.

Yvette poured water from the jug on the wash-stand into the basin, and wrung out a washcloth.

'And, Yvette?'

The maid turned. A glow of appreciation for the Frenchwoman's unwavering loyalty struck Felicity. 'Thank you for being here. I know I do not have to ask, but...'

'I shall not breathe the word, milady.'

Felicity forced her lips into a smile.

Smiles were something she must learn to fake. She felt as though she might never again produce a genuine one.

Chapter Forty-Nine

Before going downstairs, Felicity wrote a note to Charles, begging him to call upon her at four o'clock. She would take Charles when she drove her new phaeton and pair for the first time: she refused to spend even the shortest time driving in the park with Richard, making polite conversation.

Richard strode into the drawing room—where Felicity was industriously embroidering a set of cushion covers—at a little after three o'clock.

'Your business must have been important, to take until now,' Felicity remarked, glancing at him briefly before concentrating once more on her stitches.

'What, no greeting for your errant husband, my sweet?' A pair of Hessians entered Felicity's field of vision, and a finger nudged her chin, tilting her face until she had no choice but to meet his gaze. She struggled to hide her still-churning emotions.

As he leaned down to kiss her she jerked away. His lips landed by her ear.

'Felicity? What is wrong?'

'Nothing is wrong. I have the headache.'

'I am sorry to hear it. I presume, therefore, you wish to postpone driving Nutmeg and Spice?'

Felicity inclined her head, not trusting herself to speak. She felt sick, until cold fury rose up to drown her guilt. Why should *she* feel guilt? She hardened her resolve.

'Have you had something to eat?' she asked, instead of answering his question, avoiding the outright lie.

'Yes. I ate at White's with Leo. He's been having family troubles.' Felicity had no interest in the duke's problems. She had enough of her own. She stood up.

'I must go and lie down,' she said.

As she walked to the door, Richard stopped her with a hand on her arm. He tugged her round to face him.

'What is troubling you? And do not tell me it is nothing again, for I shall not believe you. What has happened? Why are you so *cold*? I should have thought, after last night, this daytime *aloofness* would be in the past.'

'Last night? I do not recall anything remarkable about last night.'

She almost quailed at the flash of fury in his eyes, but held tight to her nerve.

'You do not recall anything remarkable about

last night?' He spoke through tight lips, his voice ominously quiet. Felicity swallowed convulsively. 'You said you love me. I said I love you. And you think that *unremarkable*?'

Felicity shrugged. It almost broke her heart to do it, but she conjured up that intimate scene on Brook Street. Felicity's heart had already been cleaved in two; the worst had already happened. This denial—this lie—could not possibly hurt more.

'Sometimes, one says things in the heat of the moment. Words are cheap, are they not? It is surely actions that speak the truth. Now, if you will excuse me?'

She tugged her arm from Richard's grip and left the room.

Lying...scheming...insensitive...women!

Woman, Richard amended silently, as he slammed his study door, following a curt 'I do not wish to be disturbed' to Barnes.

Well, she had certainly taken him for a fool. She'd had him believing every word and, all the time, she...

He stamped over to his desk, grabbing a bottle of brandy from a side table as he passed. He poured a measure and drank, grimacing as the brandy burned a passage down his throat. He held up his glass, squinting at the light from the window shining through the amber liquid. Amber. The same colour as her eyes. He slumped into his chair, chewing over her words...visualizing her expression…the scorn in her eyes. *Scorn*? Where had that come from? She had been distant before…but scorn was something new.

With a muttered oath, he straightened and pulled a pile of papers towards him. He needed distraction, and there was plenty of work to take his mind off his infuriating…frustrating…*incomprehensible* wife.

Three-quarters of an hour later, Richard was tilted back in his chair, hands linked behind his head, booted feet propped on his desk, having dealt with precisely one piece of correspondence. He couldn't concentrate, and it was all Felicity's fault.

'Words are cheap, are they not? It is surely actions that speak the truth.'

Her words echoed again and again through his brain.

Actions? His actions? His *lack* of action?

Felicity had closed her mind to him again. He could *feel* her slipping from his grasp, and yet she refused to tell him what was wrong. Was he supposed to be a mind reader? Again, the thought surfaced that she had never been this shuttered, even in the very early days of their marriage. And lately, since his accident, they had been growing closer and closer. The future had shone with promise. With love.

What had happened since last night? Richard swung his feet from the desk. The chair legs crashed to the floor. Something must have happened to trigger this change in her. She hadn't withdrawn from him on a whim and, by God, he was going to find out precisely what that something was.

He took the stairs two at a time and thrust open her bedchamber door without knocking. Empty. He ran downstairs again and checked all the reception rooms, ignoring the curious glances of the footman on duty in the hall. No Felicity. Anxiety and irritation now at war in his breast, he ran down the servants' stairs. Startled faces stared as he strode into the kitchen.

'Where is Yvette? I wish to see her in my study. Immediately.'

He did not wait for a reply, but returned to his study to await Yvette.

A knock at the door and Yvette entered, head high. He never ceased to admire the Frenchwoman for the way she faced life. He also admired how she was unafraid to speak her mind. She was never disrespectful—he would not stand for that in a servant—but she was forthright. It was that trait he needed now.

'Yvette. Come in and sit down, please.'

He waited as Yvette settled in the chair opposite. Yes. Something had happened, and Yvette was aware of it. He could see by the wary look in her eyes and the set of her jaw.

'Where is her ladyship, Yvette?'

Silence greeted his question.

'Well? Has her ladyship instructed you not to

tell me where she has gone? Or do you imagine to somehow protect her by concealing her whereabouts?'

'She has not instructed me, no. She does not need another upset. It is important she is calm for the baby.'

'*Another* upset? Was she upset by something this morning? Was it because I cancelled our outing to the park?'

Nonsense. Felicity isn't petty. It has to be more than a fit of pique over a cancelled outing.

'No, it was not.'

'Then what happened? Something here, or did her ladyship go out?'

Richard fought to hide his growing exasperation, knowing any attempt to force information from Yvette would be met with stubborn silence. She would, however, respond to honesty.

'Yvette. I know something has upset her ladyship this morning. She will not confide in me, but how can I put things right if I do not know what happened? Did she go out?'

Yvette sighed. 'I will tell you because you employ me. I am fond of my lady and I want her to be happy and she is not happy, no.'

Now we're getting somewhere.

'What happened this—?'

'No.' Yvette glared at Richard. 'I tell this in my way. My lady, she is in love with you but she is scared. Then today, I do not know what she see, but she see something and she nearly swoons and Mr Durant put us in a hackney and milady cried.'

Richard's stomach knotted. He longed to pepper Yvette with questions, but forced himself to go slowly. 'Mr Durant?'

'Milady and me, we go shopping and Mr Durant escorts us. But I am told to walk ahead so I do not know what he says, but he is worried about something.'

Money. Debts. Nothing new there.

'Milady sees the Lady Brierley going into Brook Street, and she follows her but stops on the corner.'

Ice-cold fingers clutched Richard's heart. He had met Harriet in Brook Street. What had Felicity seen? He pictured their meeting. Nothing there, surely, to cause such upset.

Apart from the fact you cancelled your outing with her to meet clandestinely with your ex-mistress?

Nonsense! Felicity does not know… His brain seized, then stuttered forward, inch by agonizing inch.

Felicity did not know Harriet had been his mistress. Felicity did not know Richard and Harriet had more than a nodding acquaintance. And yet… Richard had broken his promise to Felicity in favour of meeting Harriet. They had talked and then driven off together in his carriage.

But, still, was that enough to…why did she not just *ask* him?

Charles! Damned loose-tongued… Richard recalled their conversation at the Davenports' ball. It was possible. It was the only thing that made any sense.

'Thank you, Yvette. That will be all.'

He must talk to Felicity. Explain why he had met Harriet that morning and, he knew, it was time he told her the truth about their past relationship. No other woman mattered in his life. Only Felicity.

He was overcome with a sudden urge to find her. *Now*, to clear the air, to convince her of his love.

'Yvette!' The maid returned at his shout. 'You did not tell me where her ladyship has gone.'

'She has driven to the park with Mr Durant, milord.'

Of course she has. What else would his Felicity do but try to prove she did not care by continuing their plans without him? Spurred into action, he shouted to the footman to send to the stables for his horse and to tell Dalton he was to accompany him.

Richard set a spanking pace around the park, nodding to friends and acquaintances alike, but stopping to speak to no one. At last, on the far side, he spied his target. Defying convention, he urged Gambit into a gallop, overtaking the phaeton and pair before skidding to a halt in front of them.

Felicity pulled up Nutmeg and Spice and glared at Richard.

'What are you doing?' she hissed. Richard ignored her, his eyes fixed on his sheepish-looking cousin. He nudged Gambit around to where Charles sat.

'Out!'

'Now, steady on, Stan.'

Richard swung down from Gambit and tossed the reins to Dalton. 'Take them home,' he ordered, his eyes still on Charles who, after the very slightest of hesitations, climbed from the phaeton.

'Charles? Don't, I beg of you—'

Richard leapt aboard, taking the reins from Felicity's unresisting hands. 'Say goodbye to Charles, Felicity.'

'I say…'

Richard clicked to the ponies. They set off at a trot.

'You won't forget that little matter we spoke about, will you, Felicity?' Charles's voice faded into the distance.

'Has he asked you for money?'

'Yes. Richard, why—?'

'I do not appreciate other men dunning my wife for money.'

The sharp intake of breath beside him warned Richard this conversation might not go as planned. Planned? Hell, he hadn't planned anything…had thought no further than finding Felicity, taking her in his arms and convincing her of his love.

Chapter Fifty

'And *I* do not appreciate other women making secret assignations with my husband.'

As soon as the words left her mouth, Felicity regretted them. What had come of her plan to keep her dignity and ignore Richard's behaviour? Did she *have* to blurt out the thing that was uppermost in her mind almost the second she saw him?

Richard reined Nutmeg and Spice to a halt on the side of the Row, and set the brake, twisting to face Felicity, who gritted her teeth and stared defiantly ahead.

'You saw me with Harriet.'

It was a statement, not a question. 'Harriet, is it now? It was always Lady Brierley before, whilst you were making a fool out of me.'

Felicity gripped her gloved hands tightly in her lap. As people rode and drove past, she was aware of their surreptitious glances.

'Neither of us has any desire to make a fool of you, my darling.'

Richard covered her clasped hands with his.

'I will tell you everything, and then I can do no more than hope you will forgive me. Not for anything I have done, but only for not admitting the truth when you first met Harriet.'

'I thought she was my friend.' A tear threatened to spill and Felicity snatched her hand from Richard's grasp to swipe at it.

'She *is* your friend. She is very fond of you, and has done more for you than you know.'

'*Hmmph.*' Felicity did not want this conversation. And she most certainly did not want to hear it here, in the park, in front of all these curious, prying eyes. 'I want to go home.'

Richard leaned closer, his voice low. 'First, we will have this conversation. *Then* we will go home.'

Despite her anger, a tug of awareness snaked through Felicity as his warm breath danced over her skin. She clamped her teeth tight, fighting her instinctive reaction.

'What I have to say, I will say now. And you need to hear it now, whilst you are upset and open and vulnerable. If I give you the time, I am too afraid you will rebuild those wretched fortifications around that stubborn little heart of yours, and I shall be marooned forever on the outside.'

She risked a sidelong glance. Dark-chocolate eyes burned into her. Afraid? Her strong, capable, confident husband afraid?

She inclined her head. 'Very well. It would

appear I have little choice, as you are holding the reins.'

An apt metaphor for a woman's life: someone else always in control of the reins.

'Before I decided to wed, I was a single man. Harriet was a widow.' Gentle fingers caressed her nape. Shivers cascaded down her spine. 'We had an understanding—'

'An *affaire*!' Her squirming stomach made Felicity shift uneasily on the seat. 'You were in love with her.'

'Yes, an *affaire* and, no, I was never in love with her. Nor she with me. It was a mutually agreeable arrangement. I know how cold that sounds, but it happens, sweetheart. We satisfied each other's physical needs. Nobody else knew.'

'Charles knew.'

'He did not know. He guessed, and only very recently. I suppose I should be grateful he managed to keep that much a secret. If he had not, the entire *ton* would know by now. As soon as we were betrothed, I wrote to Harriet to end our arrangement.'

'Why?' Felicity concentrated her gaze on his sensual, skilful lips. Had those lips caressed Harriet…? She shied away from the thought, miserably aware she was being unfair. She was an adult. People had *affaires*. She, of all people, knew that.

'Why did I end it?'

She nodded.

'I wanted to be fair to you, and I wanted our marriage to be content. I told myself I could always take another mistress later, after you were with child.'

Felicity stiffened. Tried to pull away from his touch. His arm wrapped around her, holding her still.

'I am being brutally honest with you, my love, because there must be no further misunderstandings between us. At that time, both you and I expected a marriage of convenience. I did not know what the future held. That is what I thought and how I felt then. It is not how I feel now.

'When we came up to town, that first time—on the very first night—I called upon Harriet. I presented her with a gift and we parted on amicable terms. That was the night I was attacked, and I stayed the night at Harriet's, in the guest bedchamber.'

'I know,' Felicity said.

'You know? How…?'

'I knew you hadn't come home that night…'

'But I sent instructions…'

Felicity felt a blush building in her cheeks. 'I looked into your bedchamber very early. I wanted…I wondered…I saw the bed was all made and yet, later, after breakfast, it was all messy and looked slept in. I suspected then you had spent the night with a woman, but I never dreamt it was…' Her voice hitched.

'But it was not, my sweet. At least, not in the way you mean.'

Felicity's brain whirled. His explanation made

sense. She had begun to trust Richard, had ceased to believe he had a mistress. And yet…

'You did not return home with the duke…'

'He had to leave early, to deal with a family crisis.'

'Harriet went out of town at the same time. Was she with you?'

'Is that what's bothering you? You saw me meet with Harriet, and then recalled we were out of town at the same time? And thought the worst of both of us? Oh, dear, Felicity Joy. No wonder… I had not even thought, until this minute, you might imagine such a thing.'

He brushed an escaping wisp of hair out of her eyes, then dropped a kiss on her nose.

'At least this has solved my quandary.'

'Quandary?'

'Harriet wrote and asked to meet me, to discuss some information she had, and whether she should reveal it to you.'

Richard released Felicity to take a letter from his pocket. 'It's fortunate I still have this with me.' He laid it on Felicity's lap. 'This is the letter I received from Harriet this morning asking to meet me. Read it.'

Her hand twitched, but she did not touch the letter. 'No,' she said. 'Please. Tell me what happened. I want to trust your words. I do not want to live my life searching for either proof of your truthfulness or evidence of your guilt.'

Gentle fingers brushed across her cheek. Deep

brown eyes fixed on her lips and she felt her body respond as her blood quickened.

'Very well. We met in Brook Street because Harriet did not want me to visit her at home, out of respect for your friendship. She said you told her about Emma.'

Misery squeezed Felicity's chest. She had trusted Harriet. 'That is true. I also told her where you had gone. I had dinner with her that night, and she made no mention of going out of town, but the next morning she had gone.'

'She only decided to go away after you left. She hoped to help you come to terms with Emma's death. She attended the same house parties as your mother and Emma that summer, and thought she could identify the wretch who seduced Emma.'

'Who is he? I want to see him. He must pay for what he did.'

'Steady.' Richard grabbed at Felicity as she turned to jump from the phaeton. 'He is not in London, which is why Harriet went into Kent, to see him. She did not tell you because she did not wish to raise your hopes if she was mistaken.

'And she told me of her discovery before telling you because of your delicate condition. She wondered if it might be better to wait—'

'Who is he?'

Richard sighed. 'Now you know this much, you must know the whole, I suppose. But understand this, Felicity Joy. There is no possibility of you going to see him. He is Sir Malcolm Poole.'

Sir Malcolm Poole? Try as she might, Felicity could not put a face to the name. 'I should like to—'

'Yes, yes—' Richard laughed, prising her fists loose '—you should like to kill him. I know that, my darling, but it won't be necessary. He is, at this very moment, paying a heavy price for his debauched lifestyle and is close to meeting his maker.'

'What did he say? About Emma?'

'He admitted to seducing her, but showed no remorse when told of her suicide, according to Harriet. The fellow has always been a rake of the worst kind—an out-and-out scoundrel. His kind live only for their own pleasure without thought of the consequences for their victims. He has been an outcast from polite society for many years now.'

'Was he...' Felicity felt her forehead pucker as her thoughts spun and she strove to weave a coherent question from them '...was he an outcast *before* he met Emma?'

Richard gathered her against his chest. 'I'm afraid so.' His voice rumbled in her ear, deep and reassuring.

'Then that means...Mama...those parties...'

'They were no place for an innocent.'

A sob built in her throat. Harriet had said the same, and she had always suspected as much, but had given her mother the benefit of the doubt.

'Your mother... You must remember she did not take Emma to those places from malice.'

'No. I know. She was just selfish and thought-less. As she still is. I *begged* her not to make me—' Felicity stopped with a gasp. How could she allow her mouth run on so?

'You *begged* not to have to marry me?'

Richard's voice quivered, and Felicity peeked up at him. Then straightened. 'You wretch!' She slapped at his chest. 'You are laughing at me.'

'No, no, I'm laughing at myself. At fate. I knew you were reluctant to marry me, but I could not fathom why. That only made me more determined to go through with it, hence the speed of the wedding. I did not want you to find a way out. Not only had you landed a bruising blow to my self-esteem, but I found myself eager to learn the truth of your reluctance.'

'And did you?'

'We worked that out together, Felicity Joy, did we not? When you read Emma's diary?'

'I suppose we did. When I knew the real reason for her suicide, I recognized my greatest fear was based on an untruth. Emma did not kill herself over unrequited love, but because she was with child and the man she loved had abandoned her.' She touched her belly. 'I do not believe that will happen to us, Richard.'

'Indeed it will not,' he said. 'I love you, Felicity Joy. I love every inch of you, inside and out.' He pulled her closer, tilting her chin. His warm breath feathered over her suddenly sensitized lips. 'Over these past few months I have fallen further and further under your spell. You fill my every waking thought and my every dream.'

His eyes darkened and awareness shivered through Felicity. She leaned closer.

'Well! Really!' The outraged female tones penetrated the sensual haze surrounding Felicity.

'Richard, no! What will people say?'

'I could not care less. All I care about is you.'

His lips covered hers, warm and seductive, as she melted into his embrace.

When they finally came up for air, it was to a smattering of applause. But they had eyes only for each other.

Epilogue

~~~~~~~~~~~

July 1816—Cheriton Abbey

'Back where it all began.'

Richard sprawled at his ease on a blanket, propped on his elbow as he gazed around with satisfaction. The Devon air was soft and sweetly scented. The melodious trill of skylarks and the hum of bees working the nectar-rich clover in the meadow were punctuated by an occasional squeal of childish delight.

The duke had thrown a family party to celebrate the birth of his new baby. He had insisted Richard and Felicity also attend as they were—in Leo's words—family, too.

Felicity caught Richard's eye and smiled, and he felt the familiar squeeze of his heart. Even after all this time, he still wanted her.

And needed her.

And loved her.

He never stopped wanting her.

'It seems like another life entirely, does it not?' Felicity said, as she cuddled baby George close to her breast. 'Do you remember the very first time we met? On the stairs?'

'I do indeed. You were a naughty minx then and you're a scandalous minx now.'

Felicty's giggle tiptoed through his heart. 'Hush, Richard. The children!'

'They are far too busy playing to worry about what their staid old parents are up to.'

Richard looked again, picking out their eldest, Emma, now four, and three-year-old Adam, Baron Durant of Fernley. His heir. And now—he regarded George with pride—the traditional spare as well. Life could not be sweeter.

Sarah, George's nursemaid, approached. 'Shall I take the baby now, milady?'

George had fallen asleep in his mother's arms, and barely stirred when Sarah lifted him, merely pursing his lips and frowning fleetingly. As Sarah carried him away, Richard made up his mind. He leapt up, grabbed Felicity's hands and tugged her to her feet. He studied her beloved face—amber eyes round with amused enquiry, soft pink lips parted on a breathless laugh.

'Felicity Joy…'

Her laughter faded. He tucked a stray curl behind her ear, and stroked her silky cheek before taking her hand again. The first time had been business. This was—undoubtedly—his heart's desire. He dropped to one knee, his gaze never leaving hers. Her eyes widened.

'…I love you more than you can ever know. You have made my life complete. Although I asked you once, and you accepted, and we are already man and wife…I ask you again. This time from my heart.

'Will you marry me?'

Felicity threw her head back and her laugh rang out across the meadow. 'I will, I would, every time!'

She tumbled to her knees, took his face between her palms, and kissed him.

* * * * *

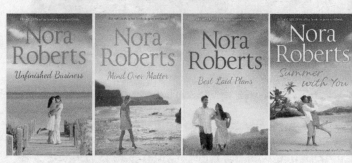

MILLS & BOON®

The Chatsfield Collection!

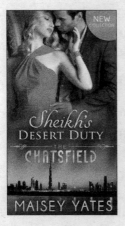

Style, spectacle, scandal…!

With the eight Chatsfield siblings happily married and settling down, it's time for a new generation of Chatsfields to shine, in this brand-new 8-book collection! The prospect of a merger with the Harrington family's boutique hotels will shape the future forever. But who will come out on top?

Find out at
www.millsandboon.co.uk/TheChatsfield2

MILLS & BOON®

HISTORICAL

AWAKEN THE ROMANCE OF THE PAST

A sneak peek at next month's titles...

In stores from 1st May 2015:

- **A Lady for Lord Randall** – Sarah Mallory
- **The Husband Season** – Mary Nichols
- **The Rake to Reveal Her** – Julia Justiss
- **A Dance with Danger** – Jeannie Lin
- **Lucy Lane and the Lieutenant** – Helen Dickson
- **A Fortune for the Outlaw's Daughter** – Lauri Robinson

Available at WHSmith, Tesco, Asda, Eason, Amazon and Apple

Just can't wait?
Buy our books online a month before they hit the shops!
visit www.millsandboon.co.uk

These books are also available in eBook format!